Moms Who Read Romance Novels

Moms Who Read Romance Novels

Moms Who Read Romance Novels

Jenifer Goldin

Moms Who Read Romance Novels
© 2023 Jenifer Goldin Feldman

Book Cover by Stuart Bache
Formatting by Alt 19 Creative

Published by Anchor Head Books

I dedicate *Moms Who Read Romance Novels* to Amy B. and Stephanie F. Not everyone is lucky enough to have friendships spanning multiple decades. Although I did not know it at the time, the idea for this book was born on our girl's trip in Clearwater.

Pool time, heart to hearts, dancing all night to a live 80's band, walking in our stylish raincoats (why didn't we take an Uber?), and one hilarious conversation that inspired the story below. Love you both to pieces. XO

Contents

KEY: Chapter Icons

    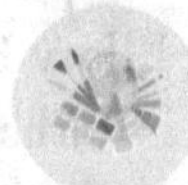

Ellory   *Tabitha*   *Faye*   *Harper*   *Ila*

New York City
Times Square Studios
February 14, 2023

Ellory Brayson

AS I WALK on set, the audience sucks in a collective breath. Everyone jumps out of their seats, applauding. The set for *This Morning America* crackles with excitement. A few women shout adoring comments, and one lady, wearing a pink cowboy hat, yells *giddy up*.

Jessica, the show's beloved host, sits across from me, smiling as I sit in a wingback chair covered in crushed pink velvet. The stage manager rushes around, ensuring the camera operators and other crew members are in place. The entire studio pulses with electrifying energy, as if the space is alive with a beating heart. *What would everyone think if they knew the truth?*

"Lights, camera, action!"

Jessica leans toward me. Her pale green suit accents the blond highlights in her hair. "Ellory, I'm thrilled to have you back for our Valentine's Day show. What a perfect day to talk to the queen of romance novels."

Jessica beams at the audience. Smiles jump from face to face as if alive. "Ellory, your fans absolutely adore you. You've sold over thirty million books and you have multiple titles on the bestseller lists. How do you do it?"

If she only knew my sales were slipping. The pressure of having to put out two to three bestsellers every year is crushing me. It's getting harder and harder to compete with romance authors like Colleen Hoover and Emily Henry. A surge of heat expands in my chest, ripping open the fresh wound in my heart.

My lips part as I attempt to answer Jessica's question, but my vision clouds with an image of Maxy's face. Last night, he admitted to another affair. The silence stretches, and Jessica softly clears her throat to help me focus.

"Yes, yes," I say, stumbling to find my words. *This is live TV, Ellory. Get it together.* I can feel a line of sweat forming under my silk Versace top.

"So, how do you do it?" Jessica eyes me carefully, surely noticing the beads of moisture pooling on my forehead. She's known for her down-to-earth personality. It's not surprising she's aware something's off. I stare at her blankly, Maxy's callous expression etched in my mind's eye.

"Why don't we start with some audience questions?" Jessica's a pro and immediately shifts the order of my interview. I feel like she's throwing me a lifeline, allowing me a few seconds to compose myself as she changes things around.

I take a huge gulp of water as the crew members switch gears. Jessica prompts the audience to raise their hands if they have questions. She continues speaking, but suddenly, I can't hear. *Is this interview going to hell? The same way my marriage is going to hell?*

Panic makes the veins in my throat pulse. I can't screw this up. I'm promoting the last book in my best-selling series, *The Prince of Silicon Valley*. Suddenly, the romance market is flooded with amazing young authors. I must solidify my status as queen bee.

Sweat drips down my back. Maxy's words beat back and forth in my mind like a ball in a pinball machine. *She's pregnant. I'm in love with her.*

"All right, let's get started." Jessica winks, but I can see the concern in her eyes. A slew of hands shoot up. The sudden burst of movement jolts me back into the moment. *This is live TV, Ellory. Get it together.*

"How about you, with the light purple top?" I choose a woman with long blond hair, dyed turquoise at the tips. She looks to be in her midtwenties. My agent's been pushing me to gain a footing with a younger audience to stay relevant.

"Hi, Ellory. My mom's a huge fan. I used to sneak and read your books when I was a little girl."

The audience chuckles.

I push my lips into a smile, fighting against an image of Maxy holding a baby girl.

"My question is this: have you ever thought about writing fantasy romance? There's nothing like dragons, sorcery, and good and evil mixed with a heart-wrenching love story."

My stomach clenches. I released a paranormal romance series called *Psychic Passions* a few years ago, but it flopped. This girl is obviously unaware.

"Hmm," I say, trying to bite back my annoyance. "I don't think so. I'm more of a contemporary romance writer."

"See, the thing is," she continues, "I want my mom to read fantasy romance, like me. If you write a fantasy romance novel, I'm sure she'd read it." She twirls the blue ends of her hair around one of her fingers.

My annoyance morphs into anger as my internal temperature soars. Suddenly, I'm burning alive. Logically, I understand it's because of Maxy, but this girl is about to become the target of all my fury.

This is live TV, Ellory. Get it together. I swallow, desperately searching for kind words. "That's flattering, but fantasy isn't my thing. I'll leave it to Sarah J. Maas and Rebecca Yarros."

The audience laughs. Insane jealousy over the success of *Fourth Wing* consumes me.

Jessica shifts in her chair. She's about to jump in and save me, but the annoying girl is talking again.

"Aww. That's a bummer." She balls her hands into fists and rotates them back and forth in front of her eyes, pretending to cry. *Is she mocking me?*

The audience laughs, but something about the gesture reminds me of Maxy's cold-hearted response to my tears last night.

Suddenly, all I can see are smears of color. I blink my eyes slowly several times, trying to capture the image of the audience. But all I see is a distorted image of the stupid girl fake crying and her insistence that I write fantasy romance.

Leaping out of my chair, I lunge toward her. "I don't get the obsession with fantasy romance!" My words are a growl. "For God's sake. Your generation can't appreciate a romance novel unless wings are sprouting from the characters' backs while they're fucking!"

Storming off the stage, my stomach drops. *This is live TV, Ellory.* Nausea engulfs me. Running to the nearest garbage can, I vomit the coffee and bagel I ate for breakfast. I've just blown up a career spanning two decades, and I'm sure that little episode is already a viral meme.

Jupiter Cove, Florida
Memorial Day Weekend
May 26, 2023

CHAPTER 1

Ellory Brayson

THE UBER HUMS as it ascends the Jupiter Key Bridge. Cars slow to a stop. Ahead, I can see the enormous drawbridge inching downward. Looking to my left, I watch as a yacht moves across the glistening blue water toward the open sea.

Cars move ahead once the bridge levels out, and Jupiter Cove comes into view. It's the first beach town on this section of the coastline. I exhale loudly. It's been years since I've been home. It's not surprising, considering my mom passed away over a decade ago. And after everything that happened, how could I face Tabby? I'll have to trust that home remains the one place that won't reject you when the world has cast you aside.

Headlines and clips from the incident on *This Morning America* are finally fading into the background. But I've got some major repair work ahead. My publicist, agent, and publishing house have devised an elaborate strategy to help me get back into the good graces of my fans. I feel like I can't breathe without getting approval from my PR team. But

I'll do whatever they say to keep my status as the world's most famous romance author. My celebrity persona has ruled my life for longer than I care to admit. It's the reason I've been unable to apologize to Tabby.

I think through the steps my publicist, Amber, and I agreed to in her high-rise office overlooking Madison Avenue. She paced uncomfortably in three-inch heels, trying to balance her swollen pregnant body. *Step one*–Maxy and I will hold off announcing our divorce until the end of the summer. *Step two*–Act like *This Morning America* never happened. *Step three*–Launch a social media campaign reminding fans why they love me. *Step four*–Show my face. The last step begins in just a few hours. I've got a book event at Jupiter Cove's independent bookstore, Blast Off Books.

MY VOICE WAVERS as I face my fans for the first time since *This Morning America*. Standing, I lean slightly forward against the back of my chair. This is the power pose I'm using to tap back into my celebrity persona. Parting my lips, I read from my latest release. This time, my voice is dense like a stone sinking to the bottom of a lake.

> "My appetite for him was insatiable. We were worn out but couldn't resist another moment of pure bliss. Clasping my hand tightly around him, he throbbed in my grip. I pushed him inside. My body contracted in pain, outlined with a perverse pleasure. I looked directly into his eyes. My body pulsed and released in an unending wave. Then my body shuddered again. But it was not from pleasure. It was from the way his eyes glowed, like truth-seeking orbs. He could never know the truth. The truth would destroy us."

Lifting my head, I glance at the women who have come to Blast Off Books to get signed copies of the last book in *The Prince of Silicon Valley* series. The audience stares back at me with their mouths slightly agape. Their eyes are glassy, and they angle their bodies forward, as if the scene I just read was a magnet pulling them toward me.

I hate reading sex scenes out loud. It's one thing to write a sex scene in the privacy of my office. And even that takes intense focus and preparation. I drink two glasses of wine to loosen up before I peck at my computer's keyboard. Sometimes I watch a steamy love scene for inspiration. The show *Outlander* has been a recent favorite. Or my classic go-to, *About Last Night* with Rob Lowe. It would surprise my readers to learn I'm not a sexual extrovert. In fact, my sex life has been nonexistent for years. If my fans knew the truth, they'd shun me as the world's biggest fraud.

"Does anyone have questions for Ellory?" My childhood best friend, Tabby, owner of Blast Off Books, steps beside the chair where I'm standing.

As the audience exhales the last bit of sexual tension coursing through their bodies, I run my hand over the charm bracelet in my pocket. Its meaning feels heavy in this setting.

A woman in the back stands, shaking her hand in the air. Tabby encourages her toward us. I notice she's younger than my average reader. Late twenties maybe? She's got a full, curvaceous body that fills the surrounding space. She moves gracefully and smiles so widely, I can't help but spread my lips out and smile. Tabby hands the microphone to the woman.

"Hi, Ellory," she says as her warm features draw me in. "My name is Harper. I'm such a huge fan. I've read all your books. Even the *Psychic Passions* series."

My muscles immediately tighten. This whole situation is triggering memories of *This Morning America*. Pushing my shoulders back, I tap back into Celebrity Ellory.

"Anyway," she continues, "my question is, do you believe everyone will experience a great love in their lifetime?" She cocks her head, thinking for a moment. "I mean, look at you. You married an actual prince and have the most incredible love story."

My mouth turns downward as Harper mentions Maxy, also known as Prince Maximilian, a royal from a small monarchy in Eastern

Europe. *Yes*, I think to myself with dismay. *It really is the most unreal love story.* Hurling the thought away, I look at Harper. I've seen her kind over and over. Lonely and starving for the kind of love that only exists in romance novels.

I inhale deeply. "I love this question, Harper. And it's one I get a lot. Everyone can have a great love story, but if you have rules about who it should be with, or a specific timeline it must happen by, or any constraints that narrow the possibilities, your great love may slip through your fingers." I pause for maximum effect as Harper nods. "So, yes, everyone can have a great love story, but most people are going to miss it." Celebrity Ellory has given this little speech at least five hundred times over the years.

"Well, you certainly didn't miss yours." Harper bounces in place, too excited to contain her enthusiasm.

An image of Prince Maxy's face flits through my mind. He's the reason I lost my friendship with Tabby. I gently shake my head to loosen my clenching jaw. "Are you single?" I ask, knowing, of course, the answer is yes.

"Yes." Harper shifts her weight from side to side but somehow remains perfectly poised.

"Well, all I can say, Harper, is stay open and see what cues the universe gives you. Don't ignore them."

Tabby gives me a side-eye, probably wondering why I ignored the cues the universe gave me. I've got to apologize to her this summer. I'm lost in thought when I hear another voice shout out. "Hi, Ellory. I love your books. So happy to see you tonight." A short woman with tan skin and overly highlighted hair smiles at me. "I love your characters, Theo and Lexi. I love your plot lines. But I have to say, I also really love steamy love scenes. You seem to write less and less spice with each new book."

The crowd laughs nervously.

Before I can respond, the woman jumps up from her chair. Rushing toward the microphone, she almost knocks over a display of Berkley Publishing's top-selling romance books. As she approaches, she passes the microphone and faces the audience. "Ladies, I love smut. Who's with me!"

Everyone's eyes lock on my face, terrified I may snap. *Get it together, Ellory.*

Shifting my gaze, my eyes settle on a large painting of the moon on the back wall of Blast Off Books. Jupiter Cove is famous for embracing the space theme. The large mural practically glows white against the purple walls. The adrenaline coursing through my body dissipates.

This woman is not wrong. It's hard to write about passionate sex when you're not having any. The love scenes in my latest books are tame compared to my earlier work. It reminds me I'm taking an enormous risk with the novel I'm working on now. My fans are dedicated romance readers. If my book doesn't have forced proximity, a love triangle, or enemies to lovers, all wrapped up with a happy ending, it's going to flop.

Heat creeps up my neck. I'm suddenly thankful I'm wearing a stylish scarf over my silky Chanel top. I can't let thoughts of my work in progress overtake me now. "I hear what you're saying, and thanks for the input."

Blank faces gape at me, and it's obvious I need to say something more to defuse the moment. From the corner of my eye, I see an audience member recording me. Just when I think I may snap, Celebrity Ellory sweeps in to save me. "I prefer the term *erotica*, but, yes, smut sells." I make myself casually laugh.

The entire room erupts with giggles.

A tall, slender Black woman, well past middle age, raises her hand. "I love smut too," she shouts proudly.

"And I love erotica," another woman squeals with a snorty chuckle.

There's more laughter from the crowd. Relief washes over me. Crisis averted.

The evening continues as more women ask me questions about love and relationships. It's as if they think I'm Cupid and can pull back my bow and solve all their love problems. I'm relieved when Tabby gives me the signal that it's time to wrap up the question-and-answer session.

Feeling like a fraud, I end the book-reading the same way I always end these events. "May you all find your happily ever after."

I almost choke as the words leave my mouth. I know better than anyone there's no such thing as happily ever after.

CHAPTER 2

Tabitha Wilson

"**T**HANKS FOR COMING to Blast Off Books," I say. "I'm happy you could be here to welcome back Jupiter Cove's Ellory Brayson. We've been friends since second grade, so it's a real treat." *Thank God no one has said a word about This Morning America.*

My eyes sweep over Ellory's glamorous image. It's hard to remember she was the one who loved climbing trees, throwing rocks, and daring boys to race her to the creek. She's traded Band-Aids for fancy scarves. I'll never get used to it.

"Ellory flew in from New York this afternoon. I'm sure she's exhausted. We're going to end here."

The group groans in disappointment.

"But I have some announcements I know you'll find exciting." The faces before me brighten. I make my voice sound enthusiastic, even though I'm feeling hesitant about Ellory's reappearance in my life. "Ellory's almost done with a new book. A stand-alone. It's different from her usual novels, but she's been working tirelessly on creating another cast of characters for you to fall in love with."

This is exactly what Ellory's publicist told me to say when we planned tonight's event. *"And don't say a word to Ellory about what happened on This Morning America.*" She wouldn't worry if she knew my relationship with Ellory was nonexistent.

And although I find it patronizing, I will play along. Ellory has agreed to sell all the hard copies of *The Prince of Silicon Valley* series through my bookstore for now. The money it will provide could not come at a better time.

The women in the crowd clap and cheer.

"And," I continue, "Ellory is renting a house in Jupiter Cove for the summer while she puts the finishing touches on this new book."

"Oh my God," a woman in the back blurts. "This is the most exciting news ever!"

"Wow, the most exciting news ever?" Ellory laughs along with the crowd. "I'm very flattered."

As I watch Ellory, I'm impressed by her ability to act as if she wasn't caught on national television cussing out a fan. "Yes, I agree. It's exciting to have a world-famous romance author living here and finishing her book." I smile at Ellory, but my chest tightens. A wave of uneasiness courses through my body. I ignore my feelings, knowing all that matters is the money. It's my last chance to fulfill my dream.

I continue with my prepared script. "But there's even more exciting news. Ellory will pick a few readers from this group to review her manuscript, give notes, and help with editing. It's a contest of sorts, called Ellory's Editors. Those chosen will be the first to read Ellory's new book, and they will help shape how it unfolds."

The women eagerly bob around in their seats. A couple of people in the audience clap. And one woman gasps with excitement.

I glance at Ellory and hand her the microphone.

"I'm so pleased to see your reaction," she says to no one in particular. "A few logistical things to know before you drop your name into the hat. You'll need to read the book between now and the end of the summer. If your life is busy and you can't meet this timeline, it's probably better not to apply."

The crowd nods in understanding.

"The editors and I will meet a few times. We'll discuss plot holes, dead-end storylines, and what ideas you have for improving my book. And my publicist will run a social media campaign, highlighting Ellory's Editors."

This was the plan Ellory's publicist came up with to resurrect her reputation as the world's most beloved romance author. It's genius, yet manipulative. But I'm not complaining, given the financial benefits of this arrangement.

"I can't wait to collaborate with my biggest fans." Ellory reaches out an arm stacked with three Hermès bracelets and hands me the microphone.

I wonder if she still has her charm bracelet. The thought momentarily derails me. Composing myself, I continue, "Can everyone who's interested raise their hand?"

Almost every hand shoots up, and I have to take a step back from the force of air molecules shifting so abruptly.

"All right then!" I laugh with forced enthusiasm. "My daughter, Ila, has been awaiting her cue. She'll hand out the applications."

"Stepdaughter," Ila replies gruffly. She peers at me through squinty eyes.

"Oh, teenagers," I say, brushing off Ila's rude response. "Return the forms to me before leaving tonight. Now, everyone, please go enjoy the delicious coffee and treats." I glance at the refreshments set up in my store's café, inhaling the scent of chocolate.

As the women sip coffee and chat, Ellory steps toward me. "That went well." She pushes back her shoulders triumphantly.

Her ability to act like *This Morning America* never happened is mystifying. But then I remember how easy it is for her to redline the parts of her story that don't fit with her desired narrative.

"I'm over the moon about this competition!" A slender woman, who looks to be in her late twenties, moves toward Ellory with her copy of *The Prince of Silicon Valley: Book Four*. "Would you mind signing this for me?" She bends her tall body toward us as she hands Ellory a black fine-tipped Sharpie. "I missed the signing before the talk. My husband was supposed to be home by five but was late as usual. I couldn't leave my kids alone."

"I remember those days," Ellory says with a conspiratorial wink. "How old are your children?"

"I have a six-year-old, twin three-year-olds, and a baby!" The woman leans back, smiling as if she's just told a hilarious joke. I suppose you get lots of big reactions after you tell people you have four young children.

As if on cue, Ellory holds her hands to her face, stunned. "Wow! How do you do it? I bet your house is nonstop."

The woman leans close to Ellory. "I'm fairly certain I'm going crazy." She screws her eyes together and shrugs as she pushes a long blond strand of hair away from her face.

"Well, we're glad your husband eventually came home. Hand me your book so I can sign it. What's your name?"

"Faye."

Opening the Sharpie, Ellory presses its black point to a blank page in the front.

To my favorite mom, Faye. Thanks for being a fan, Ellory.

"Thanks so much," Faye says as she places the book in a beat-up diaper bag. "I really need something other than being a mom right now. Here's my application."

"Thanks," I say as I take the form from Faye.

"Great, well, I have to get home. My husband has texted ten times about getting the kids to bed. He's helpless." She shrugs her shoulders and walks toward the store's door.

I turn toward Ellory, realizing the applicants not chosen will be disappointed. "How are you going to decide who to choose for Ellory's Editors?"

"It doesn't matter," Ellory says at a short clip. She lowers her voice to a whisper. "This is all for social media to repair my image. It's not like any of these women could provide input that will improve my book. They have zero understanding of what the publishing industry demands."

And just like that, I'm reminded of how much Ellory has changed since becoming the world's most famous romance novelist. She acts like she's the main character and we're all just playing bit parts in the story of her life.

An image of the peach maid of honor dress I was supposed to wear to her wedding flies through my mind. It hangs in the back of my closet, with the tags still attached all these years later.

I need to stay one step ahead of Ellory.

CHAPTER 3
Faye Carter

P USHING MY GROCERY cart toward the car, my legs wobble from the weight of baby Griffin jostling in the sling strapped to my body. He grasps at my unwashed, greasy hair, pulling tightly.

"Milo, Emma, Ezra, hold hands and stay right next to me." Cars zoom around the busy parking lot. The Florida sun glares, blurring my vision. "Slow down," I shriek as Milo and my three-year-old twins pick up their pace, running full force to my SUV. "Give Mommy a second to open the door." If only I had a minivan. I could just hit a button, making the doors slide open, and my kids could crawl into the car without my help.

But my husband, Mark, insisted on the sports utility, even though I begged for a minivan. If he thinks this bulky vehicle disguises that this is a family car, he's wrong. The dinged-up doors and smell of sour milk are beacons declaring this is a vehicle whose only purpose is to cart around children.

I grunt as I load my kids into car seats and put the grocery bags in the back.

"Mommy, we play bingo?" Ezra squeals in excitement as I pull up to the driveway of our home. My twins love to play bingo every single day.

"Bingo!" Emma repeats as I shift the car into park.

"Let Mommy put the groceries away. Then I have to make dinner. Maybe you guys can play bingo while I cook?"

"No!" Emma and Ezra yell out their opposition. My ears ring from their piercing, high-pitched squeals. Griffin, who was sleeping, wails.

The pressure of tears builds behind my eyes, but I can't give in to my emotions. I have too much to do. Needing a distraction, I reach into my diaper bag and pull out Ellory Brayson's latest book. It was a thrill to meet her last night.

Get the kids unloaded and then go read for ten minutes. The words swoop through my mind, giving me the energy I need to unsnap four sets of car seats, haul in the groceries, and put my kids in front of the TV. I plop baby Griffin into his swing.

"Mommy's going upstairs for a few minutes. I'll be down to cook dinner soon."

"But bingo," Ezra groans.

"Milo will play with you," I say, clutching Ellory's new book like a safety blanket. I quickly turn and walk upstairs to my room. Dropping my body onto the bed, I know I won't have long. Within minutes, one of my kids will need something, or the baby will fuss.

I run my hands over the pristine cover of the last book in *The Prince of Silicon Valley* series. My eyes settle on the drawing of a couple sitting at computers with their backs to each other. Whimsical illustrations of Silicon Valley's best-known high-tech campuses surround them.

I crack open the book's stiff spine, inhaling the scent of fresh pages. Excitement mixes with anticipation as I remember where the last book left off. A moment later, I'm immersed in the fictional world of Lexi and Theo.

> Does Theo really believe I've been trying to destroy his company? He's oblivious to the truth. I could never ruin him. How could I annihilate the most perfect smile, the most entrancing eyes, and the person who makes my blood alternate between a raging boil and a sensual simmer?

"I dare you, Lexi," he says, as his eyes sweep over my body. "I absolutely dare you. Take one more step toward me, and my security team will be dragging your ass out of here." He glances at my backside as he speaks, and I can tell he's pleased.

"Mommy! Mom! Mama!" My brain jerks as I hear Ezra calling from downstairs. I look at the clock. I had twelve minutes of peace. That's better than yesterday.

Thumbing down the top corner of the page, I place the book on my nightstand. Time to make dinner. Maybe, just maybe, I can read after everyone eats.

CHAPTER 4

Harper Weiss

RE: Query for *The Broken-Hearted Barista*

Dear Harper,

Thank you for submitting your manuscript to me for review. While I'm privileged to be one of the literary agents you considered to represent your novel, unfortunately, I was not as taken by your pages as I hoped to be. I am going to pass. Best of luck in finding the right representation.

MY EYES SHIFT left to right as I read the rejection from my dream agent. My heart rocks in my chest. This is the sixty-third time an agent has passed on my book. I'm losing hope. I should have asked Ellory Brayson for advice on publishing the other night. But I wasted my question on true love.

I can't help but wonder if agents would be more interested in signing me if I had completed Columbia University's writing program as I had planned. But life happened and that dream never became a reality.

"Harper, your new patient's here." My office manager, Jill, pushes her head through the door to my cramped office.

Relieved I won't have time to parse each word of the agent's rejection, I hit delete and turn to face her. Her eyelids, coated in sparkly blue eye shadow, contrast with her bright pink hair. A few coarse gray strands frame her face. My occupational therapy patients love Miss Jill and her larger-than-life personality. And she's become like a second mother to me.

Handing me a file, Jill sits on the kid-sized chair pushed up against the corner of my office. Her pink neon-colored scrubs glow against the drab beige walls. "I wanted to give you a chance to review these records before you meet your next patient, Wyatt. His dad just handed me the medical history." She smiles and the timeworn lines on her face deepen.

"Thanks, Jill. What would I do without you? Between having my back at work and babysitting for Ryder. You are my fairy godmother."

Jill stands and twirls as if she has a magic wand in her hand. "Well, speaking of fairy godmothers. Maybe I can put a love spell on you and this patient's father. He's dreamy."

I open the file only half listening. Jill is always trying to set me up with someone.

> Patient: Wyatt Silver, age seven
> Primary Diagnosis: ADHD and possible Sensory Processing Disorder (Hyposensitivity)

"And they just moved to Jupiter Cove from Miami. This dad is trying to give his son a slower way of life."

I look up at Jill, who's been talking this entire time.

She's about to walk out the door of my office. "Maybe run to the bathroom before you get Wyatt. Whoosh your hair or something. I'm telling you, this dad is cute! And he's Jewish!"

"Oh, Jill, you're on a mission to find me a nice Jewish boy. You can't force these things." I nod, as if amused, but a pang of embarrassment titters through my chest. My love life has been nonexistent for longer than I can remember. "Tell them I'll be out in five minutes."

Leaning back in my chair, I finish reviewing Wyatt's history. According to his dad, Wyatt is clumsy, fidgety, and craves constant stimulation. Closing the file, I stand and walk toward the waiting room. At the last minute, I duck into the bathroom. My heart-shaped face glows with a greenish hue from the bathroom's fluorescent lighting. Flipping my head over, I shake out my long brown curls, hoping to infuse volume into my unruly mane.

Leaning into the sink, I push my face close to the mirror. I wish I had put on mascara. My blue eyes have always been my best feature. I don't do enough to give them the spotlight they deserve.

Oh well, Wyatt Silver's dad may be a catch, but there's no chance I'm going to catch his eye. I've been a single mom for eleven years and I don't expect that to change. I'm twenty-eight and most men my age aren't looking for an insta-family. Anyway, this is about Wyatt and his treatment plan. My professional brain takes over running through the evaluation I plan to complete. I'll start with gross motor skills, I think, as I flick off the bathroom light and walk to the waiting room.

"Wyatt Silver," I say, stepping around the corner into an area filled with chairs, magazines, and beat-up children's toys. Before I can blink, a boy comes barreling toward me.

"Me!" he says, roaring his response. He runs full force, as if he's a linebacker playing in the Super Bowl. His body crashes into mine, and I stumble back. As I wobble to catch my balance, my foot catches on the edge of a stool piled high with books. My body sways back and forth, and then I'm crashing to the ground. My left foot twists as I hit the floor.

"Oh, no!" I inhale a sharp breath to ease the pain. "I think I might have broken my ankle." My words quiver.

"Wyatt!" I can hear a man's voice but can't see his face. It must be Wyatt's dad. He puts his hand on my shoulder from behind and helps me sit up.

"Is this okay?" he says. "I don't want to hurt you more."

"It really hurts," I grunt. "I may have broken it." The pain pushes tears from my eyes and wet drips fall around me.

"I'm so sorry." As Wyatt's dad speaks, he shifts his body from behind, so we're facing each other. "I'm Ben Silver, Wyatt's dad."

Like a lightning strike, my pain vanishes. The eyes peering into mine have swallowed me whole. They are deep jade and outlined with flecks of gold. As I lose myself in his soft brown curls and angular jaw, I realize that intense attraction is the most effective form of pain relief known to man.

"I'm so sorry," Ben says again. "This is exactly why he needs OT. He has a problem with space and boundaries." His eyes move away from mine. His face twists with distress.

"Can you move your ankle?" Jill looks at me with concern, and I shake my head no. "You may need to go to the hospital." She crouches on the floor and inserts her face between Ben and me.

Move out of the way, I think. I can't see Ben's eyes.

"I can take her to the hospital." Ben looks at Jill.

No, look back at me. My heart kicks in my chest.

Wyatt, who's been sitting on the floor with his legs crossed at a safe distance, slides his backside across the floor toward me. "I'm in trouble. I'm bad."

"Wyatt," Ben says calmly. "You did not hurt Ms. Weiss on purpose, but you owe her an apology." Ben's voice is the exact right combination of sternness and warmth.

"I'm sorry." Wyatt sniffles.

I do my best to smile as a sliver of sharp pain resurfaces.

"Oh, honey, you don't look so good." Jill notices as I wince. "I wish I had my car so I could take you to the hospital. But it's in the shop. Do you want Wyatt's dad to drive you?" She leans into me as a brief flicker of excitement overtakes her face.

"M-Maybe," I stammer. It seems strange to let my patient's dad drive me to the hospital, but what other choice do I have? I'm not going to call an ambulance. "Let's see if I can get to the car." I push the words out through shudders of agony.

"Don't move." Ben looks at me, then shifts his gaze to Wyatt. "Let's go pull the car around to the front. He runs his hand through his curls, and I'm desperate to know how they feel.

Jill rubs my back in a comforting motion as Ben and Wyatt leave to get the car. I wrestle through the discomfort. "I think I'll be okay," I say through gritted teeth.

Jill's face brightens. "Oh, honey, I think you're going to be more than okay. I'll come along to make sure." Her eyes suddenly gleam with mischief. "Not exactly the love spell I would have chosen to kick off this romance, but Cupid works in mysterious ways."

CHAPTER 5

Ellory Brayson

BOOKS ARE STACKED in every corner of Tabby's office. Papers lay across her desk in neat piles. A vibrant purple floor-to-ceiling bookshelf lines the entire left wall. Each shelf is organized by color, creating a rainbow of books evoking a sense of wonderment. The charm of her office overtakes me, making me believe we can discuss anything in this magical place. Even our past.

Tabby picks up the file sitting on the table in front of the oversized plush couch where we're seated. "Let's go through the applications for Ellory's Editors. It's been a few days since the event. You need to decide on the editors."

Her voice breaks my trance, and I shift back into Celebrity Ellory. This is not the time to go soft. Spending my summer in Jupiter Cove is going to save my career. I'll just keep pretending we're friends.

Tabby's motives for faking our friendship are easy to understand. I'm sure her independent bookstore is barely surviving the online competition. And she'll make a good amount of money as the exclusive retailer of *The Prince of Silicon Valley* series.

I read the first few lines of one editor's application. *"I'm an avid reader and a Jupiter Cove native. You should incorporate this town into your new book. And to be frank, we could use the tourism dollars.'* Pass," I say. "This woman has an agenda."

Tabby's eyes balloon into saucers. "Ellory, this is not the cutthroat literary world of New York. These are just regular people."

"Maybe," I say. "But once you become famous, everyone's working an angle." I can't expect Tabby to understand, so I drop it.

"Who's next?" she asks as I take out another application.

"This one says: *'Reading is my escape. And I love nothing more than escaping into a good romance novel. I'm desperate for the caring and thoughtful relationships you portray in your books. Your male characters have such emotional depth. Maybe I married the wrong man, or the men in your books don't really exist? I read seventy-five books last year, and I have a popular Bookstagram account, so this is right up my alley. Thanks for considering.'"*

"Hmmm, I like it," I say, but then notice the applicant is forty-seven years old. "I'll put it in the maybe pile. And can I get a refill on my wine?"

Tabby grabs the Prosecco, chilling in an ice bucket on the table.

I read another one as she tops off my glass. "*'Ellory, you need to add more sex and spice to your books. Erotica is where it's at!'* This must be the lady that hijacked my reading. At least she's no longer using the word smut," I say with a slight giggle.

Tabby gasps in laughter.

Tabby and I deserve Oscars for our ability to act like there's not an elephant in the room. "Wait, she wrote more," I say. "*'Ellory, have you been on TikTok? The site is overflowing with women who are begging for steamy romance novels. I'm talking SMUT. Millions of women rely on a sexy novel and vibrator. Don't miss out on this market.'"*

"Oh, my God. Hilarious." Tabby cackles.

Genuine tears of laughter spill from my eyes. The wine is forcing me to push Celebrity Ellory aside. "This TikTok thing is real," I declare, with the assurance of a world leader speaking to the United Nations. "I follow hundreds of women dedicated to reading spicy novels." Grabbing my phone, I open my TikTok app. "Here, look."

"Wait, what account is this?" Tabby asks. "I know you have your official Ellory Brayson TikTok account. Who's @KarenSmith72?"

"Oh, it's my dummy account," I say. "I use it to play around, keep an eye on what other authors are doing, see what readers in my genre are talking about."

"Oh, smart," Tabby says.

"Yeah, well, I pay for that smart in the form of a very expensive publicist. But she's the best in the biz. Her idea for Ellory's Editors is going to explode on social."

Tabby takes a tiny sip from her full glass of Prosecco. "Yes, I'm excited to see how it plays out and thankful Blast Off Books will be at the center."

Tabby's emotional honesty momentarily silences our banter. The room is suddenly deafeningly quiet. I rush to fill the awkwardness. "Here, let me show you some of these TikTok videos. You won't believe it." I type a few hashtags in the search bar: #smutbooks, #steamyromancebooks, #spicybooks, #momswhoreadsmut.

The first video I play is a mom begging for a steamy audiobook that will fog her windows on the way home from carpool.

Tabby and I fall over laughing. For just a moment, it feels like the old days, before our relationship splintered.

CHAPTER 6
Tabitha Wilson

"I CAN'T BELIEVE YOU'RE renting the Rutherford Estate for the summer." As my car slows, I admire the huge, square-shaped windows that wrap around the modern two-story house. Spacious balconies line the bright white structure. The mansion's geometric shape contrasts sharply with the gentle curve of the beach behind it. "A million-dollar view of the ocean," I say, shifting my car's gear into park.

"Remember that time the Rutherfords were having a Fourth of July party and we snuck in?" Ellory turns her head and glances down at the beach as if our past is a movie she's watching.

"Who could forget?" We grabbed the first two things we could get our hands on—two bowls filled with tiny translucent pearls of caviar—and ran out the door. We took one bite and then promptly spit it out.

My mouth waters as if I've just taken a spoonful of the slimy delicacy. Looking at the beach, I picture Ellory running ahead of me with the reckless energy of a ten-year-old girl who had done something mischievous. Orange dots trailed behind her in the beige sand as she dropped clumps of caviar on the shoreline.

"Do you want to come in and check it out?" Ellory gathers her designer tote bag and steps out of my car.

"I'd love to, but I need to get home." My shoulders sag, but I quickly push them back, hoping Ellory didn't see evidence of my distress.

"Is something wrong?"

My insides buzz as if tiny insects are crawling under my skin. I will never be vulnerable with Ellory ever again. She betrayed me. I must stay focused on my goal—help with Ellory's book launch and get the money I need to move forward. I will not share my secrets.

Loosening my jaw, I spread my lips into a smile. "I'm fine. Just tired."

"That's my girl," Ellory says, satisfied with her efforts. "I'll call you tomorrow after I think more about who to choose for Ellory's Editors."

That's my girl? My mind swirls the comment round and round as I drive away. What did she mean by that? Her remark makes my insides burn. She relied on me. Not the other way around. I barely recall a time when she wasn't present—after school, on weekends, at family dinners, and even on holidays, when her mother would join us. With her father walking out, and her mother working all the time, she orbited my family as if we were the sun tugging her along by gravitational force.

AS I PULL up to my house, I notice Ila's car's not in the driveway. I sigh, frustrated she's broken curfew again. I'm sure she's with her boyfriend, aware her dad's working an EMT night shift. *How did I become the hated stepmother?*

Between Ila and Ellory, I'm not sure how I'm going to survive the summer. Doesn't Ellory realize how insane it is that she's back in Jupiter Cove? We haven't seen each other since she got engaged over twenty years ago. Any attempts we've made at staying in touch have been superficial. A comment on an Insta post, a text here and there, a plan to talk on the phone that we cancel at the last minute because we're both terrified to say the things that must be said.

That's why it was so surprising when Ellory sent me a text this past spring that sounded borderline desperate.

> **Ellory:** Need to escape NY. Having writer's block. I'm renting the Rutherford Estate from Memorial Day through Labor Day. Can't wait to be back in Jupiter Cove and get away from all the bullshit.

As I read the words, my stomach tightened. Was she bringing Prince Maximilian? It was a question I couldn't ask. A week later, she texted again to let me know that neither Maxy (as she calls him) or her nineteen-year-old son, Cade, would be joining. Relief at this bit of information coursed through me, as if Buddha himself had enveloped me in blissful peace.

But tonight, as we spent one-on-one time together, I grew tense. It was a relief to drop her at the Rutherford Estate and head home.

Now that I unexpectedly have the house to myself, I'm certain I did the right thing by declining her invitation to come inside. We have all summer to spend time together. My skin prickles as I consider endless hours in the company of Ellory. I shrug my shoulders up and down until the discomfort dissipates.

Entering my bedroom, I know exactly how I'm going to spend my night alone. I open my nightstand and see my stack of books on infertility. My stomach knots. This is the reason I must pretend with Ellory. The money from her book sales is the only way Andre and I can afford another round of infertility treatment. It's our last hope of having a baby.

Pushing the stack aside, I find what I'm looking for, tucked inside a nondescript paper bag. My two companions for the evening. Scarlett St. Clair's *A Touch of Darkness* and my toy the Stallion Satisfier Pro. If Ellory only knew I was the queen of spicy TikTok.

Sex for Andre and I is a series of lab experiments. There's no passion, no lust, no desire. Charts, ovulation schedules, and doctor visits control us.

Laying my book and toy on the bed, I open *A Touch of Darkness* to where I left off.

CHAPTER 7
Ila Wilson

MY CAR SKIRTS along A1A. The blue ocean races alongside my window and the smell of salt hangs in the air. Taylor Swift plays. My stomach clenches as an unwelcome image of my mom invades my mind. My voice softens into a tremble as I sing the lyrics that reminds me I'm in this mother-daughter relationship with Tabby, but my motherly love is really for someone else. Someone who lied. Someone who left me and never looked back.

My car bounces around as I pull onto the gravel lot that leads to Venus Inlet. All the inlets in Jupiter Cove are named after planets. And all the businesses in town are on theme. Including the restaurant where I work part time, Meteor Café.

Opening my car door, my feet crunch along the crushed-up shells that lead down to the mouth of the water. The waist-high rocks circling this inlet sparkle in the afternoon sun.

Most in Jupiter Cove avoid this inlet, because the sand is sparse. Instead, small rocks cover the area leading up to the cool water. It's not a great inlet for lying down and getting comfortable. People my age prefer Saturn Inlet. It has the same cover of waist-high rocks for privacy but a wide expanse of sand where people can meet for a tryst under the cover of night.

I know Tabby thinks I've snuck off to be with Jackson. For a moment I picture myself grabbing Tabby's hand, pulling her close, and telling her Jackson and I broke up. I can almost feel her wrap her arm around my shoulders and comfort me about the breakup.

But I quickly shrug my shoulders, shoving the image of a loving mother-daughter interaction out of my mind. I've pushed Tabby away and now there's no turning back.

I think back to the first time I met Tabby. I was eight years old. It was hard for me to wrap my head around her sudden presence in my life. And she was so much younger than my dad. Why would she be interested in someone fifteen years older than her? I didn't understand why my dad felt a need to tangle our lives with this new addition.

My dad and I had suffered through the absence of my mom together. And although it gutted us both, we had come out stronger. We were like two elements that collided together as one after an experiment gone wrong—bonded and unbreakable.

After witnessing the way my mom pulverized my dad's heart, it was hard to let him take a chance on Tabby. I acted like a brat, throwing tantrums over silly things, tossing gifts Tabby gave me into the trash, and naming the kitten she got me Cruella. But eventually, something softened, and at age ten, when Tabby and my dad married, it thrilled me to walk her down the aisle.

Sitting on the rough ground, I push my hands through the rocks and stretch my feet out, so my toes dip into the cool water. Our first year as an official family was bliss. Poised and confident, Tabby stepped into the role of mom gracefully. There was never a moment that felt awkward or forced. It wasn't until Tabby and my dad realized they were having trouble getting pregnant that things fell apart. Suddenly, every conversation, every moment, and every effort focused on having a second child.

Our blissful life vanished. My existence, the child right before them, suddenly seemed irrelevant. My presence felt pointless, as extraneous as the unending pile of rock bits pushing against my hands.

CHAPTER 8
Faye Carter

GRIFFIN SPLASHES IN the bath while I read Ellory's book. Water trickles over the side of the tub as he pounds with more and more force. Yellow rubber ducks bob up and down as water swirls around his bath seat.

"Want out?" My words sound sharp, as if I'm a CEO who's been interrupted during an important meeting. It's not fair for me to snap at Baby G, but I haven't had one moment of peace all day. I was looking forward to getting in fifteen minutes of reading while G played in the bath. But, apparently, he has other plans.

I tuck Ellory's book in a towel and put it on the counter by the sink so it will stay dry.

Griffin's body drips with soapy water as I lift him from the tub. Thinking a few steps ahead, I call out to the twins. "Emma, Ezra, you need to get your pajamas on and clean up bingo." Drying off Griffin, I lay him on the changing table and rub lotion on his small body. I'm so tired I can barely stand. As I zip up his sleep sack, Emma and Ezra run into the room completely naked.

"Why aren't you in your pajamas?" I stare at Emma and Ezra's bare bodies as they circle me with enough energy to launch a rocket to the moon. A wave of fury sweeps through me. *"Stop!"* I blurt. "Pajamas now!"

Startled by my harsh tone, they freeze and look up. But instead of apologizing for my forceful manner, I use the opportunity to scold them further.

"And you still haven't cleaned up bingo. The cards and chips are in the middle of the hallway. Get it done now."

As they scamper out of Baby G's room, I hate myself for the way I blow up at them. This type of outburst is happening more and more lately.

After putting Baby G in his crib, I stomp downstairs. Mark sits in his leather lazy chair, drinking a beer while watching soccer. Milo sits on the floor in front of him. *Typical.*

A bloom of heat pulses through my chest. "Mark, I need some help upstairs. I can't do bedtime all by myself every night."

Mark moves his eyes away from the flat screen, looks at me, and sighs. "What do you mean? I'm helping with Milo." He quickly puts his beer down and rubs his hand through Milo's dark hair to prove his point.

Milo glances at me with a goofy grin.

"Milo can do everything he needs to do by himself. I need help with the little ones." I try to keep my tone neutral, but my voice is tight, like a rubber band about to snap.

Mark squints his eyes as if I'm a bothersome light that's suddenly turned on in the middle of the night. He looks back toward the soccer game, unwilling to engage in another round of the same fight we've been having since the twins were born.

"Be up in a few minutes," he grumbles.

"Fine." Turning abruptly, I take the stairs two at a time, fueled by irritation. Grabbing Ezra's Spider-Man pajamas, I find him sitting naked on the floor next to a trail of bingo chips. "Mommy, no. Yoda pajamas," he wails.

As the minutes tick by, I wonder how I fell in love with Mark. *Was he always this selfish? Was I always this angry?*

I picture myself when we first met. I'm perched at the desk of Sunquest Bank, attempting to get through a line of people making transactions during lunch hour. I was great at my job as a teller, and Mr. Kitler, the branch manager, said I was a perfect candidate for the bank's career advancement training program.

I carefully tallied a deposit Mark was making on behalf of the car repair shop where he was an assistant manager. He was friendly, but I honestly don't recall feeling any special thrill. He became a regular, coming in every Friday afternoon, and making the repair shop's deposit right before closing. What I remember most is how his hands were always greasy, and the money he handed over was sullied with gray streaks.

One particular Friday, he came in only minutes before closing. It was the first time I'd ever seen him out of his mechanic's uniform. I was stunned. The muscles in his arms were well-defined. His dark black hair, ordinarily slick and messy, framed his face in a neat, thick pile. My eyes could not help but settle on the perfect dimple that appeared on the left side of his face when he smiled.

I helped him with his transaction as we had a friendly conversation about Florida University's football team. We both grew up on FLA-U football. We lingered for a few moments, debating the merits of the new playboy coach that would lead the team this season.

"I have tickets to the USC game in a few weeks. It's going to be a barn burner," he said.

"Yes!" I interjected before he could continue. "I love when we play teams in other conferences."

Mark nodded enthusiastically, enjoying my passion for college football. "I'd love you to come with me."

I froze for just a moment, thrilled by his invitation. "Sure," I blurted, aware my excitement had everything to do with Mark and nothing to do with the game.

"Mommy, I can't find my bunny!" A look of panic washes over Emma's face. Before I can respond, I hear Griffin whimper.

"Mark!" I scream in frustration, realizing it's been twenty minutes since I asked him for help.

Emma tugs on my arm. "Mr. Bunny lost," she mumbles in a croaky voice.

Griffin continues to fuss. My pulse zooms through my body, almost knocking me over.

Glancing under Emma's bed, relief releases my core. "I see Mr. Bunny!" I point to where his ragged ear's peeking out.

Emma skips and embraces her favorite lovey in a tight hug.

A few minutes later, after I've settled Griffin, Mark appears. He walks toward me, but I step around him as I bend down to the floor in the hallway, picking up the bingo cards and chips the twins never cleaned up.

"Sorry," Mark says half-heartedly. "The other team scored, tying up the game. I wanted to see what happened."

"I'm at the end of my rope," I bark as I hurl a pile of bright green bingo chips into the game's plastic container. I stop for a moment and stare at the bingo cards in my hand. Suddenly, a strange thought enters my mind.

"I feel like our marriage is a game of bingo. When I feel unsupported, it's like we fill in a square. If we fill in an entire row, what does that mean?" The cards tremble in my hand.

"Oh, Faye, don't be so dramatic." Mark looks at the ceiling, too frustrated to look me in the eye.

"Dramatic? Are you kidding? Do you think I'm putting on a show? These are my genuine emotions, Mark. But I know emotions are not your thing. You'd rather I bottle everything up and just smile."

"You're being ridiculous, Faye. I just wanted to see what happened with the game. You used to be so relaxed. We used to have so much fun together, going to football games and hanging out. It's like you're a completely different person now." His words rush out in a sharp, angry burst.

"I'm not a different person," I snap back. "I'm the same person, who's trying to take care of four small children. Practically by myself! I've told you I need a nanny or to put the twins in childcare, but you refuse." Suddenly, my chest is heaving, as if my heart is a bomb only moments away from exploding. "I need to get out of here!" I push past Mark, run down the stairs, and fly out our front door.

As soon as I step outside, I take several deep breaths. This is the third "walk" I've needed to take this week. Mark and I are fighting all the time. I wish I had a friend to talk to, but I've lost touch with everyone since being completely swept away by my responsibilities as a mom. *Has Mark always been this emotionally disconnected?*

My mind races back to a conversation Mark and I had after we'd been together for over a year. It was the first time I witnessed Mark completely sidestep my difficult emotions.

"Why do you keep staring at the student section?" he asked as we cheered on the FLA-U Crocodiles.

"I don't know," I said apprehensively. "I'm a bit fascinated and a bit jealous. I always planned to go to college, but after my dad was injured at his construction job, it didn't happen. I was the only one who could take care of him." I thought about my mom dying from cancer and my dad's twisted spine. Mark knew the basics, but we never talked about it. My eyes filled with tears.

He looked at me, unsure of what to say. He quickly skipped the subject of my parents and bounced back to the topic of school. "Oh, man, I couldn't wait to get out of high school. It's amazing I even got a diploma." He chuckled.

I recall the pang I felt when I realized Mark wasn't willing to engage in a conversation with me about my parents. And then, only a few months later, when my dad suffered a fatal stroke, Mark didn't know how to get into the emotional muck with me and wade around in the mess.

As I round the block and walk to my front door, it occurs to me the difference between this version of myself and the one Mark met all those years ago is that motherhood has made me more emotional. Having children is an experience filled with highs and lows. It's not that I've changed, it's just that Mark swallows his feelings, and needs me to do the same.

Ping. My phone rings out as soon as I step back into the house. I glance down at a text from an unfamiliar number.

Unknown: Hi, Faye. Congratulations. This is Ellory. You've been chosen as one of Ellory's Editors. I know you have a lot of responsibility, so let me know if this works. Our first meeting will take place at Blast Off Books on Friday, June 16th.

As I read the words, my heart dances in my chest. This is exactly what I need, something outside of mothering. Determined to make this work, I plod up the stairs to find Mark.

CHAPTER 9

Harper Weiss

BEN SITS BESIDE me while Ms. Jill entertains Wyatt with an assortment of trinkets she keeps in her purse.

"I feel awful," Ben says as he stares ahead, pushing a hand through his luminous hair. "The nurse went to get you a wheelchair. I'll have you home soon."

Turning to look at Ben's profile, his face doubles, then triples. "Why are there so many of you?" I ask, loopy from pain medicine. I lean my head onto his shoulder and snuggle in as if he's a giant teddy bear. And then, suddenly, I'm falling face-first into his lap.

"Whoa! You okay Harper?"

I feel Ben's hand on my shoulder as he gently shifts my face to the side. My right cheek nestles into his thighs. I look out into the space before me and see Wyatt and Jill pushing a dinosaur through a pile of Styrofoam cups. The image bobs and sways. Something inside me understands it should embarrass me I've just plopped my face into a total stranger's lap in the most inappropriate way. But I'm too out of it to fully comprehend the situation.

"Here we are." A fuzzy image approaches and parks a wheelchair beside me. "Let's help her sit up, and then we'll get her into the chair," the unfamiliar voice continues.

Suddenly, I feel two sets of hands on me as I'm carefully hoisted out of Ben's lap and back into a sitting position.

"Harper, I'm Becky. I'm going to help you stand, but you need to keep your left foot off the ground. We have it wrapped up. Can you feel the weight of the bandages?"

"Oh," I say groggily, suddenly aware of the pressure engulfing my left foot.

"I'm going to have your husband help me lift you up, and then we'll get you into the chair," Becky continues.

"My husband?" My words sound slow and strange.

Ben looks at me and grins. He places an arm around my shoulders. "Lean into me."

As I push my body next to his, I can smell sandalwood mixed with soap. "You smell so good. Mmmm."

I hear Becky laugh as she steps in close to Ben. "Looks like the pain meds are hitting your wife pretty hard. Get her into bed as soon as you get home, and she'll sleep it off."

"Your wife," I mumble into Ben's ear.

"Okay, on the count of three," I hear Becky say. "One, two, three…" They magically hoist my body up and into the wheelchair.

"We did it," Becky says with enthusiasm. "Your husband is fabulous." She winks at me and nods at Ben.

"He's so gorgeous." I nod, trying to copy Becky's wink. "And he's Jewish!" I feel a bit of drool dribble down my chin as the word "Jewish" slowly drags from my mouth.

Ben laughs as Becky wheels me toward the emergency room exit.

"I SAID WHAT?"

Jill sits on the corner of my bed, giggling with laughter. "You were really out of it, honey. I wouldn't worry about it."

"This is humiliating," I say as I sit up and lean against my pillow. As soon as I shuffle my body around, my ankle throbs with pain.

"Oh no, you okay?" Jill glances at me as evidence of my discomfort consumes my face.

"To be honest," I say. "I'm kinda fuzzy on what the doctor recommended. Can you fill me in?"

Grabbing an unused pillow from my bed, Jill places it behind me against the headboard. "Is that more comfortable?"

I nod.

"The doctor said you don't need surgery, so that's great news!" She smiles widely. "But you're going to need to have this cast on for six weeks."

I can feel my eyes bulge. "Practically the entire summer." I groan.

"Well, the cast is waterproof," she replies cheerily.

"And how am I supposed to get around?" It's a question, but it comes out sounding more like an accusation.

"You have crutches. You'll learn to use them in no time." Jill points to the crutches leaning against the wall next to my night table.

"But my parents are in Europe for the summer. I can't ask my mom to help." I turn my face away from Jill and stare out the window across from my bed blankly.

Jill gently lays back in the space beside me. "I've canceled all your patients for the next few days to give you time to recuperate and get comfortable on crutches."

"But I can't drive with this cast on my leg." An anxious pang fills my chest. "How will I get to work, to the grocery store, and take Ryder to and from camp?"

Jill speaks. "It's all worked out, Harper. We've got you covered."

"We?" I ask as my body tenses.

"Remember that love spell I wanted to put on you?" She winks.

"Oh no. No. No. Tell me this has nothing to do with the cute dad I humiliated myself in front of." I can feel heat creep up my neck.

"Listen, Harper," Jill says, turning to face me directly. "Ben feels terrible. Just awful. He knows what Wyatt did was an accident, but he feels one hundred percent responsible. He's volunteered to pick up Ryder for camp and take you to work until you can manage on your own." It's hard to ignore how happily she delivers this piece of news. It's as if she has just told me I won the lottery.

"No way," I bark. "There's no way I'm accepting help from a total stranger." I shake my head back and forth like a petulant child.

"It's really not that big of a deal. When Ben pulled up to your house, he said he lives just a few blocks away. Wyatt's attending the same camp as Ryder, so it's not an imposition. I wish I could help you myself, but as you know, Howie requires my care."

A wave of guilt grabs me. Howie, Jill's husband, has Alzheimer's. He's still living at home, but Jill takes him to a memory care facility each morning and picks him up each evening.

"Speaking of Howie, I've arranged for my sister to stay with him tonight so I can be here with you. The doctor doesn't want you hobbling around on your crutches by yourself during the first twenty-four hours."

"What about Ryder?" I ask.

"He's downstairs watching *Star Wars*. He wants to see you. Can I send him up to say hi?"

I'm quiet as I mull over all the plans made for me as I slept off pain meds. "It's just that I feel really uncomfortable letting Ben take such a big chunk of these responsibilities."

"I understand. But sometimes we need to accept the help that's offered." Jill's doing nothing to hide the excitement in her voice. "Can I go get Ryder now?" she asks again.

I nod my head as I glance at Ellory Brayson's book on my nightstand. It mocks me as the plot points for a cheesy romance novel take over my life.

CHAPTER 10
Ellory Brayson

MY EYES SLUGGISHLY scan the bedroom. It takes a moment to remember I'm waking up in the grand master bedroom of the Rutherford Estate and not my New York City apartment. I've only been in Jupiter Cove for a week. I'm still adjusting.

Wide swaths of sunlight streak through the floor-to-ceiling windows, making the bright white tile floor glow. Sitting up, I grab the glass of water by my bedside table and gulp greedily.

My throat is scratchy after spending an hour late last night screaming at my agent. After a long day of working on my next novel, I went on TikTok as @KarenSmith72 to check out the newest post from my romance author nemesis, Nadine Laurel. It shocked me to see her latest book, *Love, Lies, and Little Secrets,* is being released two months early. Celebrity Ellory quickly took action, commenting on Nadine's post as @KarenSmith72—*Your new book sounds like an out-of-date eighties novel.*

"What the actual fuck?" I bellowed into the phone as my agent, Joel, muddled his way through excuses about why my next release is pushed back, while hers is launching early. I continued to bark expletives at him for the next twenty minutes. "I'm one book away from looking for a new agent," I screamed before hanging up the phone.

Curious to see if my comment about Nadine's new title has gained any traction, I grab my phone from the bedside table. I'm surprised to see several missed texts from Maxy. We've been giving each other the silent treatment since he confessed his affair.

I push my finger down on my messages and start reading. There's a string of texts. At first, I'm confused because I start reading from the most recent text to the first.

> **Maxy:** He's out, and my attorney had the charges dropped, but there are photos all over the internet, and fucking TMZ picked it up

> **Maxy:** I just don't give a fuck anymore

> **Maxy:** Is this acceptable behavior

> **Maxy:** I have my family name to think about

What's Maxy blowing up about? My temples pulse. He's the one screwing every twenty-nothing-year-old that moves. But as I keep reading the texts, the subject matter becomes clear.

> **Maxy:** He failed out of Stanford (and after we spent a small fortune getting him in!)

> **Maxy:** He's wandering around Miami without a care in the world

> **Maxy:** He's acting out since we told him we're getting divorced

> **Maxy:** Cade got arrested last night for marijuana possession!

My anger relaxes into something pliable as soon as I read the word Cade. The only person I'm soft for in this world is my son.

Pounding my phone, I type Cade's name into the search bar. Several links pop up.

> Son of royal prince Maximilian Jacoby and romance writer royalty Ellory Brayson arrested for possession outside of a Miami nightclub. More bad news for the author, who's already at the center of a controversial encounter with a fan.

Glancing back through Maxy's texts, I reread the most recent one.

> **Maxy:** He's out, and my attorney had the charges dropped

Immediately, I dial Cade's number to confirm he's okay and to figure out what the hell happened. My body bristles with fear when it goes straight to voicemail.

"Call me as soon as you get this. I know you're just being a nine-teen-year-old, but we need to talk."

A moment later, my phone buzzes with a text from my publicist with a detailed strategy for managing this event with the media.

> **Amber:** We're going to lean into America's changing relationship with marijuana. The pot Cade was caught with would be perfectly legal in states like Colorado and California. But I need to talk to Cade. I'm having trouble reaching him. Can you have him call me?

I glance at the time on my phone. *Cade, where are you?* It's ten in the morning. I'm supposed to meet Tabby at her bookstore in thirty minutes to choose my second editor. There's no way I'll make it in time. I need to call Amber before I do anything else. I dial the number.

"SHE'S ALIVE." TABBY'S organizing a table of Abby Jimenez titles when I walk through the door of Blast Off Books almost ninety minutes late.

My expression must give away my concerns about Cade, because she immediately places a stack of books with red and yellow covers to the side and steps toward me.

"Are you okay?" Tabby continues.

"Maybe you haven't seen the news," I say, "but the internet is buzzing with Cade's arrest last night." The words drag from my mouth. I still haven't reached Cade.

"What?" Tabby looks at me with worry. "I had no idea, Ellory. I'm sorry." She walks toward me and leads me to one of the café tables tucked neatly in the corner of her store.

"What happened?" she says with genuine concern. "Is Cade okay?"

I relay the details of the text messages from Maxy. "The thing is," I continue, "no one can get in touch with Cade. Maxy and I have been calling him all morning, but he's not picking up."

Tabby presses her hand over her heart. It's a small gesture, but it reminds me how comforting it is to have a friend. Celebrity Ellory hasn't allowed me to get close to anyone in over a decade.

"Cade's usually lazy about responding to me, but after an event like last night, I would think he'd call or at least text to confirm he's alive." My body trembles with worry.

"Do you know where he's staying in Miami? We can hop in the car and drive down there. It's only about two hours." Tabby grabs my hand from across the table and squeezes it reassuringly. Her touch causes my heart to swell.

"Maxy has people on the ground in Miami Beach. He's working with his connections to get a rundown of where Cade used his credit card in the last twenty-four hours." I glance away, so I don't cry. Celebrity Ellory quickly kicks in, not allowing me another moment of vulnerability. "Anyway, let's just move on to choosing the second editor. I need to get this done, so my publicist has something to focus on besides Cade's poor choices."

"Sure," Tabby says, following my lead. "So, we don't have a ton of options since your publicist is concerned about age."

I was also irritated when my publicist demanded we go with a younger demographic for this project. But she's right. I'm forty-two now, and many of my readers became fans when I was starting out twenty years ago. My audience is aging right along with me. I have to catch the attention of millennials, and even younger, if I'm going to stay relevant.

Tabby pulls two applications from the folder. "You've already chosen Faye, so that leaves us with Meg and Harper."

I pick up the applications from the table and start reading.

"I'm still concerned Faye won't be able to follow through with the commitment because of her family situation. But I really liked her," Tabby interrupts as I peruse Meg and Harper's answers.

I nod half-heartedly. I don't care all that much, as long as we're hitting a younger target. Faye is twenty-nine and gorgeous, to boot. She'll play out well on social. "How old is Meg?" I ask.

Tabby points to the field marked age on the forms in front of me. "Meg's thirty-one and Harper's twenty-eight."

"Let's go with Harper," I say.

"Harper it is," Tabby agrees. "I had my store manager print out hard copies of your manuscript. Faye and Harper should come by and pick them up in the next few days."

"Let's give them one week to read the first one hundred pages. If either of them can't meet that deadline, we'll shift and contact Meg." I push my back flat against the chair and sit up straight, still brimming with concern about Cade.

A moment later, my phone rings. "It's Maxy," I blurt as I pick up the call.

"Cade's fine!" Maxy yells into the phone at full volume.

Pushing the desperate worry out of my lungs, I breathe in the relief of fresh air. "Thank God."

"His credit card activity showed he was staying at the Eden Rock," Maxy continues. "I had an employee go into his room. He was passed out, wasted. But he's okay." Maxy speaks in the detached clinical tone I've grown used to in the last few months.

"Thanks for this information," I say, sounding just as matter-of-fact.

Tabby peers at me, astonished at the aloof nature of my conversation with Maxy. I wave my hand back and forth, dismissing her concern, and hang up.

"Cade's fine. I'm so relieved. He wasn't picking up because he had passed out. Let me call and check in." I rush out of the store, not wanting to talk with Tabby about the state of my relationship with Maxy.

My eyes narrow as they adjust to the intense Florida sunshine. I glance at the row of shops that line the street just one block from the ocean. Jupiter Cove was the setting of the best-selling romance novel I wrote while in college—*Beaches and Beaus*. The quaint storefronts, and beachtown filled with quirky characters, made the perfect location. That, combined with a classic enemies-to-lovers plot, landed me a lucky break at twenty and my career took off.

"Cade," I cluck into the phone the moment he picks up. "I was worried about you. I'm glad you're okay."

"I'm not okay!" he barks back at me. "But you and Dad are too busy with your own shit to even realize it."

I physically take a step back, as if Cade's standing in front of me screaming in anger. "I'm sorry," I say. "If I missed something, tell me." Guilt glides through my body in a wave. I've focused so much on my career, my writing, and my anger at Maxy. It's no surprise Cade feels like I haven't been there for him.

"I'm not getting into this with you right now, Mom," Cade huffs. "I've got to go." And then click. The phone goes dead in my palm.

CHAPTER 11
Tabitha Wilson

"I**T WAS STRANGE,**" I say as I scrub my face with a gentle, foaming cleanser. My long ponytail bounces from side to side as I wash away the makeup and grime that accumulated today.

"Strange how?" Andre replies, spreading a glob of toothpaste on his toothbrush. He just got home from his late EMT shift. It's twelve-thirty in the morning and he's exhausted.

"Ellory's tone of voice. It was off. It was like she and Maxy were talking about a business transaction, not their son." I pull the ponytail holder from my hair and notice a large tangle of strands fall to the floor. Stepping aside, I stare down at the brown curls laying on our white marble tile. The doctors have repeatedly explained that hair loss is a common side effect of the hormonal changes I'm experiencing from IVF treatment.

My body buzzes, thinking about the bloating, headaches, nausea, and cramping ahead. Am I ready to sink inside the abyss of IVF treatment like an object trapped in quicksand?

"Tabby?"

I look up from the floor.

Andre stares at me with a muddled expression. "Don't you think so?"

"Um, I think I zoned out for a moment," I say. "It's late. I should be sleeping."

Pushing worries about my IVF treatment out of my mind, I try to focus. Andre made it perfectly clear that we're not going through with this last round if it compromises my mental health.

He steps close to me and pulls me in for a hug. "Baby, I think I know what's going on here."

Panic pulses in my chest. I will not give up on our last attempt at getting pregnant. I recall it was the first and only thing I thought of when Ellory contacted me about getting exclusive profits from her book sales. It felt like fate intervened and handed Andre and me the financial security we needed for one last go at it. I don't care how anxious or depressed I feel. We are going through with this.

But before I can make these truths known to Andre, he continues. "Listen, it surprised me when Ellory texted and said she was coming to Jupiter Cove for the summer. Your only connection is history. She hasn't been a friend to you since she married Maxy." Andre takes a step back and cups my face in his large palm. "I totally get why you zoned out. Ellory is putting so much pressure on you, your friendship, this contest, and the whole damn town." He growls his words, but I'm overcome with relief when I realize he thinks I'm stressed because of Ellory rather than our upcoming treatment.

"You're right," I reply as I take his hand and lead him out of our bathroom and into our bedroom. "Did you see that post she made earlier today on her social accounts?"

Andre peers at me as if I just asked him if he went to the moon. "I wouldn't spend one second of my time on her. After everything you told me, and what she did, I just can't understand why you've agreed to help her." He shakes his head, displeased.

"You know why," I say. "She posted a picture of us from senior year side by side with a picture from the other night. The caption said *from high school to now—my lifelong best friend always makes everything better*." Picking up my phone, I open Ellory's Insta and shove the post in front of Andre's face.

He glances at it and then pushes it aside. "I think you need to consider that Ellory's posts are just an extension of some fictional tale she's writing about her life. Please, for your own sanity, proceed with caution."

Instead of responding, I fish around my nightstand to find my IVF medication. Andre and I are at the start of a new cycle, and this means I'll be injecting myself with hormones for the next few weeks to get my body to produce viable eggs.

There was a time when each shot felt like the promise of the future I longed for. The pain I felt with each injection pierced the longing inside me, releasing it to course through my body. But now, after so many failed attempts, the shot is just a jab that feels like betrayal.

I grab the skin around my abdomen and push the long tip of the needle into my stomach. Slowly counting to five, I take a deep breath and pull the needle out. Tomorrow is day five, and I am fully expecting the avalanche of my emotions to set in. Day seven is when my mood usually plummets, and my reactions to life become erratic.

"Did you remember to do the shot on your right side this time?" Andre gets under the covers and fluffs the pillow behind his head.

I nod yes, recalling how bruised and battered my skin became after the last series of injections we did.

Suddenly, his phone pings with a text.

"It's Ila. She'll be home in thirty minutes." His words beat with relief. "I know she's nineteen years old, and if she was off at college, we'd have no control over what she did, but I'm still not comfortable with her staying out so late."

I don't even bother to comment. Any attempts I've made to try to put boundaries on Ila's coming and goings have only damaged our relationship. I used to wish that we could sit down as mother and daughter to discuss life's ups and downs. Longing skirts through me, but I quickly remind myself that a wish is merely a desire for something that isn't attainable.

Crawling under the covers, I rest my head on Andre's shoulder. He runs his hand up and down my arm. Sex isn't allowed at this stage of my treatment, and it's a relief. Joining our bodies together only causes me pain.

CHAPTER 12
Ila Wilson

WALKING INSIDE THE house, my shoulders relax in the blackness. I love the dark. I have this memory of my dad, the first few months after my mom left. Every morning, he'd burst into my room. "Rise and shine. It's the start of a new day." Bolting to my curtains, he'd throw them open, letting in the blinding sunlight. Then, he'd sit on my bed, staring at me with a forced smile, as if our life wasn't falling apart. As if the sunlight itself was the cure for my mother's disappearance. Bright sunlight pouring in through a window feels like a false promise. A dark room allows space for the shadows in my life to make themselves known.

I put down my bag but remove my sketch pad and walk upstairs to my room.

Collapsing into my bed, the events of tonight flash through my mind. I was sitting on a rock at Venus Inlet just as the sun was dropping in the horizon. I had my sketch pad and pastels in hand as I attempted to draw the Jupiter Cove lighthouse in the twilight. It's a sketch I've been attempting for years, but it's impossible to capture the image on paper. You look down and apply a pinkish-orange hue to one area, and by the time you look up again, the sky has changed to a soft purple.

As I blended a golden yellow into the page, I heard the crunch of footsteps on the gravel surrounding the inlet. Looking up, it surprised me to see someone walking toward me. Didn't this person know this was my space? Stay away.

As the figure approached, I realized it was a guy about my age. But he wasn't from Jupiter Cove. I quickly put my sketch pad aside and grabbed my key chain. I put my finger on the pepper spray hanging next to my car key.

"Hi there," he said as he walked closer.

"Hey," I grunted, striving for an unapproachable tone.

"I like this inlet," he said, walking closer. Aviator sunglasses covered his eyes, and his hair was tucked under a gray beanie that had a stylish logo in the center.

I nodded.

"I didn't think anyone else would be here," he continued.

Knowing no one could see us from the road above, I stood and stuffed my sketch pad into my bag. I wanted to make a break for it before this random attacked me. I rubbed my finger over the trigger of the pepper spray.

"Oh!" he said with a surprised lilt to his voice. "Is that pepper spray?" He took his sunglasses off and ran his eyes up from the pepper spray to my face.

The feeling of panic I had suddenly dissolved. Smiling, his face opened into an expression of lighthearted amusement. The soft look in his eyes put me at ease. He held me in his gaze for a moment, then looked away at the ocean line.

Turning his face back to mine, he smiled again. "I love this inlet because it's the redheaded stepchild of this town. It's rocky and cramped. I've always had a thing for the underdog." He grinned and put back on his sunglasses.

"I-I don't think we've met before?" I stammered. If this guy knew enough about Jupiter Cove to know that most people avoided Venus Inlet, he was obviously familiar with my town.

"No," he said, not offering further explanation. "I didn't mean to bother you. I'm going to walk down closer to the water. Nice meeting you."

I watched as he traversed the rocky ring until he landed with a thud on the flattest part of the inlet. Taking a seat on the bed of crushed shells and rocks, he took a small notebook and pen out of his pocket and began writing. His strong, angular profile pressed against the blue of the ocean. The weight of my gaze must have been heavy because, after a few moments, he turned again and faced me. His lips spread out wide and welcoming.

I half lifted my arm, waving awkwardly, caught in my stare. Not sure what to do, but intrigued by his presence, I went back to the rock where I'd been sitting and took out my sketching supplies. The waves lulled back and forth along the shore as I continued to work on my piece. Every so often, I'd look down at the shore and watch as he continued to write in his notebook.

I'm not sure how much time passed as we both sat in our separate areas, immersed in our endeavors. Art has a way of sweeping me away and bending time in a strange way.

"Can I see what you're working on?" the voice called to me just as the sun was making its final descent into the ocean.

Looking up, I saw him approaching. He sat down a few rocks over. Instantly, a tingle ran down my spine. We sat closer than strangers, but still distant enough to make it clear we were unfamiliar with each other.

He leaned forward, taking off his sunglasses. As he pulled them away from his face, his beanie slipped off his head. Thick golden blond hair fell around his face in chunks, brushing his shoulders. A ripple of desire tickled my chest.

He quickly put his beanie back in place. "It's the only way to keep the hair out of my eyes."

"Wait? I feel like I know you from somewhere." I blurted. Immediately, my face flushed. Did I know him or was I mistaking attraction for familiarity? This guy would never be interested in someone as basic as me. I was average height, with a petite figure, and brown hair.

"No, allow me to introduce myself. My name is CJ." Shrugging, he scooted another inch closer to me. "You an artist?" His eyebrows raised as he spoke, highlighting the bright blue of his eyes.

"Sort of," I answered.

His gaze swept across the sketch pad in my lap. "Well, you don't have to show me if you don't want. I get it. I'm a writer but have a hard time sharing my work."

"Is that what you were doing down there?" Turning my head, I gestured toward the area on the rocky shore below.

"Yes, I'm writing a short story about a sea captain and his muse. I was looking for inspiration."

"Well, did you find the inspiration you were looking for?" Pushing my long, thick hair off my shoulder, I shifted my body and looked at him straight on.

He grinned shyly and nodded his head. He stood and moved to the rock next to mine. "Yes, I think I did."

CHAPTER 13
Faye Carter

HIGH-PITCHED HOWLING BLARES from the baby monitor on my bedside table. The sound is relentless. My eyes dart around in the blackness until they land on the bright red numbers on my alarm clock. It's 2:23 in the morning. Griffin is going through a sleep regression. He was up just two hours ago.

I try to get my body to move, but the fatigue I feel is beyond anything I've ever experienced. It's as if each individual cell in my body is beaten down and bleary-eyed.

Reaching my arm out toward my bedside table, I feel around for the button on the baby monitor that will silence Griffin's cry. My elbow hits the book sitting on the table's edge, and Ellory Brayson's novel plummets to the floor with a loud thud.

My mind explodes with the conversation Mark and I had when I told him Ellory selected me for her editing team.

"I need to hire a nanny ASAP," I said excitedly after I read him the text message.

"We just can't afford it right now," he insisted.

Mark shifts in the bed but quickly settles. I stare out into the darkness, anger bubbling in my gut. Stalling for a moment, I hope he'll feed Griffin the bottle I have filled with fresh breast milk. But he's perfectly still.

Mark doesn't get up for the middle of the night feedings, especially during the workweek. He thinks it's easy for me to nap during the day since I'm at home with the kids. The truth, however, which I've explained many times, is that I absolutely cannot rest during the day while at home with our four children. It feels like I'm treading water every single day, barely able to come up for a breath. Sometimes I wish the water would swallow me whole. I feel scared when these types of thoughts invade my brain.

Yanking the covers off, I use enough force that the blanket also falls off Mark's body. It's Saturday, and there's no reason he can't get out of bed and give me the night off. He shifts for a second but then curls back into himself and goes back to sleep. His methodical snoring mocks my anger as I stomp down the hall to attend to the baby.

I enter Griffin's room quietly and shut the door behind me. His cry is sharp. I don't want to risk disturbing the other kids. The smell of baby powder and stale urine fills my nose as I step over to the changing table to activate a small nightlight.

As soon as I approach the crib, Griffin turns his head and lets out a loud whimper. My heart thumps heavily in my chest. This sleep regression has been going on for weeks. Each time he wakes, I go through a standard routine: diaper change, cuddling, feeding, burping, rocking, and pacifier. But nothing soothes him.

Reaching down into the crib, I remove the sleep sack that's wrapped snuggly around his small body. It's supposed to help him get through the night comfortably. So many of the baby products I buy are snake oil, but it's impossible not to try any product that claims it can improve the dismal sleep issues that plague Baby G.

Pulling Griffin up, we look directly at each other. His shrill howl becomes a quiver as soon as our eyes lock. I am reminded his face reflects my own and feel a gentle warmth spread over me. By the time I nestle him into the crook of my neck, he's calm. I'm grateful for this small victory. Compared to how things have gone this week, it feels like progress, or at least the promise of this phase ending soon.

Breathing in the soapy scent of his bald head, I pace around the space between his crib, rocker, and changing table. He calms quickly in my arms and falls back to sleep. I'm overcome with relief, realizing I'll be back in bed soon.

As I place him in his crib, I hear the door to his room squeak.

"Mama." Emma stands in front of me, clasping her beat-up stuffed bunny in one hand while she rubs her eyes with the other. "Griffin waked me up." Her soft voice spills out of her in the surrounding quiet. "Mama, come lay down with me."

A wave of furious energy crashes through my body. *No, no! I need to go back to bed.* "Emma, Mommy's tired. I'll tuck you back in, but I'm not going to lay down with you."

"Mama lay down with me. Mama in my bed." Her voice turns wobbly.

If I don't do what she asks, this will quickly devolve into a meltdown. I'm stuck between a cliff and the pitch-black sea. I resentfully accept I'll have to do as she says if I hope to get any sleep tonight.

Grabbing her hand, using more force than necessary, I lead us into her room.

Her eyes look up at me and fill with water. "Mama mad." Her face twists up in the most heartbreaking expression.

Guilt engulfs me, squeezing my neck and making it hard to inhale. "Mama's not mad, honey," I say in a soft, whispery voice. "I love you. Mama's just tired."

I put Emma in bed and fold her small frame into mine. Pulling her pink and white polka dot sheets around our bodies, I rub my hand over her back in a comforting motion, lying with her until she goes back to sleep. As soon as she drifts off, I drag myself back to my bed, falling asleep before my head even hits the pillow.

A few hours later, I hear Griffin gurgling noisily through the baby monitor. I glance at the clock. It's 5:45. The crack of dawn. I've got about fifteen minutes before Griffin's tender coos turn into a hungry cry. Then, I remember it's Saturday. I'm going to stay in bed. Mark can get up and deal with the baby.

Rolling over, I face him. He's sleeping peacefully. His ears are deaf to the noise spilling through the baby monitor. I wonder if the neurons in my hearing system have a unique sensor that causes them to snap into place whenever Baby G makes the slightest sound. Mark's hearing system is missing this particular sensor.

"Hey, can you get Griffin? It's Saturday. I'm going to sleep in," I say. I gently push his arm to wake him.

His nose crinkles as if he has suddenly smelled rotten food, but he doesn't move.

I sit up on my side and tap his shoulder. "Mark, it's Saturday. Griffin needs to eat. Can you get up and deal with him and all the kids? I'm sleeping in today." The soft tone of my voice evaporates with each new syllable.

"Yes, yes, I'm getting up in just a minute." Mark shuffles his legs around. He sits up and turns his back away from me. "You know, I'm tired from work, too. I'd love to sleep."

His words sting, and my heart constricts. Suddenly, an image of the bingo card invades my mind. After ten years of marriage, Mark and I have definitely filled in a few squares. I know the grim statistics. About fifty percent of marriages end in divorce. *Will mine be one of them?*

I can't help but wonder if other moms with young children are struggling like I am. I wish I had an actual friend to talk to. None of the moms I meet at the playground ever complain. Are they happy? Do they feel supported? Or are they keeping their turmoil a secret like I am?

Closing my eyes, I try to relax and fall back asleep. After ten minutes, I give up. I'm too riled up with frustration to calm down. Wanting to escape from these miserable feelings, I lean over and grab Ellory's book from the floor. All my problems fade away as I lose myself in her words.

CHAPTER 14

Harper Weiss

P*ING.* GLANCING AT my phone, I see a text from Ben.

> **Ben:** What kind of coffee do you like? I'm running through Starbucks on my way over.

Is this guy for real? He's offering to pick up coffee. He can't be real. Clearly, I'm still suffering from the effects of pain meds.

> **Harper:** That's okay. You're already doing enough.

A moment later a Bitmoji of Ben holding a steaming cup of coffee overtakes my phone's screen. I laugh out loud at the cartoon image bearing a bizarre likeness to Ben's handsome face.

> **Harper:** Okay, okay. I can't argue with your Bitmoji. I'll have a venti iced coffee with two pumps of vanilla syrup, four pumps of caramel syrup, extra ice, whip, and extra caramel drizzle.

Three dots flash for a moment before Ben responds.

> **Ben:** My God, Harper. You're a monster feared by baristas across the world.

A smile consumes my face. This is so on the nose, considering I wrote a book called *The Broken-Hearted Barista*. I make a note to myself to work this text exchange into my next edit. I wish I could find more time to write, but single mom life is all-encompassing.

> **Ben:** And by the way, I'm not sure all those ingredients will fit into a coffee cup. Sounds like you need a trough.

I quickly text back a laughing emoji and then steady myself on my crutches.

"Ryder, are you almost ready for camp?" I hobble down the hallway of my bungalow. The bright blue sky peeks through my dormer windows. It's going to be a beautiful day.

"I'm ready." Ryder steps out of his bedroom dressed head to toe in Under Armour apparel. Even his socks and sneakers boast the popular athletic gear's label.

"You look handsome." I beam.

"Mom, stop." He holds a palm out in front of my eyes, embarrassed.

"Ben will be here soon to take you and Wyatt to camp. Thanks for being ready on time."

"I'm the blueprint." He smiles, proud of himself.

"Um, yeah," I respond. "You're the blueprint." It's impossible to keep up with all his pre-teen slang.

Making our way toward the kitchen, Ryder pulls down a bowl and fills it up with Cocoa Krispies.

"Hey, that's only for the weekend," I protest.

"But you'll let it slide this one time, since I'm on time for Ben." He winks, and for just a moment I see his dad's face.

I take an extra breath to clear the image from my mind. "Just this once," I say, using my mom voice.

"What are you doing today?" he asks between slurps of cereal.

"I'm not sure. I'll keep practicing on these crutches. And I'll probably read." It's the perfect time to get a good start on *The Prince of Silicon Valley*'s last book.

"You should get one of those knee scooter things," Ryder says as he stands and puts his bowl into the sink. "I could ride it down the hill in the park. That would be *dope*."

"Um, I know you want to live your life like you're in Dude Perfect, but it's not happening."

Ryder shrugs me off. "You should work on your book," he says just as the doorbell rings.

He's right, I should work on my book, but as much as I love writing, I can't deal with the rejection. Each no fills me with questions about who I'd be if I hadn't slept with my high school boyfriend and ended up pregnant. I still have my acceptance letter to Columbia in a box tucked away in my closet—the road not taken forever preserved in black and white letters.

"I'll get it." Ryder runs from the kitchen to the front door.

Mom guilt instantly fills every cell of my body. I love Ryder more than life itself, and if Columbia had happened, it would mean I wouldn't have Ryder. I recall how heartbroken my parents were when I deferred my acceptance, as he swings the door open.

"Yo!" he bellows.

"Hey, Ryder," Ben says as I totter on my crutches toward the door.

"I've got your trough of sugary syrup." Ben chuckles, holding up a large Starbucks as if it's evidence in a trial. "Consider this my mitzvah for the day."

I never realized a Hebrew word could be so sexy. My stomach twists with desire as I lean into my crutches. He pushes the drink toward me, and I lift my hand from its position on my crutch. He steps in close, and his hand brushes my side. I feel the hairs on my arms lift.

"Oh, um." We both laugh, quickly realizing I won't be able to take the drink and walk on my crutches.

"Why don't you go sit down, and I'll bring you the coffee." He gestures to my couch.

"Right," I say. When I reach the couch, it suddenly seems like it's at the bottom of a pit, hundreds of feet from where I'm standing. I stare at it, contemplating how I'm going to get myself seated.

"Mom, I'm out. I'll see you after camp." Ryder skips out the front door to Ben's car.

"Guess he didn't realize I could use his help," I mumble.

"Eleven-year-old boys. What can you do?" Ben shrugs. He takes a step forward. "Can I help you?"

"I don't think I have any other choice," I say, somewhat thrilled.

Ben leans into me. Wrapping my arm around his shoulder, he removes one of my crutches. I can feel his solid muscular arms under his shirt. I look away, praying he doesn't see the red bloom probably overtaking my neck.

"There you go. All set." He steps away and places the coffee on the table next to me.

"Thanks."

"Sure. Is there anything you need before I go?" He pushes his hand into the pocket of his well-fitted jeans.

My mind races with a steamy thought about what's under those jeans. "I think you've gone above and beyond. I'm good." I nod my head for emphasis. But then I remember Ellory's book. "Oh wait. There's one thing. I hope this isn't too awkward, but there's a book on my nightstand in my bedroom. Would you mind grabbing it?"

"Anything for the coffee monster." He grins as I point him down the hall toward my bedroom.

Theo's eyes scrunch together. He's irritated. "Now that I know you're the anonymous venture capitalist who's been pouring funds into my start-up, I thought it was important we start over fresh."

I turn his words over in my mind. I had my reasons for remaining anonymous. Now he's one step closer to the truth, and I'm terrified. "A fresh start," I repeat, hoping he doesn't detect the slight shake in my voice.

"Yes," he continues. His voice sounds off, far away. "What happened between us was a one time thing. I would never have let that night happen if I knew you were providing half my company's funding. I think you'll agree the best course of action is to move forward with our professional relation-ship...and nothing else."

My heart nose-dives off a cliff, rushing towards the ground at lightning speed.

Glancing at the clock, I realize I've been reading *The Prince of Silicon Valley* for well over two hours. Ellory's ability to pull readers into her stories is legendary. There's even a hashtag on Insta where readers can brag about how fast they read her books—#ElloryBraysononedayclub. Maybe I'll finish it in bed later and join the club. But now, it's time to do something else.

Feeling inspired, I close the book and decide to take Ryder's suggestion. I need to work on editing my novel. Leaning forward, I grasp the table next to me and steady myself with my crutches. I stuff my phone in my pocket and make my way toward my desk. Despite my ankle, it certainly feels luxurious to read and write on a weekday.

Ping. I hear my phone alert me to a new message. Sitting down at my desk, I'm proud of how well I moved across the room. I'll be fine on these crutches. I pull my phone from my pocket and see a text from an unfamiliar number.

Unknown: Hi, Harper. This is Ellory Brayson. I've chosen you as one of my editors! First meeting will be Friday June 16th at Blast Off Books. We'll meet a few times over the next six weeks. You'll

> need to read the first hundred pages this week.
> Let me know if you can commit.

Letting out an excited squeal, I type:

> **Harper:** Yes, I'm in! So excited.

> **Ellory:** Great! You'll need to go by Blast Off
> Books as soon as you can. Tabby has a printed
> copy of my manuscript. And the nondisclosure
> you'll need to sign.

Suddenly, I remember my inability to drive. My stomach sinks. My finger hovers over my phone's type-pad as I consider the situation. I have a book of my own. I love to write. Maybe Ellory's the mentor I need to take my novel to the next level. Maybe Ellory and this editing group are the universe's way of making up for my lost chance at Columbia. There's no way I can pass up this opportunity.

> **Harper:** Sounds great!

I respond as my heart thumps. I have to make this work.

CHAPTER 15

Ellory Brayson

"I 'VE CHOSEN MY editors for the social media campaign. They're both under thirty." I stare into the camera of my laptop as my publicist, Amber, forces a grin. Her newborn baby sleeps in a swing, gently rocking in the background. She's angry I insisted on Zoom for tonight's after-hours meeting. But Celebrity Ellory needs the face-to-face interaction to confirm the plans for repairing my image are on track.

She glances at the notes in front of her. "I'm going to send you a document with some ideas for photos. They'll be sort of staged, but only so we can capture you and your editors working together in a way that translates well on your social platforms. We need to get things rolling. We're already into June."

"Do me a favor," I say as she turns her face away from the screen and coos at her baby. "Copy Tabby on that email. She's taking the photos, so I need her in the loop."

"Um, uh…" she stammers for a moment as she turns back to look at me. "Tabby?"

"Yes, Tabby, I say. She's my right-hand person here. An old friend of mine. You've already been talking with her." My words push through my lips, short and clipped. *Doesn't she understand my status as the world's most famous romance author is on the line?*

"Yes, right." Her voice is still a coo. She's having trouble shifting gears between mom and publicist. A moment later, her baby whimpers.

"Oh my!" she says, crinkling her nose. "I think Bennet just had a diaper explosion. I'm so sorry, Ellory. I need to go. Melinda isn't here tonight to help. I hope you understand."

"Right," I say. Melinda is Amber's wife, and she's a bigwig at Amazon. She's always traveling. "We can pick it up from here in a few days," I say with as much compassion as I can muster.

"Thanks, Ellory." Her voice trails off as I snap my laptop shut.

Standing, I walk to the kitchen's large island. The green marble countertop pops against the white base. Abstract paintings in bold primary colors line the kitchen's long wall. The entire home makes me feel like I'm living in a museum of modern art. It's not my taste, but it's a relief to be somewhere that feels so different from my apartment in New York.

Searching through the refrigerator, I find the bottle of sparkling rosé I picked up to enjoy after another long day of writing. The subject of my new book has my mind swirling with the past.

As my glass fills with bubbling liquid, I wonder how Tabby's adjusting to my presence in Jupiter Cove. I did what was best for me all those years ago. I didn't fully understand that my decision to put myself first was also a decision to sacrifice our friendship. It was an error in critical thinking. I want to apologize, but Celebrity Ellory is not used to being vulnerable. I'll have to hope the money Tabby will make from my book sales will ease our past.

Taking a long sip of wine, I bury my thoughts of Tabby deep within. Relief courses through me as they sink into my subconscious. I've got things to do tonight, I remind myself.

Walking toward the front door, I pick up the Amazon package sitting in the entryway. It's Nadine Laurel's most recent release, along with a pack of fine-tipped red markers. Nothing's as satisfying as finding the places where her novels fall short.

As I tear open the packaging, headlights beam through the full-length windows flanking the door. *Who in the world is that?*

I lean toward the window and peer into the darkness. I glimpse someone stepping out of the car from behind the driver's seat just as the car headlights go out. Everything outside disappears into blackness. A few seconds later, there's a knock and a muffled voice I can't distinguish through the heavy wood of the door.

Holding my breath, I push my ear against the grainy dark mahogany.

"Open up. It's me." The voice is still hard to make out, but something about it's familiar.

Turning the lock, I pull on the handle and open the door a few inches.

"What took you so long?"

Blinking a few times, I step back and let my visitor inside.

"Hi, Mom," Cade says, dragging a suitcase behind him.

CHAPTER 16

Tabitha Wilson

ANDRE HAS HIS poker game tonight, and Ila is once again missing in action. I find myself alone, thinking about Ellory. We've perfected our act, but it's starting to eat away at me. I can't help but wonder if she will ever let down her walls and discuss our past.

Picking up my phone, I open Insta and scroll to the graduation photo she posted. We hold each other tightly, with our arms clasped. Bright blue robes hang over our slim bodies. Ellory's cap sits slightly askew, drawing attention to her dazzling sapphire-colored eyes. Her tan skin shimmers next to my pale complexion.

Studying my face in the photo, I wonder why I'm glancing at Ellory rather than straight at the camera. She must have cracked a joke, because my smile is so wide it looks like my face may split in two. My charm bracelet hangs from my wrist against her robe. There's magic in our smooth skin and bright, fearless eyes. Our youth was an elixir, but it failed to protect us from what would come as the years rolled on.

An image of Ellory's relieved face after speaking with Cade the other day flits through my mind. For a moment, the creases around her eyes relaxed, and her expression softened. It reminded me of a young Ellory and our childhood, dancing on Main Street with our yellow Discmans and crimped hair while listening to New Kids on the Block.

How do I break away from someone who's one-half of every childhood memory? How do I let go of the person woven into the fabric of every high school and college moment? If I pull her thread away, won't it all unravel? Letting go of her will create holes that can't be mended.

Suddenly my phone pings with an alert from TikTok. One of my favorite users, @Smutbooklife12, has posted a new recommendation. I slide my finger over the app, thankful for the distraction. @Smutbooklife12 appears on my screen in a light pink sweater set, cupping steaming tea. Her blond hair is half up and half down. She looks like a kindergarten teacher and makes her spicy book reviews seem like a lesson on the golden rule. Holding up Jennifer L. Armentrout's *From Blood and Ash*, she rates the volume of spice and the book's tingly factor. She ends by giving the book five out of five red peppers.

For a moment, I consider grabbing my current spicy book. But the urge passes quickly. My sex drive drops off during IVF treatments. And I'm stressed about my upcoming ultrasound to monitor when my eggs will be ready for retrieval.

Instantly, I'm transported back to six months ago when my doctor called me to report that the embryos we hoped to implant had stopped growing. He continued with a medical explanation about the lack of symmetry of cells and too much fragmentation. But as he continued to talk, his words morphed into a deafening white static. This was our third attempt, and we hadn't even made it to embryo transfer, the step where things went wrong last time.

I recall how I left my bookstore and walked in a trance-like state toward the ocean. I stared ahead at the crashing waves and considered what would happen if I swam out deep, until I was so exhausted that the water would fold around me and take me under.

My spiraling thoughts are abruptly interrupted when my phone rings. It's Andre.

"Hey, babe," he says quickly. "Is Ila home?"

"No, but her car's in the garage. She must be out with Jackson."

"Shoot." He exhales the word as if he is pushing out musty air.

My body tenses. "What's wrong?"

"I just ran into Jackson's mom at the gas station. She was wondering how Ila was doing since the breakup." He pauses.

"The breakup?" I ask, confused.

"Exactly," Andre says in a tight voice. "They broke up a few months ago."

"What? Are you kidding me?" A wash of guilt rams me in my gut. "But how did we not know? How did we miss that?"

"I don't know. It's just a shame…" He starts to say something, but then stops.

"What?" I say. "It's just a shame, what?" My composure is crumbling.

"It's just a shame she refuses to talk to us. To confide in us. It breaks my heart. You're her mother. She should want to talk with you about this kind of stuff." His voice is thin.

Silence stretches for a moment as tears streak my cheeks. Ila's rejection cuts deep. "But we've made mistakes, Andre."

"How long can she shut us out because of the time and energy we've put into having another child?" I can hear the pain in his voice. "And we don't even know who she's out with tonight. Is it a friend or a new boyfriend? Or is she roaming around by herself, trying to cope?"

"Have you tried calling her?" I ask hopefully.

"Yes, I called and texted a million times in the last ten minutes. She's not picking up." I can practically see the look of concern on Andre's face as he speaks into his phone.

"I'll try her as soon as we hang up," I say. I make it sound like I'm confident Ila will respond to me, when Andre and I both know, if she won't pick up for her dad, there's zero chance she'll pick up for me.

"Thanks, baby. I'll be home in about fifteen minutes."

Hanging up, I hold the phone in my palm. I try typing out a text that will convince Ila to respond, but I end up deleting each attempt before hitting send. It's difficult to connect with her when I have to approach every interaction delicately. She needs me to stay firmly behind the line she's drawn. I never discuss her emotions, I never pry into her personal life, and I absolutely never, ever refer to myself as her mother.

Something suddenly clicks inside me. Maybe I need to cross the line to grab her attention. My fingers type fast, as if they are moving on their own accord.

Tabitha: Ila this is your mother. Text me back immediately. Dad and I want to make sure you're okay.

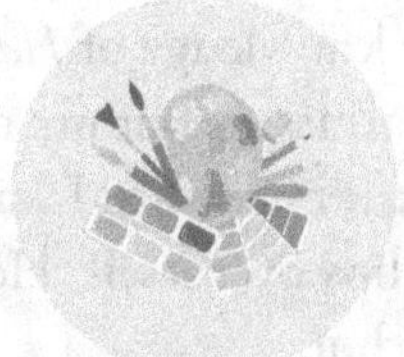

CHAPTER 17
Ila Wilson

THE SOUND OF lapping waves surrounds me. I push my hands through the rocky sand, noticing the pink hue of the moon hanging in the distance. *Again?* Although I set my phone on silent, it's hard to ignore the way it lights up in the darkness. My eyes glance at the screen.

Tabitha: Ila this is your mother.

My buzz is the only thing keeping me from feeling hot rage. How dare she refer to herself as my mother? I push the off button, throw my phone back down on the blanket, and watch as it shuts down.

CJ looks at me. "Everything okay? Your phone's blowing up."

"Yup," I say. "Everything's peachy."

"Peachy." He smirks. "Have we been transported back to 1950?"

"I wish," I say as I take another can of the hard seltzer we picked up on the way to Venus Inlet. Although CJ has been texting nonstop since we met a few nights ago, it surprised me when he asked me to do something.

I want to show you how I get into the head of my main character, the sea captain, he'd said.

I agreed, not really knowing what to expect.

"If it was the 1950s," CJ continues. "I would definitely be the Fonz." He lifts his hand and pretends to smooth down the sides of his hair. "A leather jacket, a motorcycle, the coolest guy in town."

"Wow," I tease. "Your knowledge of *Happy Days* is impressive."

"Ha, I should be embarrassed, but my mom loves that show and made me watch it on Nick at Nite when I was growing up." He smirks at me, and my stomach flips over itself. He's got this boyish charm that's as endearing as it is hot.

"My dad's wife also loves *Happy Days,*" I say. "I've probably seen every episode." I'm so thrilled by this strange connection that my words fly out too fast. Suddenly, I realize I sound eager. I'm embarrassed.

"Did your dad just get married?" CJ asks.

I'd rather avoid this conversation. I don't want to get into the whole sob story of my mom running off, and I refuse to even mention Tabby's name in front of CJ and ruin my mood.

"So what song is this?" I ask, ignoring his question.

"Oh, shhh!" CJ jumps up, oblivious to my discomfort, and starts swaying to the beat of the music playing on his Bluetooth speaker. "This one slays. Tell me you've heard it."

It's hard not to grin as he moves his body to the rhythm of a song my dad probably loves.

"Shh," he says again. "This is the best part." His eyebrows rise in anticipation.

I let the words and beat of a song about Brandy and a sailor wash over me.

Before I can protest, CJ has me up. Our hands clasp as we dance around to one of the Yacht Rock tunes he's listening to as research for his character. As we spin and sway, my body feels like it could float away. I'm suddenly gliding. Everything that seemed impossibly complex is instantly simple. *This is joy,* I think. *This is joy.*

As the song ends, CJ pulls me in close. His hands circle around my back. A slight tremble radiates out from my spine to the rest of my body.

"Can I kiss you?" he whispers into my ear.

Turning my head, I look at him. There's something mischievous, yet tender, about the way he looks back. He's like the cute boy in middle school who makes harmless jokes that even the teacher can't resist.

I lean into him instead of answering. Our mouths meet. The kiss starts sweet and innocent. But, after a moment, it intensifies. CJ may have boyish charm, but there's certainly a man in that body.

After a few minutes, he pulls away. I'm momentarily confused.

"This is another great one!" he bellows happily.

"You really take your short story research seriously," I tease.

"Yes, I do. In fact, I'm planning to rent a boat for a half-day excursion around Fort Lauderdale sometime soon." CJ takes a step toward the water and lets his feet sink into the crisp ocean. He looks deep into the blackness as the song he loves says to make a wish, because you're the biggest part of me.

Taking a few steps, I move toward him until we're standing side by side with our feet submerged. He slowly swings his left arm around my hip. We both turn our bodies, so we're facing each other. My insides flutter in anticipation of another kiss. But instead of moving his plump lips toward mine, he talks.

"Why don't you come with me on the boat?" he says.

There's so much tension between our bodies that his words smolder with heat. When his warm breath caresses my ear, my entire body vibrates. I take a step back, afraid of what will happen if we continue to stand so close.

Feeling awkward, I sit back down on the rocky beach. He's oblivious to the way my body is screaming for his touch and casually sits down next to me. Taking a deep breath, I inhale, loosening the knots of desire that have stiffened my body into a ramrod.

"You should come sailing, Peach."

"Peach?" I raise my eyebrows questioningly.

"Yes, I'm going to call you, my peach." He says the words nonchalantly, as if we've known each other for decades. It thrills me.

"I've hired a captain. We're going to boat around historic Fort Lauderdale and through downtown. The boat also cruises by

Millionaire Row." He turns to me with his sly grin, and I feel as if I'm rocketing to the moon.

My head buzzes with happiness for a moment, but then I land back on Earth. "So, the…the thing is," I stammer. "I don't even know you. Who exactly are you? Where did you come from?"

"Fair," he says as he pushes his hands through the perfectly golden blond hair hanging over his eyes. "Go ahead, ask me whatever you want. I'll give you three questions, and then I get to ask you three." He's smirking now, enjoying this game we're about to play.

"All right, let me think for a minute," I say as I consider exactly what I want to know. "Number one," I start. "I'm trying to figure out how you have the entire summer to play around in Jupiter Cove and write. Are you in college and taking the summer off from classes?"

"Good first question, Peach." He winks. "I was in college until this past March. I dropped out. College may still be in my future, but now's not the right time."

"Where were you in college?" I ask.

"Do you want this to be your second question, Peach? There are probably better questions you could ask."

He's not wrong about this. So, I continue trying to figure out as much about CJ as I can. "No, I retract that question as my number two," I say playfully.

CJ nods with an adorable smile.

"My second question is, where are you from? Where did you grow up?"

"Ah, my place of origin. This is a good question, Peach. I was born in Southern California but mostly grew up in New York."

My head continues to spin with this additional information. "Give me a minute," I say. "I have one final question, and it has to be good."

"I've got all night," CJ says as he stretches his legs out before him and leans his head back onto his hands.

"So how are you able to stay here all summer, write, rent a boat, listen to your Yacht Rock music? How are you paying for this fabulous lifestyle?"

"Lay down here next to me, Peach." CJ gently grasps my arm and pulls me next to him. "To be completely honest, I'm just winging it. My friend, who lives on the other side of the bridge, in Jupiter City, is letting me crash on his couch for free. And I've got enough money saved up to get me through the summer. Once fall hits, I'll need to figure out my next move."

We're both looking directly up at the sky. The stars twinkle around us, making the moment feel surreal. Can I trust this guy? Is he telling the truth? Do I want to get involved with someone who's only here for the summer and has such a carefree attitude about life? My logical brain says no, but I cast it aside.

"And how do your parents feel about your choices?" I ask, hoping to get a bit more information.

"Are you trying to sneak in a bonus question?" he says playfully. "My parents don't have time to care about what I'm doing." Immediately, his light, cheerful energy shifts. "And anyway, Peach, you're out of questions. It's my turn." His voice sounds slightly irritated.

I sit up and grasp his hand. "Did I upset you?"

"Nah." He waves his free hand back and forth, dismissing the sudden change in his demeanor. "Family can be tough. I'm sure you get it, with the way your phone was blowing up earlier."

"Yup, sure do." We're both silent. Suddenly, I'm desperate to move us back to the fun banter we were having only a moment ago. "So, what are your three questions?" I ask.

"Right." CJ sits up and lifts his knees to his chest. "Question one. How do you plan to pursue your art? I looked at the link you sent me with your portfolio. You're talented."

My stomach sinks. Can I trust CJ with this? I ponder for a moment and then decide why not? He's leaving here when the summer's over. He's the perfect person to tell.

"I applied for FLAD last fall but got wait-listed. I never got in. I've spent the last year working at Meteor Café while my friends started college and moved on to other things." Warmth engulfs my neck. Admitting my failure feels scary.

"FLAD?" he says questioningly. "Is that the Florida Art and Design School in Miami?"

I nod my head as shame constricts in my throat.

"I have a friend from New York who tried to get in. It's so competitive. The fact that you were wait-listed is impressive."

"Maybe," I say half-heartedly. "Or maybe I'm just not good enough."

CJ pushes a stray piece of hair away from my face and tucks it behind my ear. "If you're putting yourself out there creatively, you're going to be told no almost every time. Anyone who makes it in art, writing, acting, or music is just someone who refused to give up." He speaks his words confidently, like the beat of a drum.

"Maybe," I say again. *Am I going to give up?* "Anyway, FLAD encouraged me to reapply, and I was wait-listed again for this September. I'll find out at the end of the summer if they change my status to an acceptance." It's hard to admit this and keep looking him in the eyes. I shift my gaze toward the rocky sand beside him.

"Amazing! You're still in it!" He lifts his hands over his head and cheers. "Second question," he continues. "Why doesn't someone as beautiful as you have a boyfriend?"

My heart slams against my chest. *Did he just call me beautiful?* "Wow," I say. "I didn't fully appreciate how hard this game would be until this very moment. Your second question cuts right to it. Can I pass?"

"Hmm," CJ ponders my question. "Unfortunately, the rules on passing had to be agreed upon before the game began, so I'm sorry, the answer is no." He shrugs his shoulders teasingly.

"Next time we play this game, I want to amend some rules." I flip my long dark hair over my shoulder and take a long breath. "I had a boyfriend until a few months ago. We were together for three years. We tried to stay together after he left for college, but it was a miserable year, so we ended things."

"Oh, so this was, like, your high school boyfriend?" CJ asks curiously.

"Is this your third question?" I shoot back playfully.

"Um, no. Clearly, he was your high school boyfriend. I'm sorry it didn't work out, but high school relationships are doomed from the start. It's a real Romeo and Juliet scenario."

"I suppose," I say. "It was time for us to move on. It's sad, but we both know it's the best thing."

"Well, that sounds very mature and healthy, Peach. It's okay if you're sad about it."

"I'm okay. I really am."

CJ leans his body toward mine. The smell of salt in the air mixes with his clean, soapy scent. I brace myself for another kiss. But, again, instead of kissing me, he speaks. For a moment, I wonder if he's doing this on purpose. Drawing it out, so I want him even more.

"My last question," he says with an impish smile. "Is there anything more enjoyable than a ripe peach on a summer evening?"

He leans in to kiss me, but I can't help but laugh. "That was so cheesy." But before I can continue to make fun of him, his lips are on top of mine and the moment turns from something sweet to something pleasingly tart. My lips pucker as I succumb to the exhilarating tang coursing through me.

CHAPTER 18

Faye Carter

PUSHING ASIDE BROKEN crayons and uncapped markers, I lay three bingo cards on the kitchen table. The twins rush over. I promised them we could play after getting Baby G down for his morning nap. Milo stares at his tablet in a trance. It's Saturday, but Mark's out playing soccer. *Ping.* I hear the sound and jump up from the table to find my phone.

> **Mark:** We won our game! We're moving to the next round.

Heat flies through my chest as I read the words.

> **Faye:** You didn't even tell me that was a possibility! You said you'd be home by 2????????

How many question marks will it take for him to realize I'm about to explode in anger? Three dots appear and disappear. I stare at the phone and wait. After another few seconds, he replies.

> **Mark:** I know I told you. Wish us luck.

"What the hell!" I scream.

Emma and Ezra quickly scamper. I rush into the bathroom, slamming the door behind me. Tears slide down my cheeks. My back slides against the wall as I drop to the floor. *Soccer all day on Saturday?* The thought stabs through my brain again and again.

I can't believe I felt guilty about sneaking to Blast Off Books the other day to pick up the manuscript for Ellory's Editors. I'm taking advantage of this amazing opportunity, whether Mark agrees to let me get a nanny or not.

"Mommy? Mommy?" A moment later, I see Ezra's little hand slip under the bottom of the bathroom door.

"Mama." I hear Emma's sweet voice, and now there are two sets of tiny hands pushing through the crack.

Inhaling deeply, I wipe the tears from my eyes, stand, and open the door.

"Here," Ezra says as he hands me Ellory's book. "Mommy is happy when she reads."

For a second, I'm confused, but then realize the twins must have gone upstairs to get my book. It's no wonder with the way I'm always carrying on about Mommy needing her reading time to relax. I take the book from Ezra's small hand and pull both him and Emma in for a tight hug. "You guys are the sweetest," I coo.

"Mama, you read. We play bingo." Emma looks at me with a prideful grin.

"Wonderful!" I say. "What a great idea."

Making myself comfortable on the couch, I open Ellory's book to where I left off. As the twins sit on the floor a few feet away, playing, my mind fills in another square on my marriage bingo card. I force the image away by getting lost in my book.

Theo glares at the note in his hand. "Why would you write this? You're putting my entire business at risk. No one can know about us. We've been over this." His eyes smolder in anger.

My pulse quickens. "Maybe I'm sick of acting like we're just business partners. Maybe I'm tired of watching you attend business dinners with tall, skinny blonds who want you to fall in love with them."

"But we've discussed this, Lexi. For God's sake, you're the one who told me to always bring a date to events." He exhales, out of breath, and the room goes quiet.

But instead of silence, all I can hear is the beat of my heart throbbing in my ears. After a moment, I feel a pressing need to explain myself again. "I wrote you that note so you would understand how I feel. I put it all on paper so you can't twist my words and make them into something else. Now you know how I feel and what I need. There's no more pretending you don't understand."

A strange feeling suddenly courses through my body. Maybe I need to write it all down for Mark. What I need…and how I'm feeling.

LATER THAT DAY, while Mark's still playing soccer, I sit down during Griffin's afternoon nap to type up my letter. Like Lexi, I may not have done a good job explaining things. Maybe Mark doesn't completely grasp how hard it is for me to be home. Maybe seeing each task spelled out in black against a stark white background will force him to grasp how hard my days are.

Dear Mark,

Being at home with the kids is hard. I don't feel like myself lately. I need to go back to work or start painting again. I want to do something that enriches my life beyond caretaking. The Ellory's Editors group is exactly the outlet I need. I'm at a breaking point.

I appreciate how hard you work to keep this family going. You work long days that are often stressful and thankless. You provide a good and secure life for this family. We appreciate everything you do.

I thought I would provide an account of the work I do during the week. I work REALLY hard, too, and unlike you, I do not get a break from my work on the weekends. My job is twenty-four hours, seven days a week.

I thought breaking everything down in numbers may help you better conceptualize what I am doing. I read somewhere that if a stay-at-home mom were to make a fair salary, it would be over $100,000! This makes sense to me. I'm on call every minute of every day. Below is a list of how I spend my time.

Per Week
I empty the dishwasher 4 times
I do 10 loads of laundry
I clean the house 12 times
I make plans and arrange social activities 7 times
I bathe 28 bodies
I make 18 beds
I sweep the kitchen floor 15 times
I brush 26 sets of teeth
I clean the highchair 30 times
I strap kids into car seats 48 times
I change 65 diapers
I prepare and serve 76 plates of food
I dress, undress, and put the kids in pajamas 52 times

This is what I need
1. A part-time nanny or part-time daycare for the twins
2. Two to three days a month to sleep in.

3. Two evenings a month where you pick up, plan, or prepare dinner.

4. A three- to four-night family vacation once a year. I've sent you links and tried to discuss vacation plans countless times over the past several years. It never seems to happen.

Hope this helps you understand more about where I'm coming from.

Love,

Faye

The printer spits out a single sheet of paper, but it's my heart on the page. I hold it in my hand and read it over again. My stomach knots when I consider how weird and desperate it is to copy an idea I read about in a romance novel.

Folding the letter in half, I ask Milo, Emma, and Ezra to come upstairs. I peek in on Griffin. He's sound asleep.

"Let's see what's on TV," I say to the twins.

I turn the television on. A funny-looking man in a tight orange costume is singing and dancing while a cartoon version of the letter F bounces around the screen. Emma sits on the floor and claps. Ezra rests his head on her lap.

"Milo, can you do Mommy a big favor? Can you watch the twins while I take a quick shower?"

"Yes, Mommy. I'm a big boy. I'll babysit them."

"You are the best babysitter, Milo!" I place the letter under Mark's pillow, enter the bathroom, and undress.

My body relaxes into the steam of the shower. As the water beats against my back, I wonder how I ended up being an unhappy stay-at-home mom who feels disconnected from her husband.

I recall after Milo was born, how I took a few months off, but then went back to work at the bank. I was assistant manager and on track to managing my own branch.

Two years later, just as I was getting ready for my promotion, Mark and I discovered we were having twins. We were overjoyed at the unexpected news but disagreed about how we would handle childcare. I wanted to go back to work after my maternity leave. The bank had finally given me my own branch. I researched the cost of both a nanny and daycare.

Mark felt differently. "Now that my parents have moved to Key West, we don't have anyone to help. The money you bring in from your job after we pay for childcare doesn't make it worth it for you to work."

The guilt I felt about not wanting to stay home with my children, combined with the negligible amount of money I would bring in after the cost of childcare, pushed me to accept Mark's suggestion. "Only one year," I told him.

However, one year later, when I approached Mark about returning to work, he insisted it still didn't make financial sense. "Plus, how great is it you get to be at home with Milo and the twins?" he said enthusiastically.

I was stunned by his words. How could he be so oblivious? It had only been a week since he'd come home to find me crouched in a corner, drinking wine, and sobbing about how badly I was failing at motherhood.

Then, before I even had the chance to tell him I would go back to work, whether or not he agreed, we found out I was pregnant with Baby G.

It's hard to understand how Mark is utterly ignorant of my struggles. I have to wonder if all the conversations I've had with him are a figment of my imagination. It's been close to four years since I agreed to stay home with the twins.

Drops of liquid stream down my face, but I'm not fooled. The wet drops sliding down my cheeks are not shower water. They are tears.

CHAPTER 19

Harper Weiss

THE DEEP PURPLE wood walls of Blast Off Books surround me. Sunlight shines through the store's large windows onto a painting of a gray shadowy moon, surrounded by the words "Reading can take you places." Hobbling forward, I take balanced steps on my crutches to a table of new romance releases in the center of the store.

Tessa Bailey has a new release, but so do Carley Fortune and Christina Lauren. Maybe I should get Ashley Poston's new one? But I've also heard amazing things about Sara Goodman Confino's *Don't Forget to Write*.

I spend a solid five minutes creepily caressing beautiful book covers, unable to choose just one.

A thin scraggly teenager walks over. His Blast Off Books badge sits cockeyed on his chest. "Ma'am, can I help you?"

"Um, yeah, that was weird," I say, embarrassed by the way I've been stroking the books on the store's center display table.

Tabby appears defusing the awkward moment.

"Harper, I saw you come in." She steps next to me as her employee grabs the misplaced Caroline Peckham smash, *Zodiac Academy*, moving it back to the TikTok's bestsellers table. Luckily, Tabby's employee doesn't call me out for fondling Meghan Quinn's latest.

Tabby smiles. "Let me run back in and get you Ellory's manuscript."

"Great," I say, watching as she disappears to the back of the store. Looking down at the table in front of me, I'm still overcome with the desire to thumb through as many of the books as possible. Over the past few days, I've gotten better on my crutches.

I wonder if I can do it. Leaning my weight on one of my crutches, I pitch my body forward and scoop up Jean Meltzer's *Kissing Kosher.* I rise proudly, as if I've just won gold at an Olympic event.

"Impressive." I hear Ben's voice and slowly maneuver my body to face him.

"Thanks again for agreeing to bring me here to pick up Ellory's manuscript. It's the middle of the day. I'm sure you have work to do."

Ben adjusts the tortoise-shell glasses on his face and grins. His smile is effortless. I half expect a twinkle of light to appear from the corner of his sultry mouth as a bell dings, signaling his perfection.

"This actually worked out great." He smiles again, and a rush of heat pulses in my thighs. "I need some books. I haven't had time to drive down to Miami and pick up my odds and ends."

"Odds and ends. I'm offended," I say teasingly. "Books are exactly the opposite of odds and ends. Books are essentials."

"Books and sugar-filled caramel iced coffees," Ben banters back.

"You really get me." I beam. But then feel embarrassed. "Anyway," I say, moving on. "Show me what you've picked out."

Ben holds up a paperback, with two historic, stoic faces set against a black background.

"*Nicholas and Alexandria,*" I read the title out loud. "Is this a book about the Romanov family?"

Ben nods. "Yup."

"That sounds heavy," I say.

"Well, sort of. But Robert Massie has such a talent for making history readable. I just finished *Peter the Great.*"

Before I can respond, Tabby appears. "Harper, I apologize. I just noticed the copier messed up. It printed every other page. Can you wait about ten minutes while I get everything straightened out?"

I glance at Ben. "It's up to him," I say. "He's taking time out of his day, so it depends on whether he needs to rush back to work."

Ben glances at his watch. "I've got something in about an hour. If you can have the manuscript ready before then, we're good."

Tabby smiles and nods her head. "Yes, be back in a few. Why don't you both have a seat and order a snack? It's on me." She gestures toward the café and then turns and rushes away.

"I owe you big," I say.

Ben chuckles.

"Can I add another favor, as long as I'm going to be forever drowning in debt?" I inch my crutches toward him, desperate to inhale his intoxicating scent.

"Sure." He winks. "Let me just get out my phone, so I can add to the list I've been keeping." Ben pulls out his phone. "Let me find it on my notepad," he teases. "Here it is, Harper Weiss Owes Me Big." He stares at his phone's screen as if he's reading something. His glasses magnify the long lashes of his eyes, drawing me into the jade green pools behind his frames.

"So, what's the favor?" He offers me round three of his perfect smile.

I don't know how much more I can take before I throw my crutches to the ground and thrust myself at him. I swallow and steady my voice. "Can you grab a few of these books and bring them over to the café?" I point to Danielle Steel's *Nine Lives* and *The BodyGuard* by Katherine Center. "Oh, and this one too." I tap the cover of Annabel Monaghan's *Nora Goes Off Script*.

Ben collects the brightly colored paperbacks. "I thought romance novels had pictures of half-naked muscle men embracing women in low-cut gowns?" His eyebrows arch questioningly.

"That's so 1980s," I say. "Women tote these books around in public as prize possessions. It's all about eye-catching modern drawings. Readers of romance no longer have to feel judged for carrying paperbacks with R-rated images on the front." I gesture toward the table to prove my point.

Ben's eyes bounce around, taking it all in. He picks up Ali

Hazelwood's, *The Love Hypothesis.* "Interesting," he says as he studies the cover intently.

I can't help but wonder what it would feel like to have his eyes focused on me—studying me, exploring me, for the first time.

"Um, Earth to Harper?"

I quickly snap out of my fantasy, realizing I must have missed what Ben just said. "What?" I ask as I try to slow down my rapid breathing.

"Let's go find a table," he says as he walks toward the café.

Sitting down, I inhale the scent of brownies and coffee. "It smells like heaven in here."

Ben nods in agreement. "I'm going to order a latte. Do you want your coffee monster signature drink?"

"That would be wonderful." I squeal as if I'm five and he's offered me a lifetime supply of candy. "Oh, and you should probably get one of those frosted brownies," I add.

A few minutes later, Ben's back and seated across from me. We're sipping coffee (in my case, almost pure sugar) and sharing bites of a large decadent brownie.

"So Russian history?" I ask as Ben picks up his steaming cup.

"I know lots of people think it's lame, but it's fascinating. I researched my family tree and found out all my ancestors are from a tiny shtetl in Russia." He pushes his Romanov novel toward me so I can check it out.

I catch it just as it teeters on the edge of our table. "I can see how this could be interesting," I say as I thumb through the pages, glancing at images of the Romanov family.

As we both get comfortable in our seats, I suddenly realize this has turned from a quick errand into something that feels like a date. Here we are, face-to-face, sitting across from each other, eating, bantering. A line of sweat prickles my back.

"Right now, I'm on a Russia kick," Ben continues. "I've been reading everything I can get my hands on—the Romanovs, Rasputin, the Russian Revolution." He pauses for a second and catches my eye.

My entire body contracts under his gaze.

"I did the same thing with China last year," he continues. "I binged on everything about the red dragon." His glasses slip a bit.

I watch as his hands push them back in place. *His hands*, I realize. I want them on my body.

"So why do you like romance so much?" Ben tilts his head to the side and his curls fall gently with the motion. "I remember that movie *Fifty Shades of Grey*," he continues. "That was a book, right? A very steamy book." His eyes flick with a mix of curiosity and amusement.

My gaze dips to his lips, and all I can think about is what it would be like to kiss him. Trying to focus, I think about Ellory's book. "I always get swept away by it all," I admit. "The tropes are familiar, yet reinvented each time. Opposites attract, work adversaries, forbidden love, soulmates, small towns, fake dating, and of course, the bone-thin blond skinny ex who is always wearing pointy expensive high heels in said small town." I pause for a moment and feel my lips curl up into a smile. "And there's contentment in knowing it will have a happily ever after."

Ben's forehead scrunches up as his eyebrows furrow together. "Hmm, soulmates and happily ever after."

His words remind me of the loneliness I've felt over the years.

My chest pangs with longing. "I'm not sure I believe in all that either, but it's sure fun to read about and fantasize."

"Fantasize?" Ben's demeanor quickly changes from cynical to buoyant. "Tell me more. What does Harper Weiss fantasize about, other than artificially flavored coffee?"

I squirm in my seat under his intense gaze. "Oh, I don't know. My fantasies are boring. Just someone to share the load and occasionally do the heavy lifting. I wouldn't mind being pampered every so often. I'd love to be with someone who wants my dreams to come true, as if they were their own. And I would love to have another child…" I let my voice trail off. I suddenly feel as vulnerable as a butterfly in the hands of a small child.

"But what about all the romance stuff? The roses and grand gestures? The moment Lloyd Dobler from the movie *Say Anything* shows up with the boom box blasting the song *"In Your Eyes?"*

As he waits for my response, my attraction intensifies, causing my heart to beat wildly in my chest. He must notice the blush taking over my face because he quickly changes the focus back to himself.

"You're right. None of that big romance stuff matters," he says. "I just want to give my son what I had growing up. A few more siblings, Jewish summer camp, a solid example of a loving marriage."

"Yes!" I practically yelp, finally able to focus. "Jewish sleepaway camp is the best. I bet you had your first real kiss at camp. Who needs fake dating and horrible skinny ex-wives? Jewish sleepaway camp is the only thing necessary for an amazing whirlwind romance."

Ben's face contorts strangely as I finish speaking. He's quiet for just a moment too long.

Have I said something wrong? I notice he's looking past me now, over my shoulder, and into the main part of Blast Off Books. I track his gaze and land squarely on a bone-thin blond with stick-straight long hair. She turns her head and begins pounding toward us. Her expensive pointy heels click and clack as she storms through the café area right to our table.

"Thank God, I still have that app that tracks where your cell phone is. I've been waiting at your house for twenty minutes to get Wyatt." Each word she speaks is as sharp as the point of her heels.

"Well, you're early, Cassidy. Very early." Ben crosses his arms and his entire body stiffens.

The evil woman, now identified as Cassidy, huffs and turns her eyes at me. "Hello," she says in a voice lined with irritation. "I'm Cassidy, Ben's wife."

"Soon to be ex," he says under his breath.

"We'll see about that." She turns and looks at me. "We're in the process of reconciling."

Ben shakes his head, cupping his mouth with his hand as if he's trying to keep himself from saying something he'll regret.

My face twitches into a strange smile as I stare down at the pile of romance novels in front of me. The absurdity of this situation is unreal. I almost laugh out loud, but quickly take a sip of my coffee instead. I'm trapped in one of these books.

CHAPTER 20

Ellory Brayson

A S I WALK toward the kitchen, my eyes focus on the large marble statue of a greyhound nestled beside a cobalt blue ottoman. The bold décor of the Rutherford Estate is getting under my skin. I can't relax. Grabbing a white mug from the open shelving by the kitchen table, I step to the whistling kettle on the stove.

I add organic loose-leaf tea to the large mug. As I pour the water in, steam rises and tickles my face. It's hard to prepare proper tea without thinking about Maxy. We were living in Paris when he taught me how to add a hint of fresh mint and steep the leaves for the perfect amount of time.

Unwelcome thoughts of the night we met invade my mind. I was twenty-one years old and had just graduated from college. I was living in Paris, doing research for my second release—*We'll Always Have Paris*. Unbelievably, my first novel, *Beaches and Beaus*, was number one.

One night, a few weeks into my three-month trip, I found myself at a glamorous party hosted by one of Paris's top socialites. She was an avid romance reader. When she learned I was in town, she contacted my agent and invited me to her party.

I can recall standing on the posh balcony of her villa in Le 16, French high society's chosen mecca. A man wandered over and introduced himself as Prince Maximilian Jacoby. He was from a small nation I'd never heard of on the eastern European border. His family's status was like the royals in England. They gave honors, advised, and pranced around their country as human morale boosters. Prince Maximilian explained he was the fourth and youngest child of the king and queen. He was thirty years old and fourth in line for the throne.

"I'm the punch line of many jokes in my country," he said indifferently, with a raspy accent dripping with sex appeal. "But the joke's on them. I have all the benefits of being royalty, with no chance of responsibility." His eyes twinkled with amusement.

I should have excused myself at that very moment. Prince Maximilian was clearly a man with wealth, influence, charm, and good looks that would lead to nothing but trouble. But, then again, he was a man with wealth, influence, charm, and good looks. Extreme good looks, if I was being honest.

It wasn't long before we were gallivanting across Europe. I was suddenly living in a romance novel, and the press couldn't get enough. My agent encouraged me to step into the limelight and let the public be part of the budding relationship. "It's so on brand," she insisted. "Your fan base is going to explode."

It was hard to argue with her. And it thrilled me to showcase my great love and good fortune with the world. He proposed with an eight-carat stunner just three months after we met. The news exploded with headlines like "Romance Author Gets Her Happily Ever After" and "Ellory Brayson is a Modern-Day Cinderella." Katie Couric even interviewed me on the *Today Show*. Bookstores could not keep my first book on the shelf.

The problem was, once you've announced to the world your life is perfect, you can never ever be anything but. So, when Tabby begged me not to marry Maxy, I had a choice to make. Was I going to abandon my growing fame and fortune, or was I going to embrace my rising star and success despite the price?

The choice wasn't as hard as one may think, but in doing so, I replaced my genuine self with my celebrity self. It was the only way to survive.

Picking up my steaming mug, I sip the delicate floral liquid, feeling the warmth spread through my body.

"Morning." I hear Cade's voice before he steps into the kitchen.

"Hey, good morning," I reply, making my way to the kitchen table. With so many thoughts of Maxy still swirling in my mind, it's hard to look at Cade without feeling momentarily unnerved. He has the same angular jaw and entrancing eyes. Inhaling deeply, I let the thought fly away. Cade is not Maxy.

"How did you sleep?" I ask.

"Great. The bed's really comfortable." Cade walks to the fruit bowl, grabs a banana, then joins me at the table. His skin is sun-kissed. He's been here almost two weeks, and I haven't questioned him about his plans going forward. I know, as his mother, I need to broach the subject, but I'm afraid to do anything to push him away. I start with something simple. "So, what are you doing today?"

He breaks off the banana where it's brown and soggy and puts the overly ripened piece of fruit on the saucer that holds my mug. "I'm not a hundred percent sure," he says. "I may check out the pier and go to the beach."

An anxious twang makes my stomach clench. He's not in school, he doesn't have a job, he was just arrested, and he has no long-term plans. He doesn't have a care in the world. He might as well be on that balcony in Paris telling me how he gets to have all the fun with no real responsibility.

"The pier is nice," I begin before I pivot to his plans for the future. "Tabby and I used to spend a lot of time there as kids."

"Tabby? Your best friend?" He makes air quotes as he says the words *best friend*. It irritates me.

"Yes, my best friend," I snap.

"It's just weird you've had this best friend I've never heard of until a few weeks ago. Where has she been all my life?" He drops his banana on the table and leans back in his chair. His broad shoulders spread out, taking up the surrounding space.

"She's been around. We've kept in touch here and there. You know how my life is. I'm always writing, editing, and promoting. I have to put out two or three books a year if I want to stay on top."

"Oh, yes, I know." His lips pucker into a pout, and suddenly he looks five years old.

"I don't like the way you're talking to me, Cade." I peer at him, wondering how this conversation went south so quickly.

"Well, it's true. When I was a kid, you were always busy. You never had time for me. You just said it yourself. All I did was agree." He quickly gets up from the table. His chair makes a discordant squeak as he stands.

"Wait, Cade," I call, fully expecting him to ignore me. We've played this scene out a thousand times. But instead of stomping off as he usually does, he stops and turns toward me.

"I'm not like your, quote-unquote, best friend Tabby," he says gruffly. "I'm not going to just let you pretend nothing's wrong because you suddenly have time for me." His face twitches slightly in anger.

For a second, I'm silent. I want to point out that he's staying in this beautiful house because of me. I want to shout that he's had every opportunity, every privilege, and the freest ride in life because he's my son.

But as soon as I open my mouth, his expression changes, and all I can see is Maxy explaining away Tabby's concerns about our relationship in a way that makes me powerless to argue with him. Suddenly, it's as if Maxy is standing in this kitchen, gaslighting me for the millionth time. He's Maxy, the one I chose over Tabby.

Guilt overtakes me, and I blink several times, bringing Cade back into focus. Then I realize Cade's right. Why would Tabby let me back into her life so easily? Why hasn't she called me out for the way I treated her? Is the money she'll get from our arrangement really enough for her to push aside our past?

My heartbeat picks up. I instantly realize I'm in a risky situation. Would Tabby turn on me? I'm still trying to recover from *This Morning America*.

"I have to go Cade." My words come out with sharp edges.

"Typical," he sighs.

"I'm sorry. You're right about a lot of things, but our conversation reminded me of something I need to do. It's important." Standing, I walk past him. I need to get dressed and get to Blast Off Books immediately.

"Exactly, Mom, there's always something more important than me."

I cringe for a moment at his comment, but I can't respond. My genuine self would hear Cade out and make things right. But my genuine self no longer exists. I take long strides toward my bedroom, my celebrity self in full control.

CHAPTER 21

Tabitha Wilson

MY BODY BUSTLES with pangs of excitement as I slice open the box I received from Anchor Head Books. It's a small publishing company, but they have a talent for picking entertaining novels mixed with heart and soul.

Pulling out their newest title, I read the book's description and am reminded of why I wanted to order this one. It's contemporary fiction with a nod to the '80s. A whimsical drawing of two girls with big hair and off-the-shoulder fluorescent-colored tops makes the cover pop. I can't wait to get started.

"There you are."

Glancing up, I see Ellory standing before me. Her lustrous long blond hair is in a messy ponytail. And it doesn't look like she's wearing any makeup.

I purse my lips into a forced smile. "Hey, I wasn't expecting you. The first meeting for Ellory's Editors is two days from now. We're all set, right?"

Ellory breezes past me and sits on the couch in my office as if she owns the place. "Yes, everything starts in two days, but did you get the email from my publicist with details about the photos I need for social media?"

Ellory and I already texted about this, so I'm confused. But my confusion quickly turns to concern. I get the sense Ellory's up to something. I'm reminded of what Andre said the other night. That I need to keep my guard up.

"We texted about that already," I say, trying to keep my voice balanced. "Remember, you'll meet with Faye and Harper in my office, but we'll stage the pictures out in the store at the table in front of the big bay windows."

"Yes, I know, but I wanted to talk with you about getting some shots of us around town. Maybe in front of the Picture Planet. The old-time movie theater marquee would make a great backdrop." Ellory taps her foot, unable to be still.

Is she nervous? I can practically hear alarm bells ringing in my ear. Before I can respond, she's talking again.

"Or maybe at the pier? Cade and I were just discussing the pier this morning at breakfast."

Her words come out too fast. Something's going on. Maybe it has to do with Cade. It certainly surprised Ellory when he showed up at the Rutherford Estate, unannounced, with plans to stay for the summer.

"Is everything okay?" I ask, treading lightly.

"Yes, why?" Ellory's eyes shift back and forth uneasily.

"You seem agitated," I say honestly.

Ellory sinks back into the couch and lets out a sigh.

Is she going to be vulnerable with me? I'm not sure she's capable of letting down her shield. She transformed into something hard and inflexible after she married Maxy. It surprised me the other night when we shared a laugh over TikTok, but I quickly realized her edges softened because of the wine.

"Yes, it's Cade," she says. "We had a fight. He's angry I've been wrapped up in my career for his entire life." Her eyes widen and surprisingly prick with tears.

Her honesty is so unexpected that I find I'm moving to the couch and putting my arm around her. But as soon as our bodies connect, I pull away. *Keep your guard up*, I remind myself.

"I bet that's hard to hear," I say. But as the words leave my mouth, I also feel a twinge of satisfaction. *That's what you get for putting your career before everything else.*

"Tabby." The voice draws my eyes toward my office door. One of my employees peeks in hesitantly. "Sorry to interrupt, but the register just crashed, and I can't get it back online."

"Again?" I say frustrated.

"Yes, and there's a line of people waiting to pay five deep," my employee continues.

"Okay. I'm coming." I turn to Ellory. "Sit tight. I'll be back in as soon as I deal with this."

WOMEN WITH ENORMOUS bellies shuffle around me in the waiting room of my obstetrician's office. It's hard not to feel as if they're showing off their good fortune. This is the top fertility specialist in Jupiter City. And even though I know all these women have had a hard road, I can't help but feel jealous. *Why not me?*

I need to stop thinking like this, or I'm going to spiral quickly. I shift my thoughts to earlier today when Ellory stopped by the store. The whole thing was strange. And then, before we could discuss Cade, I was called away. The problem with my register ended up taking longer than expected, and Ellory left before we could continue our conversation. It was a relief. Why should I support her when she so easily dismissed me?

Sighing, I think about being stuck with Ellory all summer. I wish I had pushed back on the whole Ellory's Editors plan when she suggested it. But I couldn't resist the money and how it would allow Andre and me one last opportunity to go through IVF. I just need to make it to Labor Day.

"Mrs. Wilson." A medical assistant wearing scrubs adorned with baby rattles calls my name. Fear crashes over me. This appointment must go well. I won't be able to handle bad news.

Standing, I follow the assistant to the ultrasound room. A paper robe sits on top of the exam table.

"Go ahead and get undressed. The ultrasound technician will be in shortly."

I nod but don't meet the assistant's eye. I don't want my emotions to get the best of me.

As I pull the flimsy paper robe around my body, I hear a knock at the door.

"Come in," I say.

The ultrasound technician enters. I notice her scrubs have teddy bears all over them.

Enough with the baby-themed scrubs. I rest my legs in stirrups for the millionth time. This process has hurled my sense of modesty into outer space. As she places the probe inside me, the cold gel causes me to shiver.

"Dr. Feldman will come take a look as soon as I'm done."

I wonder if she can feel my desperation. It must be hard to work, day in and day out, with women praying for a modern miracle.

My body throbs with worry as the minutes drag on. Nothing is worse than knowing I have no control over what my future will hold. I feel helpless.

"All set. I'll be right back with Dr. Feldman."

This moment is always excruciating. The ultrasound tech knows my fate but must remain silent. She's like an all-knowing god who's unable to reveal her powerful knowledge.

Moments later, there's a knock at the door. Inhaling a sharp breath, I prepare myself as best I can.

"Come in," I say again.

"Hey, baby." Andre peeks his head in and then enters the room.

"Oh," I blurt, surprised he's here.

"I know you said I didn't have to come, but I wanted to be here." He steps toward me and grasps my hand in his large palm.

My body relaxes when our hands connect. "That's sweet of you." I'm instantly reminded of why I love this man.

"I know we've been through it all before, but I'm part of this just as much as you." He leans over me and brushes the hair out of my eyes as Dr. Feldman enters the room.

"Hi there," Dr. Feldman says with a wink. "So great to see you both."

It's hard not to read between the lines of every single thing Dr. Feldman does before he delivers the update.

"I'm going to take a quick look myself, if you don't mind." He picks up the probe and locks his eyes on the ultrasound machine's screen.

My mind spins. Was that wink to let me know everything looks good and to relax? Why is he squinting toward the screen? Why is he pulling the probe out so fast?

"Great news." He beams, turning toward me. "Everything looks wonderful. Let's get some blood work. But I think you're ready for your trigger shot."

All the muscles in my body relax as if they're thawing after a deep freeze. Hope gently puts its hand on my shoulder and squeezes. A calm whirl settles over me. The fact that I'm feeling hopeful is its own kind of miracle.

CHAPTER 22
Ila Wilson

THE SKY IS exploding with colors that leave me breathless. Oranges and pinks hang over the buildings of the Fort Lauderdale skyline like a canopy. I wish I had my sketch pad and pastels to capture the moment.

"This is beautiful," I say as I lean back into CJ's broad chest. We pulled onto a shoulder on A1A so we wouldn't miss the sunset on our drive back to Jupiter Cove. CJ parked his car in a small circle beside a line of palm trees. We're shielded from the cars whizzing by.

Leaning back, he wraps his arms around me as we both look into the distance. I was unsure how things would go today when CJ picked me up from Meteor Café after the breakfast shift. As I entered his car for the sailboat excursion, my body fluttered with nerves. An image of CJ's naked body over mine caused my skin to prick with sweat. *Did I really have sex with CJ the other night while we were at Venus Inlet?*

Until then, Jackson was the only person I had ever been with. And our sexual relationship unfolded as if under the guidelines of an after-school special. We dated for over a year. We were exclusive. We said we loved each other.

Sleeping with CJ was not only an act of rebellion, it was also the knockout punch that slammed my past with Jackson closed. But it was more than a moment of pure pleasure. Everything in the world faded as soon as CJ wrapped his naked body around me. Everything ceased to exist but CJ.

But this morning, as we drove to Fort Lauderdale, there was a sinking feeling in my stomach. *Would today reveal that the other night was a mistake?*

We didn't talk much while on the boat. Instead, CJ wrote furiously in his notebook, capturing every detail he felt. I tried my best to relax and enjoy the wind in my hair and the beauty of where the horizon met the ocean. But as the silence dragged between us, my worries expanded.

Standing, I walked away from the deck where CJ and I sat and moved toward the back of the boat. A few moments later, CJ appeared. His body bobbed slightly from side to side as he took carefully balanced steps toward me.

"Hey, Peach. Sorry I've been ignoring you. When I write, I get swept away into a black hole." His hair swung over his eyes.

I knew the feeling. When I'm zoned into my art, the world stops. Often, hours go by before I pause and realize the day is ending. Even so, I felt vulnerable, considering we had just had sex for the first time. I nodded half-heartedly, feeling unconvinced by his explanation.

"Here, do you want to read a few of the disjointed thoughts I've written?" He pushed his notebook toward me.

"Sure." It surprised me that he would let me look over his work in such a rough state. I never let anyone see my drawings until I'm past the first five shitty drafts.

"It's unpolished. I'm just brainstorming. Don't be too judgmental." He blinked back a bashful smile.

> The breeze breathes life into me
> The salty air infuses my body with vitality and power
> The rhythmic movement of the boat is like a trance

The pages continued with notes about his character, Captain Nicholas, and his life on the sea. Reading his words was like a window into his inner thoughts. I felt like I was being pulled away from my past and toward something new and wonderful. The misgivings I had about our night on the beach suddenly felt unfounded.

And now, the silence between us, as we watch the sun disappear from the sky, fills me with unexpected contentment. Just as I relax into the moment, my phone buzzes.

"Again?" CJ asks. "Why don't you just answer your dad's call?" CJ untangles our bodies and turns me so I'm facing him.

"He has too many questions," I say, ruffled. "It's like I tried to explain to you on the phone the other night. Now that he knows Jackson and I broke up, he's in full-on investigation mode. He's desperate to find out all the details, but it's none of his business." I step away from CJ, needing some breathing room.

"Hey," he says as the corners of his lips fall. "I didn't mean to upset you. But did you ever think your dad's interest is coming from a place of love?"

I shrug as if my shoulders can make his words roll away.

CJ continues. "I wish my parents wanted to know what was going on in my life, but they're always running around focused on their own stuff. I just think you should consider your dad's motivation."

An irritating buzz beats in my chest. This thing with CJ is just starting. I don't want to tarnish the shiny beginning with my family problems. Thoughts are piling on top of each other as I try to come up with an excuse for us to drop this topic of conversation. But before I can say anything, CJ is talking again.

"And I think you should think about your dad's wife's motivation as well." He says the words *dad's wife* with emphasis, to point out that I refuse to call her my stepmom. "From the little you've told me, it sounds like she also keeps attempting to connect."

"Clearly, I've already told you too much." Hot, angry words spill out of me.

"Really, Peach?" he asks, keeping his composure. "I don't even know your stepmom's name." His voice is soft. He's approaching this gently, with kindness. His eyes lock with mine, and my insides turn to jelly. He is breathtakingly beautiful in the fading light.

Reaching his hand out, he pulls me back into an embrace. "Let's not fight. This is silly." He cups my chin in his left palm and turns my face up to his. "I shouldn't be getting involved in your family stuff. I'm sorry." His lips meet mine, and all my anger rushes out of me as if swept away by a sudden gust of wind.

A moment later, we're making our way to his car in the twilight. Our bodies collide in the back seat. His hands travel over every inch of me.

"Not here," I say as he sits me on top of him. "It's too open. It's still too light out."

"I don't think I can stop," he pants. "I want you too much." His eyes search mine for permission to continue.

As much as I want to be with him, I feel exposed. The line of palm trees next to the car barely camouflages our presence. I cross my arms over my body and look away.

"Okay," he whispers in my ear. "You're right. Let's head home. We can go to Venus Inlet. And it will be dark when we get back." He caresses my arm with his palm as he slides me off his waist.

"Or," I say, "we could go to your friend's place in Jupiter City. It's on the way home."

CJ's eyes flit from side to side. "Oh, but my friend will be there. It's a good idea, but maybe another time."

I lean in and kiss him fully. "Yes, definitely another time."

Moving apart from our embrace, I crawl from the back seat to the front. My phone buzzes again, this time with a text notification. I pull it out of my bag and read the words from my dad.

> **Dad:** Tabby's made it through the next step of IVF. I need you to do everything you can to keep her stress level down.

What exactly does he mean by keeping Tabby's stress level down? I'm practically a ghost in that house. I toss the phone back into my bag angrily.

"Everything okay?" CJ asks, as he settles in the front seat.

"Family stuff. Let's just drop it." I slide my hand onto his thigh and up to the waistband of his shorts.

"Hey," he says in a sultry whisper as I lean into him and kiss his neck. "I thought we were going to find somewhere more private."

But before he can continue, I'm on top of him.

CHAPTER 23
Faye Carter

CRAWLING UNDER MY covers, I sink into my sheets. An enormous pile of clean laundry sits in a basket on the floor. I know I should fold it, but the first meeting for Ellory's Editors is coming up, and I need to finish the first hundred pages of her manuscript. I'm not sure what to think so far. This book differs from her usual. There's not a central love story, and I have a feeling it will not have a happy ending.

Flipping through the printed and bound pages, I drop the bulky manuscript on the floor. This is exactly why I love reading romance. Reading books about women with unhappy marriages and heart-breaking stories is not an escape. It hits a little close to home.

I pick up *The Prince of Silicon Valley* and continue to read about Lexi and Theo's love affair. He's about to announce his company's IPO, and all hell is going to break loose.

My eyes scan the pages, but the words disintegrate into nothingness before my brain can process them. My anger about tonight is still a sharp pulse in my throat. I was not expecting to feed, bathe, and get the kids ready for bed on my own again tonight. Mark was supposed to come home after his playoff game. But he called to say he was going to hang out with his teammates for a bit.

"You've got to be joking." I practically spat my words into the phone. "You promised you would do bedtime tonight so I could have a break."

"Awe, babe. I'll do bedtime for the next few nights. I promise. We came back and won. Everyone's pumped!" In the background, I could hear the boisterous shouts of men who had not a care in the world. And then the phone went silent.

Now, two hours later, my body still burns with furious energy. I think about the letter I wrote to Mark last week. It took every ounce of my courage to put it under his pillow. But he hasn't said a word about it. It sits unopened on his bedside table. *Should I just rip it up?*

Closing my eyes, Ellory's character, Lexi, pops into my mind. Her long shiny auburn ponytail sways back and forth as she angrily considers what to do about the unread note. When I open my eyes, she's sitting on the corner of my bed.

"Oh!" I gasp.

"It's okay," she says. "I want to talk to you about Mark."

Squeezing my eyes shut again, I open them slowly, hoping her image disappears.

"Make him read the note, so you have a fighting chance." She stomps toward Mark's side of the bed and shoves the letter under his pillow.

"But how are you here?" A strange tingle spreads through my body.

"I'm here because you need me. I want to make sure Mark reads your letter."

Shaking my head, I expect Lexi to fade away. But instead of vanishing, she continues to talk. "And why don't you think about a happy memory of Mark to keep your mind from spinning with anger?"

My mouth gapes open.

"Just do it," she insists. She sighs impatiently, and I can't help but sympathize with Theo. She's relentless. And although I know it's crazy to follow advice gleaned from a fictional character, I decide to try.

Lexi nods triumphantly, somehow aware I'm giving in to her suggestion.

I think about the first time Mark told me he loved me. It was after FLA-U had just won a big rivalry game in overtime.

"We got the W!" I said as we huddled around a bonfire with Mark's brothers and a small group of exhilarated FLA-U fans.

"Yes," Mark cheered as he pretended to throw a long pass to one of his brothers. "If my soccer team wins tomorrow, it will be the perfect weekend. Are you coming to my game?"

"I wish, but I'm starting my painting class on advanced watercolor techniques. I'm excited."

As Mark and I fell into each other's arms, I felt like I was finally in a healthy adult relationship. We had our shared interests, but we also gave each other space to pursue other things.

"Will your class be over in time for you to come to the barbeque at my parents'?" Mark pulled me close to him, and we snuggled under a blanket close to the fire. "My family loves you."

"And I love them," I said without hesitation. I treasured the way Mark's parents opened their hearts to me. His mom, Elaine, was incredibly kind and somehow walked that delicate line of being motherly without trying to star in the role. The warmth I felt from the Carter family was incredibly comforting since my parents were gone.

"Come here," he said as the fire crackled around us. He pulled me onto his lap. "It's so hard for me to say this kind of thing, but I just can't keep it to myself anymore."

I can recall how my heart skipped a beat before he spoke again.

"I love you," he whispered into my ear.

Something inside me softens at the memory. Maybe Lexi's onto something.

CHAPTER 24
Harper Weiss

"**T**EXT ME WHEN it's over, and I'll come to get you." Ben swings open the door to Blast Off Books and waits for me to hobble inside.

"Are you sure? I can easily call an Uber." I think back to the awkward moment last week when Ben and I left the bookstore along with his almost ex, Cassidy. As I got in his car, I could feel her eyes blazing into me as if they were laser beams.

"You're not taking an Uber. My job is super flex. I got this." He smiles and I melt.

"Okay, thank you." I make my way past him, hoping he doesn't catch me inhaling his amazing scent. *Stop pining away for this man,* I tell myself. He's not emotionally available. He made that clear last week when he called to apologize for Cassidy's behavior.

"She's holding up the divorce with every excuse possible. She wasn't ready to see me with another woman, even if we're just friends." *Just friends,* I say over and over in my head as I approach Tabby.

"Follow me this way," Tabby says excitedly as she leads me through shelves of books until we reach a door. "You're going to meet with Ellory in my office, so everything you discuss remains private. Ellory doesn't want any leaks about her new book." She winks at me as she opens the door to her private office.

The interior is spacious and cozy. A distressed wooden table is centered between a plush floral couch and two oversized gold velvet chairs. A gorgeous purple bookcase lines one wall. Several small-framed black-and-white posters hang on the wall behind the couch with sayings such as "Crazy Book Lady," "Just One More Chapter," and "Reading Is My Jam."

"What an amazing space." I walk inside.

"Thank you." Tabby beams with pleasure. "You're the first one to arrive." She gestures for me to take a seat.

I pull out Ellory's manuscript and a pen as I get comfortable on the couch.

"I'm going to grab a tray of snacks and some water. Would you like some coffee?"

"I'm good," I say nervously. "If I drink coffee, I'll be even more jittery than I already am." I tap my pen back and forth, trying to dispel some of my revved-up energy.

"Oh, don't be nervous," Tabby says as she turns. This is going to be fun!"

As I sit and wait for the first Ellory's Editors meeting to begin, I review the notes I made in the margins of the manuscript. Will I be brave enough to tell famous author and icon Ellory Brayson what I really think?

I circle what I feel is my most insightful comment just as Ellory enters the room.

"Hey, Harper." Her eyes travel to the crutches leaning against the couch beside me. "Oh, no, did you break your leg?"

I wonder for a moment if I should tell her how my life is a failed romance novel, but then think better of it. "It happened at work. I fell over a stool. It's my ankle, but I'll be okay."

"Well, I'm sorry to hear that." Ellory steps toward one of the velvet chairs and places an enormous designer tote bag on the table between us.

As she pulls out her copy of the manuscript, my body tingles with electric energy. I'm so grateful to be part of this, it feels as if my chest could burst with delight. *Will my brush with Ellory be the steppingstone to fulfilling my lifelong dream of becoming a published author?*

"Let's see. It's five minutes past. Let's give Faye a few more minutes, and then I guess we'll get started." Ellory puts on bright red reading glasses and pushes her perfect long blond hair away from her face. "So, tell me about yourself," she says as she sits back in her chair.

I grin like a silly schoolgirl. "Sure. I've got an eleven-year-old son. I'm an occupational therapist. I'm originally from Boca Raton, but moved here when my son was three years old."

"An eleven-year-old?" Ellory's face makes that surprised expression that everyone makes when they find out I have a tween.

I'm well practiced in how to respond, but because it's Ellory, I feel a bit off-kilter. Swallowing my nerves, I tell her the short and sweet version. "I know. I'm so young, right?" Clasping my hands together, I continue. "I had a serious boyfriend in high school. I found out I was pregnant my senior year. My boyfriend and I loved each other, but it didn't work out. He went to college, and I lived at home with my parents. I finished high school, went to a local college, and then went back to school for my masters in OT. My mom was an OT, and it was a practical career choice."

"Wow!" Ellory says. "You're obviously determined and know how to achieve your goals."

"I appreciate that," I say, wondering if I should tell her my true passion is writing, and my real goal is to be a published author. But nerves make my limbs jumble with a tingly sensation, and suddenly I can't speak. Luckily, Tabby walks in with an assortment of baked goods.

"Did you see Faye out there?" Ellory asks.

"No. Hopefully, she'll be here soon," Tabby says.

"I think we need to get started without her."

I can sense the slightest bit of irritation in Ellory's voice.

"You know what, Tabby. I can't believe I didn't think of this before, but why don't you jump in as a third editor? I'd love your feedback. You're clearly well read."

Tabby stiffens, and I can't tell if it's because she's nervous to accept or uncomfortable. "Ha," she responds, laughing off Ellory's comment.

"No, I'm serious." Ellory's face pinches as if she's been pricked by a pin. "You're already halfway through my manuscript. Please, I insist you jump in."

"Well, it's just—"

"I'm here. So sorry I'm late." Faye bounds up to the door, pushing a stroller, and cutting Tabby off. "My childcare fell through, so I've got the baby, but he's asleep. I hope that's okay. Milo and the twins are out in the children's section. One of your employees said they'd keep an eye on them." Faye avoids looking at Ellory. I guess she's hoping she can still participate.

"Um, sure." Ellory shifts around in her chair. I can tell she's not thrilled. "Let's get started. Tabby, have a seat."

Tabby's eyes widen. I guess she wasn't going to agree to Ellory's offer.

Ellory reaches her arm out toward the empty spaces around us, encouraging Tabby and Faye to get settled.

"So, thank you again for participating. As explained in the non-disclosure, everything we discuss is confidential."

I nod my head as Ellory continues.

"Today, I want to talk about the first hundred pages. Did you have time to read that far?" Ellory looks directly at Faye.

"Yes!" Faye blurts anxiously.

"Great. I wonder what your initial thoughts are. Faye, why don't you start?"

"Sure." As Faye pulls her manuscript out of a large diaper bag, a pacifier rolls to the ground. "Sorry about that," she says, leaning over to grab it. She stuffs it back in her bag and continues. "My first impression is that this book is not like your others. This doesn't feel like romance."

Ellory nods. "You're not wrong. It's not romance. How did you feel as you read? Did you wish you had known it was something different, or were you glad to be along for the ride?"

Before Faye can answer, her baby lets out a whimper. Faye peers into her stroller, but the baby settles on his own. "Sorry. Next time, I'll have backup childcare. I promise."

She closes her eyes for a moment and then comes back to Ellory's question. "For me, reading your books is all about escaping the problems of everyday life. So, I was confused when your book touched on some serious subject matters. I guess I would have liked a heads up you were trying something new, that this wasn't romance."

Ellory nods her head and makes a note in her manuscript. "This is good information, Faye. My team is deciding whether to tell readers my new book differs from my usual romance novels or not." Ellory turns and looks at me. "Harper, what did you think?"

"Hmm, let me think for a moment." I consider my thoughts as I read the first chapters of the manuscript. "I think, like Faye, I was surprised, but I'm a pretty go-with-the-flow person, so I feel like I'm along for the ride, as you said."

"Okay, we've got one of each," Ellory says. "Tabby, any thoughts?"

Tabby stares at the ground, as if the correct answer is written on the floor. "I'm not sure I can answer this one fairly," she says. "The inspiration for this story…" Tabby's voice quiets before she finishes her thought.

My muscles tighten at the sudden tension in the room.

"Fair enough," Ellory says as she taps her pen against her thigh. "Let's move on to the opening. Did it work? Did it pull you in?" She looks around at the three of us.

I have the answer to this question. It's the insightful comment I circled just a moment ago. My leg bounces. *Am I brave enough to say it?* The room is uncomfortably silent.

"Hey, listen, everyone, take a deep breath. Put the fact that I'm the world's most famous romance author aside. I love that Faye was honest about my genre change." Ellory glances at all of us. "Someone say something."

Suddenly, I hear words spilling from my mouth. It's as if I'm a doll and someone has pulled a string to make me talk. "I actually have a comment about the beginning."

"Well, let's hear it," Ellory says encouragingly.

"See this part here that I highlighted?" I flip my manuscript around so Ellory can see the page number. She takes a few minutes to read my highlights.

"I think this would work better in chapter one. This scene where the girls steal the caviar from the party is fun. It's so visual. I could picture the girls running down the beach, holding hands, thrilled about their crime. I would start with that."

Ellory cocks her head. I know what she's doing from my experience writing novels. She's taking chunks of text in her mind, reordering them, and then piecing them back together as if it's a puzzle.

"Hmm, I like that, Harper. I think that works." She makes a few notes in her manuscript and smiles at me. "That was a great edit. I'm impressed."

My face flushes with a mix of pride and excitement.

"I think you may have missed your calling being an OT," she says with a laugh.

My body trembles slightly. Ellory has given me the perfect opening to tell her about my writing. Should I take it? I have to take it. I pull together courage from all my edges.

"Well, I actually write on the side. I've written three romance novels, although none are published." I exhale the words. My lifelong dream is now flying outside my body. Free to roam.

"Oh, wow!" Ellory says excitedly. "That's fabulous. I'm so glad we chose you to be one of my editors."

My stomach rolls as she speaks. I'm dying to ask her to read some of my work, but I'm going to take things slow. Hopefully, the opportunity will present itself.

CHAPTER 25
Ellory Brayson

"**I LOVED THE PART** where Emma and Tish were in the bathroom getting ready for the middle school dance." Faye's face brightens. "Piling on too much makeup, doing each other's hair, singing into their hairbrushes as they listened to music. It brought back so many memories."

Nodding my head, I'm suddenly assaulted by the most horrid smell. My nose bristles in response.

"Oh, no!" Faye jolts up from the couch in Tabby's office. "I'm so sorry. I think Griffin needs a diaper change." She lowers her head, defeated. "Is there somewhere I can change him?"

Tabby stands, her eyes glued on the baby with a fervent stare. "Let me show you to the restroom. We have a changing station there."

Faye scurries out with Tabby, and I'm left with Harper. My head swirls with irritation. *Why in the world would Faye agree to do this if she couldn't find childcare?* Her presence is a disruption. And even though Harper's feedback is good, is she going to turn into one of those desperate writers who wants me to be her champion?

"The baby years can be so challenging." Harper breaks the silence with a comment meant to defuse the situation.

"Yes," I say, although I can't really relate. I had a full-time live-in nanny when Cade was young, and then a house manager who oversaw Cade's entire life when he was older.

"Do you mind if I catch up on a few emails while we wait for them to return?" Harper asks. "I've got some work things that need attention." She fishes inside her bag.

"Sure, good idea," I say as I take out my phone and open Gmail. The draft I wrote to Tabby last night sits at the top of my inbox, unsent.

> I saw you read my manuscript when I was in your office the other day. I specifically asked you not to read it until we talked about it. Surprised you would go behind my back.

On the night of the book signing, I gave Tabby my manuscript on a thumb drive, but I told her we needed to talk before she read it. I hoped a conversation about my work in progress would inspire me to apologize. I guess curiosity got the best of her.

And it was my curiosity that led me to the discovery. When she was dealing with the broken cash register, I was snooping around her office. It was wrong, but I was unhinged about her motivations for helping me.

I rummaged around her desk, and that's when I saw she was reading my book.

She certainly looked stunned earlier when I called her out and insisted she join our editing group.

"Look what I have!" Tabby returns with Faye's baby snuggled against her chest. Her face shimmers. From scrolling through Tabby's emails, I also know about her treatments for infertility. I saw an appointment reminder. I had no idea she was struggling to get pregnant.

Tabby has always wanted a baby. Practically every charm she chose for our friendship bracelets related to being a mother—a rattle, a teddy bear, tiny baby shoes. The fact that she never told me about her infertility is a harsh reminder of our lost friendship.

My heart pangs. Losing Tabby from my life is not something I've ever allowed myself to face. I quickly shove my regrets away and snap back into my world's most famous romance author persona. "We really should get back to editing," I say with a bit of a snap to my voice.

Tabby sits on the chair next to me. She's completely intoxicated by Faye's child. I'm not even sure she heard what I said. But before I can say anything else, Faye's twins come running into Tabby's office, holding a game.

"Mommy says we play bingo right outside the door while you finish." A little girl with Faye's lanky body and shiny yellow hair looks at me, smiling.

"Okay." I stammer, annoyed by how my editing session has morphed into a daycare.

"Emma! Ezra! I told you not to come into the office!" Faye rushes in after them. She leads her kids to the area just outside of the office door. "Stay here and play bingo. Give Mommy a few more minutes. I'll take you to Rocket Ship Ice Cream if you behave." There's desperation in her voice. Her shoulders slump as she takes her baby from Tabby. "I'm so embarrassed." Her voice wobbles. She turns and looks at me. "I promise this won't happen again."

A knot of frustration forms in my core. But I know I have to make sure Ellory's Editors is a success. Smiling, I stand. "Being a mom is hard. I understand. Why don't we go into the store and take the photos we need for social media? I think we've discussed enough about the book today."

Faye's eyes shine with a hint of tears. "Thanks, Ellory. I'm really—"

Suddenly, Cade appears. He looks at me with a piercing stare. "Mom." The word *Mom* stretches with trouble.

"Cade?" I walk towards him, confused by his arrival.

He looks at me, his expression a mix of worry and anger. "It's Dad. I have to talk to you about Dad."

CHAPTER 26

Tabitha Wilson

SWIVELING MY HEAD around, I catch Ellory's eye to determine her reaction to Cade's concerns. She doesn't look the least bit rattled.

She walks to Cade and places her hand on his shoulder. "Let us get a few shots for my social media, and then we can talk."

"Really?" Cade's voice vibrates with irritation. This is the first time I've seen Cade in person, and I can't help but study his face for elements of Ellory. He's the spitting image of Maxy. It makes me uneasy.

Faye's eyes bulge in surprise at Ellory's response to Cade. Sadly, I'm not the least bit stunned Ellory has put her career needs over Cade.

Our group walks toward the scenic bay window in my shop, and I assemble everyone into the configuration Ellory's publicist, Amber, has specified.

As Faye, Ellory, and Harper take seats at the table in front of the window, Cade sulks off to a far corner of the store. Despite the negative energy, the scene is bright and welcoming. I arrange Harper, tucking her cast neatly under the table. Each woman holds their manuscript. Bright pink highlighters and the trendy-looking coffee mugs Ellory's publicist sent add to the ambiance.

"Just talk about anything, but try to be natural." My hands shake as I snap images from different angles, hoping a few will hit the mark. I'm rattled. Ellory discovered I'm reading her manuscript. *The book is about us. It's about me.* Why in the world wouldn't she tell me? And how can she expect me to participate in the editing process when the subject matter makes my insides twist into a knot?

"Great, we also need to get some video footage." I force my voice to sound upbeat as I hand Faye and Harper a printout of the lines suggested by Amber. They read the information and then tuck the loose papers into their manuscript.

"Okay, on the count of three…one, two, three…"

Faye and Harper make general statements about the compelling characters in Ellory's book, as I record. Ellory ends the staged exchange by writing some notes in her manuscript and saying, "This feedback is wonderful." The tone of her voice bounces unnaturally, but it's not something anyone else would notice.

"I think we've got everything," I say, reviewing the detailed instructions Amber provided. "We'll meet again next week."

"Try to read the next one hundred pages." Ellory stands. "Thanks for your time today," she says as an afterthought as she wanders away to find Cade.

Faye hops up and pushes her stroller toward her twins, who are still playing bingo in front of my office. "See you at the next meeting."

Harper's still seated and tapping on her phone.

"Do you need help standing back up?" I ask.

Harper shakes her head. "I'm good. My ride is on his way." Her phone pings with a text, and she giggles like a schoolgirl.

"Did you see where the young man who was in the history section went?" I hear Ellory question one of my employees. I walk over to join her. We need to talk.

"The guy in the gray t-shirt?" my employee asks.

Ellory nods.

"I think I saw him leave."

Ellory's face flickers with guilt, but then she quickly composes herself. "I've got to go," she says, looking at me.

My lips turn downward. We need to discuss her book. We need to talk about the way she forced me into the editing group. We need to talk about so many things, if I'm being honest with myself. But instead of saying any of this, I just say, "Okay, go find Cade."

A SHARP STING pierces my eyes as I slice onions for tonight's dinner. Today is Andre's birthday, and I'm making his favorite, French dip with onion soup. Wiping tears from my burning eyes, I continue to chop. The rhythmic motion, combined with the Otis Redding playlist I have on in the background, lulls me into a trance-like state. I'm feeling positive, although a bit jittery. I'm giving myself my trigger shot tonight.

Recalling the way Faye's baby curled into my neck earlier today, I swell with longing. I quickly redirect myself to the joy of the music and tap my foot to the beat of the song. "Try a little tenderness," I sing, determined to stay optimistic. Suddenly, I'm moving my hips to the soulful yet energetic tune. I'm dancing freely, when I realize Ila is staring at me.

"Oh," I say, embarrassed.

She peers at me, her mouth slightly open in surprise. I see the car keys in her hand.

"Are you going somewhere?" I ask as I move back over to the cutting board and dump the onions into a pot. "Your dad will be home soon. Dinner will be ready at seven."

"I have somewhere to be. Not sure I'll make it back in time for dinner."

I notice she's wearing makeup, and her long brown hair bounces from the touch of a curling iron. "Where are you going? It's your dad's birthday. We're having his favorite meal for dinner to celebrate." I pick up the pot of onions and thump them onto the stove with a bit too much force.

Ila lets out a huff. "I'll try to be back in time." Her eyes roll forcefully as she turns and walks to the front door.

Anger curls in my gut as I follow close behind. "No," I say sharply. "Tonight's your dad's birthday, and that comes first."

Ila places a hand on her bony hip as her facial features contort in annoyance. "You're not my mother. You can't tell me what to do."

Not this. Is she really starting the *you're not my mother* routine? I want to remind her that her mother left. I want to scream that I'm the one who has raised her since she was eight years old. I want to tell her that everything with our little family was great until she decided that Andre and my desire for a second child meant we didn't love her.

Pushing aside my anger, I take a sharp breath, pausing before I speak. "I know you're upset your mom left. I would be too. But I'm here for you, Ila. I always have been." My voice cracks as the hurt I feel about the state of our relationship overtakes me. My eyes find hers, but I can't tell if she feels the same pain I do.

Moving her gaze away from mine, she takes a step toward the door and opens it. "I need to go." She walks out without turning back.

Otis continues crooning in the background as my body pulses with sadness. I stare blankly at the closed door, recalling the first time I cooked a meal in this house. Ila was a kid and eager to help me make spaghetti and meatballs. I put her long, unbrushed hair into a ponytail to keep it from falling into the bowl of ground beef and breadcrumbs. She was thrilled to be my assistant, and I was thrilled to connect with her.

Andre had told me the full story about Ila's mom leaving, and it broke my heart. She suffered from long bouts of depression and coped by drinking. She vanished the day she was supposed to start rehab.

She sends a letter once or twice a year. Sometimes her letters brim with a hopeful vigor, detailing how long she's been sober and what her plans are. Other times, her letters are a series of chicken scratch sentences that make little sense.

The odor of burning food suddenly interrupts my thoughts. *Shoot, the stove was on.*

I run back to the kitchen and twist the heat down. I never added water to the pot with the beef broth and onions. Black slivers of burned, shriveled onion line the bottom of the pan. The soup is ruined.

CHAPTER 27
Ila Wilson

WIND WHIPS MY hair around through the open window of my car as Taylor Swift's song "Breathe" beats around me. It's an older song, but it has always captured the sadness I feel about my mom, as if my hurt is a firefly that can be contained in a mason jar.

Pulling into Venus Inlet, I'm surprised to find CJ's not here. I'm fifteen minutes late because of the dust-up with Tabby. My heart sinks. *Where is he?* I need support from someone who understands me. And Tabby's not that person.

An image of her wounded face when I left the house flies through my mind. I've been thinking a lot about Tabby since discovering a letter from my mom in the mailbox the other day. A letter clearly written when she was drunk or high. At nineteen years old, I'm just coming to terms with the fact that my mom will never be part of my life. *Why did I hold a space for her all this time?* Tabby wants nothing more than to fill the void, but I push her away at every turn.

Looking back, it's easy to see the part I played in our strained relationship. I was young, struggling with the loss of my mother, and feeling abandoned. The thought of having a sibling to compete with terrified me. Tabby, my dad, and I were a unit of three, and I did not want that to change.

I was awful to them. Especially to Tabby. I perfected my surly attitude and avoided interacting with her. What started as a crack widened into what we have now—a boundless void between us.

Lately though, since my breakup with Jackson, I've had a strange desire to repair our relationship. And after receiving my mom's letter, these feelings intensified. But why would Tabby want to fill the space I left for my mother after all these years? It seems easier to just keep pushing her away.

Suddenly, I hear a car slowing its pace, pulling in beside me. He's here. My body instantly burns with desire.

"Hey." CJ looks at me as he steps out of his car. It's a breezy afternoon, and his hair blows around, making him look even sexier than usual.

"What happened to 'hey, Peach'?" I say playfully.

"Right. Hey, Peach," he says, but his words sound forced.

Instantly, I know that something's off. "Are you okay?" My palms perspire. Maybe this whole thing with us is over.

"Yes, yes. Sorry. Just have a few things on my mind." He bounds up to me and wraps me in a bear hug.

Fear releases from my body as I push myself against his chest. I'm falling for CJ too quickly.

Grabbing my hand, he leads me down to the alcove in front of the water.

We stretch out on a blanket, and I lay my head on his chest. He hugs me close as we listen to the sound of waves crashing in and out.

"So, what did you want to talk with me about?" CJ interrupts the silence.

Sitting up, I hug my knees into my chest as I pull my mom's letter from my pocket.

"What's that?" he asks.

"It's a letter from my mom. My real mom, who left me." My voice trails off as I finish the sentence.

"Oh." CJ searches my face for clues about how I'm feeling. "I know you said she writes to you sometimes. I can't imagine how unnerving it is to hear from her."

"It is," I agree as I glance at her nearly illegible handwriting. "What did she say?"

Instead of answering, I push the letter toward him. He places his hand over my hand and pauses for a moment before taking it. Something about the way he does this makes my insides dissolve. True connection is born in the smallest, most infinitesimal moments. Anyone else may have taken the letter and started reading. But CJ paused and joined me in my emotional space before proceeding.

"She doesn't say a whole lot," he admits after reading it.

I nod slowly, unsure of what to say.

"It doesn't make a lot of sense. But she left a phone number. Will you call?" he asks.

"I don't know. She's never given me a phone number before. And anyway, it seems like she's drunk or high," I add as I push my feet through the rocky sand.

He drops the letter on the blanket and moves toward me. "I'm sorry, Peach. I hate knowing how sad this makes you."

"The thing is," I say with a bit of hesitation. "After reading her letter, all I can think about is how I've ruined my relationship with my stepmom." Regret pools in my chest.

"Really?" CJ asks, moving closer to me. "I think that's a good thing. A great thing, actually."

"You do?"

"Yes, sometimes things happen that force us to let go of people that are hurting us and embrace the people that are showing up."

"But I think it's too late to fix my relationship with my stepmom."

The wind gusts and CJ's hair rustles, then falls gently back into place.

"From what you told me, your stepmom hasn't given up on you." His face twists for a moment as an unexpectedly powerful gust of air shoves past us.

Suddenly, the envelope with my mom's letter is blowing toward the ocean.

"The letter!" I shriek. CJ and I jump to our feet, running after it. It moves quickly, rising and falling to the ground with each gust of wind.

Reaching out, CJ's fingers brush the note just as it floats above the water. Undeterred, he rushes into the ocean, waist-deep, just as it drops to the surface without so much as a splash. He grabs the wet paper and holds it up like a prize. "Got it!" he says with a huge grin.

I hurry toward the water, submerging my toes. "Thank you. But you're all wet. I'm sorry."

He pushes through the swirling waves and meets me on the shoreline. "Here," he says, handing me the letter.

As our hands brush, I'm overcome with a whirling mix of desire and gratitude. I take the letter from him, walk over to the blanket, and place it in my bag.

Spinning around, I pull off my clothes as I rush back toward him. Our eyes connect. He pulls off his soaking jeans and shirt. His seductive smile draws my eye upward from his perfectly glistening body.

As we submerge in the cool water, our naked bodies find each other for warmth and pleasure.

CHAPTER 28

Faye Carter

GRIFFIN SMILES AS I put him in a baby swing dotted with images of fluffy sheep. Mark's busy shuffling around the kitchen, filling his soccer bag with an enormous Gatorade and PowerBars. The cabinets hang open at odd angles as he searches for his favorite water bottle.

"Found it." He holds it triumphantly, as if it's a trophy. "I'm leaving for the championship game in a few minutes." He raises his fists in the air and pumps them in excitement. "I won't be home until after dinner," he says. Then he slings his bag over his shoulder.

It's Saturday, and I'm on my own with the kids again. And to make matters worse, it's been several days since I put—or Lexi put—the letter under Mark's pillow again. I saw it opened on his bedside table, but he hasn't said a word about it. My stomach clenches as I realize maybe he's just going to ignore it.

Suddenly, I feel as if my entire body is overheating. I glance out the window as a realization falls over me like a heavy weight. There's no lock on the door keeping me here. My body begins to move on its own.

I snatch my car keys off the table. The engine of my SUV revs as I pull out of our garage before Mark even realizes I'm gone. The car, usually filled with squirmy kids demanding snacks and a crying baby, is strikingly silent.

I drive along the highway without a destination in mind. The open road spreads out before me. A stream of steady tears caresses my face as a smear of green trees flashes through my window. Before I know it, I'm sobbing. Inhaling deeply, my chest expands. I let the systematic hum of my car soothe me.

Suddenly, I hear Lexi's voice. "Drive to the townhouse you lived in when first married."

My body jumps in surprise. "Not again," I say. You're a character from a book. You can't really be here." Lexi puts on stylish sunglasses from the passenger seat."Just do what I say," she says.

Turning onto Devonshire Lane, the stumpy tree that sits on the lawn outside the townhouse Mark and I shared appears like a doorman at a fancy hotel. Its only purpose is to welcome me back.

I pull my car to the side, in the parking area across from the townhouse's entrance. I stare ahead at the three white wood steps that lead to the door. How many times did I climb up and down those steps? How many times did I sit on the rocking chair on the front porch?

"I want you to retrace your steps. Were you genuinely happy when you lived here?" Lexi stares out the windshield, pointing.

Closing my eyes, I'm easily transported back inside to the full-sized bed Mark and I shared on the second floor in the master bedroom. The bed was too small for two adults and left little room for us to spread out. Mark always said he loved that we had to be squished up next to each other all night. I mostly remember the relief that would course through my body in the mornings when he would get out of bed, allowing me space to spread out comfortably.

I recall the week after we were engaged. It was the first time I seriously questioned our relationship.

"I don't want a big wedding," I said as we walked inside the townhouse. "I want to elope." The entryway was full of boxes, bags, and hangers, as I was moving in. Stepping over to his large beige couch, I relaxed into its soft fabric. I was tired after tailgating all day. The annoyance I felt over Mark's refusal to understand why I didn't want a traditional wedding exacerbated my exhaustion. "The only family I have left is Aunt Sandy. There aren't many other people I'd invite."

"I know." He nodded. "But this is every girl's dream. I think you'll regret it."

"I actually won't," I said as I peeled off my sweaty socks. "Don't you understand? Both my parents are gone. I'll spend the entire day wishing they were there, looking for their faces. It will take all the joy out of what's supposed to be the happiest day."

Mark stepped over to the couch, gently put his hand on my face, and pulled me close to him. "But my family is your family. My mom and dad, my brothers. We will all be there. We love you so much. All of us."

No matter what I said or how I explained it, I couldn't get him to understand the pain a traditional wedding would inflict. It was as if the words I spoke disintegrated into the air before he heard them. In that singular moment, I realized Mark couldn't grasp my point of view. The same way he can't grasp my point of view about motherhood.

"Well? Any thoughts?" Lexi's question pulls me back into the moment.

"Some," I say meekly.

"Care to expand? I have a meeting with a start-up. I need to get back to Silicon Valley." Lexi removes her sunglasses and her perfectly groomed eyebrows arch high.

"I've lost myself in motherhood," I say. I picture the disastrous moments at the Ellory's Editors meeting. Humiliation tears through me. "And no matter how I try to explain it to Mark, he doesn't get it."

"Communication is key to a good relationship," Lexi says.

"But it's not just that he doesn't get it," I continue. "Mark does what he wants, when he wants, and moves through the world, unencumbered by the very family he created. He never considered giving up his career. He hasn't put his hobbies aside to care for our children." Tears slide down my cheeks.

Lexi grabs my hand. "This is hard, but I'm here for it."

"It's nice to have someone in my corner." I turn and face Lexi directly, all the while knowing she can't possibly be real. "I keep thinking about my relationship with Mark as a game of bingo, and once we fill up a line, it's over. But is this really Mark's fault? He didn't create this culture that arranges everything to cater to the needs and wants of men."

Lexi pulls *The Prince of Silicon Valley* out of my bag. "You just read about this last night." She thumbs through the pages and points to a section of text.

My eyes scan the words as I reread the argument between Lexi and Theo.

> Theo snarled. "You should have admitted you were the venture capitalist behind the funding for my company. Our entire relationship is based on a lie. I don't know if we can come back from that."
>
> I nodded as tears streamed from my eyes. "I didn't tell you because men are fragile. They can't take it when a woman has more power and wealth than them. But you're right, I'll never cater to a man's needs again. I'm no longer living in a man's world. From now on, I'm a person living in a world of people."

Yes, I think. I need to get home. It's time to confront Mark about my letter. I will not cater to his needs anymore. I will not blindly accept that it's a man's world. I need to be sure he understands my world and what needs to change.

I turn to thank Lexi, but she's gone.

CHAPTER 29
Harper Weiss

"**T**HAT'S A PRETTY shade of lipstick." Ms. Jill smirks as she glances at my freshly applied makeup. She knows Ben's on his way to pick me up.

My cheeks blush, and I pray she doesn't notice. "We're just friends," I say, dropping my head and rummaging through my bag as if I'm searching for something.

"Almost all romances start with the same sentiment." Her eyes shine with a playful spark.

"Like I already told you. He's still going through a divorce. His wife's convinced they're going to reconcile." Hearing the truth of it spoken out loud depresses me.

Standing, she places an arm around my shoulders. She knows I spent my twenties raising Ryder and going to school instead of dating. She knows Ryder's dad broke the part of me that believes in love.

"Listen, honey, it's Thursday afternoon on a beautiful summer day. A gorgeous, kind man is coming to pick you up. Both of your kids are camping out tonight at the Jupiter Cove Community Center. He likes you. Take advantage of it!"

"He likes me?" I ask, confused.

"Don't you see it?"

"See what?" I ask puzzled.

"All week, I've watched as he picks you up. That man lights up like the North Star when you walk into the waiting room."

I can feel my heart soar in my chest. "Huh, really?"

The front door to the clinic suddenly scrapes against the floor. Ben's fit body pushes through the opening. He's wearing a navy blue Henley shirt and khaki shorts. His eyes, tucked behind his glasses, are luminous against the color of his top.

Jill's comment whirls through my mind.

"Hey." He waves at Jill and me. "Sorry, I'm a few minutes late. I got stuck on a call."

"No problem," I say, feeling jittery. *Is it possible he likes me?*

"Well, you both go on and get out of here," Jill says. "Have some fun while your kids are away for the night."

My eyes widen. I'm mortified Jill has suggested Ben and I spend time together. But before I can say anything to make light of her comment, Ben is talking.

"Actually, I was thinking the same." Ben smiles at me. "We should grab some dinner or something and take advantage of our kid-free evening."

Is this for real? I think, as my nervous energy skyrockets into panic.

"I mean, if you don't already have plans," Ben continues.

Suddenly, I feel parched and unable to speak. I swallow and try again. "Sure, I'm free. We should grab some dinner or something and take advantage of our kid-free evening." I awkwardly repeat exactly what Ben said as Jill observes the entire embarrassing conversation.

MY SECOND GLASS of wine has done the trick. My body relaxes as the waiter drops a dessert menu on the table.

"You're clearly going to pick the caramel brownie with vanilla ice cream and caramel sauce. It's your favorite coffee in disguise." Ben cocks his head and gives me a sly grin.

"Ha!" A laugh escapes my throat. His comment is funny, but I'm secretly thrilled he got the answer correct. Knowing what someone will order is prime relationship territory. But, as much as I want to continue our sort-of date, I don't want to set myself up for a major heartbreak.

"I'd love dessert, but I can't eat another bite. Sun and Moon Sushi never disappoints." I need to get home. I need to stop hoping we can be more than friends. I'm not even sure his almost-ex is out of the picture.

Ben leans back in his chair, taking up all the surrounding space. "Okay, I'm pretty full myself." He rubs his hand over his perfectly sculpted stomach. "So, tomorrow, I'll pick the boys up after the breakfast cookout at ten. I'll drop Ryder off right after. He told me his dad's coming to visit." Ben's eyebrows raise, begging me to elaborate on the visit.

My stomach tightens at the mention of Noah. It's not a subject I want to discuss with Ben, but Ryder has already spilled the beans.

"Yup," I say, hoping to brush it off.

"Do you get along?" Ben pauses.

Is he wondering about this because he likes me? Hope bubbles in my gut.

"I guess I'm just wondering if there's any hope for Cassidy and me to have a friendly relationship down the road."

The bubble quickly pops when I realize it's a practical question born from his own situation.

"One thing's for sure," Ben continues. "Next time around, I'm going to be sure to find someone that isn't self-absorbed. I hope your divorce with Noah was easier than what I'm going through."

I hate talking about Noah, but the wine makes it easier. "Noah and I were never married," I say quickly, before I lose the nerve. "We were high school sweethearts. Our parents begged us not to have the baby. But, instead, Noah and I deferred our college acceptances, to see if it could work. But Noah was incapable of growing up in the way that was necessary when Ryder was born, and our relationship fell apart."

Ben leans toward me. "I don't understand men who can't step up when they have a child. I was lucky my dad was hands-on. A real mensch." He winks.

No wonder Ben's such a stand-up guy. A stab of worry beats in my chest as I realize Ryder doesn't have a strong dad figure in his life.

Ben reaches out his hand, almost placing it over mine, but rests it on the table instead. Disappointment swirls in my gut.

"I'm sorry Noah couldn't be who you needed him to be."

My mind races back to the moment Noah told me we would both be miserable if we built our life around a baby we hadn't expected. My parents infused me with strength and convinced me to let Noah go. But the abandonment I felt when he left slashed my heart. It's the reason I've never pursued another serious relationship. The gash he inflicted when he showed me how easily someone could leave has never healed.

"Noah was just a kid back then. We both were. It was hard. But he's married now. He lives in Hamilton Beach, California, so he's not close by." I get back to the facts of the story.

Ben nods. "Does he have other kids?"

"No. He visits over winter break and then spends a month in Boca with his parents during the summer, so he can see Ryder. His summer visits are the reason Ryder hasn't gone to sleepaway camp yet. He'll be here for the next several weeks." The lengthy explanation kills my buzz.

"Well, that's great for Ryder. I'm sure he loves having his dad close by during the summer."

I nod, purposefully skipping how disruptive it is to have Noah show up and insert himself into my life. He's never been good at respecting my boundaries.

I'm relieved when the waiter returns and drops the check after we decline dessert.

Twenty minutes later, Ben is using the key I keep under the flowerpot to help me open my door.

"You've gotten so good on those crutches," he says as we step into my entryway.

"Fingers crossed I get the walking boot soon, as planned." I smile.

"That's great!" Ben replies as we stand facing each other.

We're only a foot apart. I so badly want to know what it would be like to kiss him. Thankfully, my broken ankle and crutches are keeping me from doing anything impulsive.

"Unfortunately, I still can't drive with the boot. But, since Noah will be close by, he can help. And then my parents will be back from Europe, so you'll be able to get back to your day-to-day without the hassle of driving me around." As soon as I say this, I realize how much I'll miss seeing Ben daily.

Ben's eyes fall on me and linger. The intensity of his gaze makes me feel exposed. I look away through the open door into the twilight sky.

He takes a step forward, shuts my front door, and closes the gap between us. "Hey," he says softly. "Look at me." His palm cups my jaw and lifts my face toward his. "What if I don't want to get back to my day-to-day? What if I look forward to seeing you?"

Our faces are so close together. All I can see are his eyes, and I'm drowning in them.

"I'm going to kiss you now," he whispers.

Our mouths brush each other's, tenderly at first. And then, after a moment, we ignite like a match dropped on dry branches. Ben pulls me closer, but the weight of my cast and crutches makes us unsteady. We wobble for a moment before steadying ourselves. Laughing for a brief second, he pushes me up against the door for balance. My crutches fall to the ground as he kisses me deeply. Feeling stable, I wrap my arms around him, pulling him closer. I want him to melt into me.

"Is this okay?" he asks in a raspy voice between kisses.

I don't want to answer. I don't want to think. I just want to feel his body against mine. If we talk, we will lose the moment and end up saying all the reasons this is a bad idea.

Ben pulls away from me and waits for me to respond. But instead of answering, I glance toward the hallway where my bedroom door is.

"Are you sure?" he asks again. But I put my finger over his lips, so he doesn't continue asking questions. He nods in understanding.

Lifting me up, he scoops me into his arms and carries me down the hall into my bedroom.

Laying me on my bed, he pulls off my shirt and kisses my shoulders. I unhook my bra, needing to feel his body against mine.

"Do you want me to finish undressing you?" he says. "Or do you need to do it yourself because of the cast?" His lips push against my ear, and his breath is hot.

I guide his hand to my skirt, helping him remove my clothing. My body tingles as his palm brushes my thigh. His naked body hovers over mine, and then I free fall, down, down, into pure bliss.

ROLLING OVER, I curl into Ben's broad chest. His arm circles my shoulders, but he hardly stirs. Suddenly, I wonder what time it is. Ben and I were so wrapped up in exploring each other last night that we hardly slept.

Turning away from him, I glance at my phone. It's after seven. We have some time before he needs to leave to get the boys.

Turning back, my gaze settles on his slumbering body. My mind reaches back to the moment last night when my eyes blinked open. The blackness outside was just beginning to crack with a hint of light. Ben immediately woke up, our rhythms perfectly in sync. As we collided together, I suddenly felt like I needed to protect myself.

"Nothing happens between us after tonight," I said. "This is a one-time thing."

He leaned into me and kissed my chest.

Inhaling deeply, I fought my need to give in and spoke again. "You're not in the right space for this," I whispered as pleasure coursed through my body.

But instead of responding, Ben thrust himself inside of me. Now, as I lay here next to him, I'm convinced I did the right thing. He didn't disagree with my plan, so he must approve. I'll savor this bit of time before he leaves, and it's all over. I move my body over his. *One last time,* I tell myself as I wake him.

"WHAT'S THAT NOISE?" I hear Ben's groggy voice and realize we must have fallen back asleep.

My neighbor's lawn company fills my bedroom with a sound as loud as a jet plane. "Ugh, I know." I groan. "It's my neighbor's lawn people. They always come early in the morning."

"There's only one solution," Ben says as he sits up and leans his back against the bed's headboard. "You're going to have to move." He smirks at me, and my insides tangle into a knot. "Do you have any coffee around here?" he yells over the thunder of the mowers outside. "There's no chance we're going back to sleep."

I nod instead of attempting to talk over the deafening rumble. Hobbling out of bed, I throw on my underwear and his navy blue Henley. As I pull it over my face, the scent of sandalwood engulfs me. I'm going to miss his smell, his eyes, his body. It's imperative that this ends today. I'm already in too deep.

Ben gets out of bed and puts on his briefs. He grabs my hand and helps me hop to the kitchen. Stepping over to the coffeepot, I fill it with water and scoop grounds into the filter.

"You're adorable in the morning," he whispers in a grainy voice. I can hardly hear him over the roar of the yard work.

He pulls me toward him as we wait for the coffee to brew. I fall into a deep kiss with him for several moments before pulling away.

"What's wrong?" he whispers into my ear as he moves his body back toward mine.

"We agreed last night. This is a one-time thing." I can feel water well up in my eyes. *How can I be this upset already*? He can't know I'm about to cry. I push my face against his shoulder so he can't see me.

"What?" he says. "I didn't—" But before he can finish, Noah is standing in my kitchen, his eyes wide with shock.

"Noah, what the hell?" I shout. Pulling at the hem of Ben's shirt, I try to cover my underwear.

"I'm sorry. You didn't hear me. I was knocking over and over. I used the key under the flowerpot. I wanted to surprise Ryder." Noah backs up with each word he speaks, but his eyes fix tightly on Ben.

"You can't just walk into my house, Noah. We've talked about this before." My voice pulses with anger.

He shifts around in his joggers, pushing his hand through his thick hair. "I know. You're right. I apologize." Noah looks from me to Ben as he takes another step away.

I'm not sure if I'm feeling fury or shame. I've been caught having a one-night stand. "This is my boyfriend, Ben Silver," I blurt. As the words fly out of my mouth, I'm desperate to pull them back. Ben and I are nothing. We barely know each other.

But before I can say another word, Ben places his hand on my shoulder and steps behind me. "Can't say I expected to meet you quite like this, but I've heard a lot about you."

My muscles tighten as soon as I realize Ben's playing along. I don't know whether to laugh or cry. Fake dating—it's the most common plot device used in romance novels. I'm a living, breathing trope.

CHAPTER 30

Ellory Brayson

"THE PHOTOS AREN'T selling me. We may need to hire a professional photographer to get it right." Amber peers at me through my computer screen. "Bookstagram is going to explode with comments once we launch Ellory's Editors, but it needs to be perfect." She's working from home again as she continues to juggle her career and motherhood.

"But," she continues, through tired eyes, "I really want one more editor who's even younger than Harper and Faye. With Nadine Laurel's new release gaining steam, we need to expand your audience. Were there any younger women at your book event that you can reach out to?"

Irritation creeps through my chest. Nadine's newest book is already number one on the *New York Times* Best Sellers list. "No, Harper and Faye were the youngest out of the group."

Amber rubs her right hand against her temple. She seems frustrated. Or maybe she's just tired. "Okay," she says. "I'm not going to launch Ellory's Editors for another few weeks, so keep your eye out for any prospects."

Before I can respond, Amber's wife, Melinda, is on screen in the background, pacing back and forth with their fussy baby. "I'm sorry to interrupt, Ellory. Our little guy is having a meltdown. Amber is the baby whisperer. She's so much better at this than I am." She hands the baby to Amber, and his large bald head takes over my computer's screen.

"We were just wrapping up, anyway," Amber coos in her baby voice. "Call me if you find an additional editor."

At any other moment, her brevity would anger me, but I want to avoid talking with her about the drama with Maxy. "I'll speak to you soon," I say, slapping my laptop shut.

I rush into the kitchen. Cade is sitting at the table, slurping cereal as he stares at his phone.

"I hope you're not still watching clips of your dad's arrest." I walk over to the table and take a seat across from him. "How are you doing with everything?" I say, attempting to keep the edges of my words soft. It's only been a few days since Maxy was arrested with a bunch of mob types for illegal gambling. Guilt about the way I blew Cade off when he came to the bookstore to tell me, shoots through my core.

"All the media about it has disappeared," he says. "I guess Dad's family pulled every string they had to get the story out of the public eye." Cade drops his phone on the table and looks out the window, as if searching for something.

I reach my hand out and place it over his. I can't imagine how hard it was for him to see the video footage of his dad being slammed up against a wall, handcuffed, and thrown in the back of a police car.

"Yes, your grandparents certainly have enough power and money to do that," I agree.

"The thing is," Cade says as his eyes drift back toward my face. "They can't do anything about an FBI investigation. What if Dad goes to jail?" His voice quivers.

"I don't know what's going to happen," I answer honestly. "Your dad may have been there with those mob guys, but it doesn't mean he's wrapped up in anything more."

"But these are the people we hung out with when Dad took me to the Cayman Islands a few months ago. He's obviously close with these criminals." Cade slouches in his chair.

"Close doesn't mean criminal," I say, hoping and praying that Maxy was not stupid enough to put himself in a position where he could go to jail. It would devastate Cade for the rest of his life.

"Well, Dad called and asked me not to say anything about the trip if the FBI contacts me. So, it sounds to me like he's in trouble."

"What?" I shriek. "I'm going to kill your father." Fear breaks over me. "You need to cooperate with the FBI and be honest with them. I will not have you lying to them or leaving things out to protect your father. He got himself into this mess, and it's not your responsibility to get him out." My heart beats wildly.

Pulling out my phone, I call Maxy, but it goes straight to voicemail. "Call me immediately!" I screech. "We need to talk."

"Shoot, Mom. Don't call Dad. You'll only make things worse." Cade jumps out of his chair, his face twisted in anger. "I'm outta here."

"Cade, wait!" I yelp as he grabs the keys to his rental car and walks out the door.

NODDING MY HEAD, I can see Faye's lips moving, but my brain can't process the words. The books on Tabby's purple bookshelf morph into a blur. It feels like that moment on *This Morning America*. My fears about Cade and my anger at Maxy are taking over.

Suddenly, Faye's staring at me. I push my back against the chair until it's uncomfortable, hoping the pressure will keep me focused.

Faye continues. "I love how Emma and Tish add charms to their bracelets to represent things that happen in their lives. It's a cute detail and very visual."

Taking a deep breath, I swallow my concerns. "Thanks, Faye," I say. "That was good feedback."

I quickly glance at Tabby, but she avoids my eye. *Is she angry I've written a book loosely based on our relationship?* It's the closest I can come to apologizing.

I decide to move on to Harper. "And what feedback do you have on that scene?" I ask.

Harper shifts her body slightly, adjusting her leg. "Sorry, I'm still getting used to this boot. It's obviously more comfortable than the cast, but it feels different." She flips a few pages ahead in her manuscript. "So, on page two hundred and twenty-two, the girls are now adults and back at the inlet. So much has happened between them. It's unclear if their relationship will recover."

I notice Tabby pulling at the spiral curls of her hair. She seems uncomfortable.

Harper continues. "You're missing out on an opportunity for symbolism here. I think you could work in a whole thing about the inlet eroding. Describe how different it looks from when we were first introduced to it at the beginning, when the girls are young. Let the scenery do some of the work, helping the reader visualize the way the relationship between the two characters has eroded."

Immediately, my mind spins with ways I can use the setting. My writer's mind is moving on its own, connecting scenery and plot points. My thoughts are twisting, turning, and tumbling, as if they are speeding down a steep hill. I can't control what's happening inside my head. This is the part of writing that's mystifying. I don't know where the energy and momentum come from, but once it takes over, I have to stand back and let it consume me.

Everyone must sense I'm locked up in my head, because no one says anything for several minutes. "Yes!" I finally squeal. "Harper, this is perfect. Wonderful, just wonderful." An electrifying surge of excitement courses through my body.

"Great!" Harper says proudly.

"Your writer's brain is on fire!" Suddenly, an impulse overtakes me. I have an unexpected desire to help Harper. "Why don't you email me the first four chapters of the book you're sending to agents? Maybe I can provide some feedback."

"Oh, my gosh. Really?" Harper nearly falls out of her chair with excitement.

"Yes." Pulling out a scrap piece of paper, I write my email address and hand it to Harper. Her eyes shine. My heart feels open and light. I'm thrilled to help her, I realize.

"We've only got ten more minutes, and we need to get our next round of photos done." Tabby interrupts the moment to keep us on track. She stands, and we follow her to the table by the bay window. Everything's set up.

As soon as Faye, Harper, and I take our places at the table, one of Faye's twins, Emma, comes running over crying. Faye brought a mother's helper today, who entertained her children during our meeting, but I guess she could only keep them from interrupting us for so long.

"Mommy, Ezra cheat at bingo. He's not fair." Emma pulls at Faye's top.

"Sorry, Mrs. Carter." A teen girl trails behind Emma. She shows Emma a lollipop and motions for her to come and get it.

Emma wipes her snotty nose on her palm and skips happily toward her babysitter.

"Sorry about that." Faye's cheeks redden as she straightens out her top.

"No worries," Tabby says. "Let's get these photos, and everyone can be on their way."

Ten minutes later, Harper leaves with her ride, and Faye is shuffling out the door with her entourage of kids.

My heart is still surging with a good-natured hum. I look at Tabby. "Can we have a cup of coffee together before I leave?" I ask, unsure of what I'm trying to do. It's almost the end of June, and I haven't made any attempts to unpack the mistakes I've made.

Something shifted inside me after learning about Tabby's infertility. I should support her. I should take care of her. But I'll need to apologize, or there's no chance she'll let me in.

Tabby's eyes scrunch together as if she's trying to solve a hard math problem. She looks at her watch. "I've got about ten minutes. Give me your coffee order," she says.

Tabby tells the employee working in the café to bring our coffees to the bench outside the store. "It's warm outside, but I need some fresh air."

I nod in agreement and join Tabby on one of the benches that line Jupiter Cove's main street.

"How's Cade?" she asks, turning to look at me as our coffees arrive.

My stomach sinks. "He's struggling," I say honestly. "He's afraid Maxy may go to jail. And if Maxy goes to jail, what will that do to Cade?" I don't want Tabby to answer. I just want to move away from any conversation that involves Maxy. She doesn't even know we're getting divorced.

Instantly, I realize I'm not ready to apologize. My mind scrambles for a second, trying to figure out how to shift the conversation, when a young woman walks across the street and toward the bench.

"Hi." She looks at Tabby as she brushes long, thick, wavy hair over her shoulder. Her skin is sun-kissed, and she's beautiful in an understated way.

Tabby smiles. "Ellory, this is Ila, my stepdaughter. You met her last month at your book event."

Yes, it suddenly comes back to me. She was rude and left early, but maybe she was having a bad night. "Nice to see you again, Ila," I say.

"Nice to meet you," she replies and then looks at Tabby. "Do you want me to go inside and start unpacking the new shipment?"

"Sure, I'll join you in a few minutes."

"Okay." Ila gives us a small smile as she heads toward the store.

"Sorry to cut our conversation about Cade short, but I want to spend time with Ila. When she asked if she could come by to help me today, I almost fell over. We've been struggling to connect for a long time." Tabby glances at the ground and then lifts her head and grins.

"Well," I say, "maybe things are changing." The call I had this morning with Amber comes bursting through my mind. "Actually, do you think Ila would be interested in joining my editing team? It would give you a reason to spend time together."

Tabby leans back and stares at the historic Picture Planet movie theater across the street. Red and yellow trim surrounds a marquee displaying the title of the summer's blockbuster *Robotic Island*. "That's an interesting idea," Tabby says. "She loves to read, so maybe? But why?"

Tabby's body tenses, and I realize she's wondering what's in it for me. Our history has taught her it's always about me. Not wanting to lie, I tell her the absolute truth.

"Well, my publicist wants me to find a younger woman to add to the team. But I'd also love to help you and your stepdaughter reconnect." In my heart, I know what I've said is the truth. I owe Tabby this and so much more. It's time for me to apologize.

CHAPTER 31
Tabitha Wilson

A S I WALK toward my shop, the sun glints off my store's bay window. The books displayed shimmer in the light. I step toward them, enticed by the beautiful colors. As soon as everything comes into focus, my eyes land on Ellory's last book in *The Prince of Silicon Valley* series.

I'm surprised she invited Ila to join her editing group. Andre would tell me to decline, and maybe I should. He made it clear I should exile Ellory from my life. But, unlike love relationships, there's no formula for how to end a friendship. So instead of a breakup, our friendship has thawed from a solid block of ice to a trickle of water—an annoying drip that's not worth repairing but won't go away.

But Ellory's right. It would be nice for Ila and me to have something to connect around that's outside of our family life. A neutral place to start over. My nerves swell like a building wave, wondering why Ila is here today.

When she came home, hair soaking wet, the night of Andre's birthday dinner, I was still upset about the way she lashed out at me before disappearing. *You're not my mom.*

Andre and I were midway through our French dips when she arrived. She slunk into the kitchen and apologized for being late. Sitting down, she was quiet as Andre and I continued to discuss the large shipment of books I was expecting. They would need to be unpacked, priced, and put on the shelves of my store.

Ila listened but was quiet. Perhaps it surprised her that neither I nor Andre reprimanded her for being late or questioned her about why her hair was soaking wet. But Andre and I had decided we would not ruin his birthday by arguing with her. The next morning, I was stunned when Ila offered to help me unpack and shelve my book order.

Swallowing hard, I move my gaze from my shop's window and peek inside. Ila is wheeling a cart full of books toward cash out, where we tag them for the floor. Her face glows with contentment, and I can't help but wonder what's happening in her life to bring about such a positive shift. I'd love to ask, but as I enter the store, I decide I'll just follow her lead. I don't want to push too hard. Ila will set the pace.

Walking toward her, I smile. "Looks like you're off to a great start."

Ila nods as Lisa, my store manager, jumps in. "Maybe you two can work on unboxing everything. I can get these books tagged."

"Sure," Ila says. "Should we head to the storage room?"

"Let's do it," I reply.

The next thirty minutes pass quickly. Ila and I open boxes and sort the books into piles based on genre. Ila has a Taylor Swift playlist going, and we can't help but shake our hips and dance around. It reminds me of when Ila was younger, and we first discovered the song "Tim McGraw." The moment takes me back to the time when my relationship with Ila felt like happiness.

"I can't wait to read this one." Ila holds up Colleen Hoover's latest and swoons.

"Me too," I agree. "She has a special talent for heartbreak and tortured love, mixed with happy endings."

Ila flips the book over, reading the blurb. She looks up and starts to say something, but then quickly quiets.

"Everything okay?"

Ila puts the book down on the cart and sighs. "Yeah, the book's description reminds me of my relationship with Jackson. Some things just aren't meant to be…" Her voice trails off.

My mind stumbles. *Should I continue this conversation or just nod?* I don't want to blow this moment. I choose option two.

"I guess I never told you what happened. Or even that Jackson and I broke up."

Drawing in a breath, I nod again.

"We just grew apart—with him being away at college and all. I'm okay. I'm sorry you and Dad didn't find out from me." She grabs another handful of books and fills the cart.

I need to say the right thing. Pausing for a moment, I decide on something neutral. "I'm so glad to hear you're okay."

Ila presses her lips together in a satisfied smile, and my heart fills with happiness. We remain silent for another few minutes as we put the last of the books on the cart. The presence of Taylor Swift's voice makes the moment even more gratifying.

As we stand and break down the empty boxes, the ping of a text interrupts the music. Ila puts down her box cutter and looks at her phone to see who it is. Reading the incoming texts, her entire face lights up with excitement.

I will not ask who it is. I will not ask who it is. I repeat this in my head, determined not to ruin the amazing interaction I've had with Ila today.

After a moment, Ila sets down her phone and floats back over to me as if she's walking on a cloud. I do my best to keep my face blank, even though I'm filled with curiosity.

As we wheel our carts to the cash wrap, Ila picks up the Colleen Hoover book. "Can I have this one?"

"Absolutely!" I say, happy I can easily fulfill her request.

Ila sets the book apart from the others and beams. "I'm starting to believe in happy endings."

AS I WALK into Dr. Feldman's outpatient surgery center, fear replaces the excitement I felt earlier about my time with Ila.

"Over here." Andre waves his arm and pats the seat in the waiting room next to him.

Sitting down, I grab his hand and thread his fingers through mine.

"Happy egg retrieval day," he says with a glint of humor. He's always been great at lightening the moment and saving me from my crushing emotions.

A moment later, we're escorted into a room, and I'm undressing. "Dr. Feldman is hoping to get at least fifteen eggs," I say as I take my place on the examining table.

Andre nods, used to the way I state and restate the details we already know.

"Save the best for last," Dr. Feldman says as he enters the preop room. "It's been a long day, but I'm happy to see you all and get things rolling."

Andre and I smile.

"Do you have questions before we begin?" Dr. Feldman motions for me to scoot down to the end of the table as he begins the ultrasound.

"Nope," Andre says. "I think we're pretty much experts at this point. Just looking forward to you getting those fifteen eggs."

"Okay, the anesthesiologist will be in soon. The embryologist will tell us how many eggs we got as soon as we're finished. I'll see you in about thirty minutes when it's all over." He squeezes my hand and leaves.

"It's time for you to go back to the waiting room now." The nurse looks at Andre, who promptly gets up.

"Good luck, baby. I love you." He kisses the top of my head as the nurse wheels my bed toward the procedure room.

My eyes open slowly, but I'm aware of where I am. It's impossible to escape the intensity of emotions around IVF, even with powerful drugs that send you to Neverland. The IV in my arm stings and I notice the outline of Andre and Dr. Feldman behind the curtain surrounding my bed. They're talking in low whispers, and my heart drops. But before my brain can spin out with disaster scenarios, the curtain opens.

I can already feel the well of tears in my eyes.

Andre grabs a tissue, leans over, and hugs me. "There's no need to cry, baby."

A sob escapes me, and he squeezes me tight.

Dr. Feldman steps next to Andre and places a hand on my arm. Andre releases me.

"Is it bad news?" I say in a breathy cry.

"No, not at all, Tabby. We got seven viable eggs."

I can feel my face sink in as more tears come.

Dr. Feldman looks at me with a slight smile. "Listen to me, Tabby. Seven is great. Seven is a great chance that we're going to have a viable embryo. Stay positive. I know it's hard, but you have to try." He squeezes my arm. "The nurse will be in with discharge instructions. Call me if anything comes up."

My thoughts come like a tidal wave. We only got half the eggs we wanted. *Half.* And while I know half is part of something, and half is equal to the remainder, in this particular case, half feels like nothing. Half feels like exactly nothing at all.

CHAPTER 32

Ila Wilson

CLOSING THE LID of my pastel case, I tuck the crayons into my bag behind my sketch pad. Slinging the bag over my shoulder, I wince. I worked the breakfast shift at the diner this morning. I must have tweaked something as I carried a heavy tray of omelet specials.

Collecting my things, I'm excited to meet CJ at Venus Inlet. He's bringing a picnic lunch. I plan to sketch as he continues to write. There couldn't be a more perfect plan for the day.

I take a step toward the front door, but then turn back around. Tabby is here. I should say goodbye. It's something I haven't done for years. But I'm trying to dismantle the wall I've built brick by brick.

Peeking my head into the kitchen, I see Tabby. "I'm headed out. Not sure exactly when I'll be home."

Tabby lifts her eyes from her phone. They're glazed over. Something seems off. She attempts a smile, but her lips only curl at the edges. I'm sure it has to do with her recent doctor's appointment. But I don't feel comfortable asking about it.

"All right, see you later," I say as I leave.

When the door shuts behind me, regret blooms in my chest. Looking back at the door, I consider going back inside but decide against it. We need more time before we can be vulnerable with each other.

Ping. CJ texts me as soon as I arrive at Venus Inlet.

> **CJ:** Running late be there in 30

> **Ila:** All ok?

> **CJ:** We need to talk…

A crushing surge breaks over me when I read his words. He's breaking this off. It's the only thing that makes sense. My eyes well up as I take a gulp of air. But the air feels like a sharp blade as it travels down my throat.

The pain is strangely familiar. For a moment, I wonder why, but realize the despair is similar to the hurt I feel about my mom. She left me, and now CJ's doing the same. Logically, I know it's not the same at all, but feelings don't give a damn about reason.

My mom. The thought of her feels like a stone in my chest. Scrolling over to my phone's keypad, I type in the number she gave me. It's something I've done several times in the last few days, but I never hit send. My heart pumps in my chest. There are just ten numbers between us. Ten simple symbols are the only thing keeping me from hearing her voice.

Suddenly, my overwhelming emotions ignite in a groundswell of restless energy. I hit send, calling the number.

"Hello." It's a woman's voice. *Is it my mom?*

"Um, yeah…" My voice quivers. "I'm looking for Cecily. Is this Cecily?" Every inch of my body is thumping and pounding.

"Cecily hasn't been around for a few days," the voice responds. "Not sure when she'll be back."

I can hear music and voices in the background.

"Want to leave a message?"

Instead of answering, I quickly hang up. I'm so stupid. Of course, she's disappeared. That's what she does. I push my phone into my pocket and run toward the water. Lying down on the rocky sand, the sharp edges of minuscule shells jab at my skin. I feel every tiny prick. My body burns, and I welcome the physical discomfort. It's much easier to understand than emotional distress.

"Hey."

I hear CJ's voice and my eyes shoot open.

"What are you doing?" he asks as he sits down next to me.

"I just called my mom, but she wasn't there."

"Really?" CJ leans over me, his mouth agape.

"Yes, really," I say, my tone on the edge of anger.

CJ cocks his head, confused.

Sitting up, I face him. "So, what did you want to talk to me about?" I ask. There's no need to drag this out.

"Oh," CJ says, as if he's surprised. But he's the one that texted those exact words only a short while ago.

"The thing is…" he says, but then stops. "The truth is…" he starts again, but his voice instantly fades away.

"What is it, CJ? Can you just say it?" My words rush out, kicking my throat as they leave my mouth.

"I haven't been completely up front about everything, Peach," he says. "There are some things I need to tell you." He wraps his pinky around mine but looks away.

"What?" I say, immediately releasing my hand from his. "Do you have a girlfriend or something? Or a wife? Now it suddenly makes sense that I've never seen your place." As I jerk to a stand, my phone falls out of my pocket. I turn to grab it, but CJ gets to it first. He reaches out to hand it to me, but I'm already five steps ahead, rushing toward my car.

"Wait!" CJ lurches toward me, grabbing my arm. "That's not it at all," he says. "No, there isn't anyone else. I really like you, Ila. I mean, I didn't expect this whole thing, especially to meet someone I really liked while I was taking a break from life this summer."

Although my body should fill with relief after hearing his words, I'm still shaking. "What haven't you been up front about?"

"I wanted to tell you—"

But before he can finish, my phone rings and the display lights up. The name Tabby scrolls across my screen. CJ's eyes focus on the letters until they disappear, and my phone's screen turns black.

"Tabby?" he asks. His tone is uneasy.

"Yes!" I shout as I grab my phone from him. "Tabby is my stepmom."

"Wait, your stepmom is the owner of Blast Off Books?" CJ looks at me with a puzzled expression.

"Yes, what's going on? Do you know her?"

"Not really," CJ says. "I've been to her bookstore a few times this summer."

"Why do you seem so freaked out?" I stammer, confused. My entire body shudders, afraid of what he's going to say. He's going to break my heart.

CHAPTER 33
Faye Carter

FLIPPING TO THE next page, my eyes skip ahead, eager to know how Theo will respond to Lexi.

> "Are we going to fight for this? For us?" I say as my eyes trace the line of Theo's muscular body.
>
> He stares at me, but doesn't say a word.
>
> I step closer, closing the space between us. "Answer me," I say, my lips only inches from his.
>
> The moment extends, but instead of answering, Theo places his palm on my cheek. I see tears in the corners of his eyes.
>
> "It's over," he says in a hushed voice. Taking a step back, he releases his hand from my face and walks out the door.

"Argh!" I screech as I throw Ellory's book to the floor. Lexi and Theo have to make this work. Their love must overcome every obstacle. "I want my goddamn happy ending!" I scream out into the silence of my bedroom.

Sitting up, I close my eyes and take a deep breath. When my eyes open, Lexi is standing in front of me, pacing.

"Kind of a dramatic reaction." She looks at me. Her lips round into a grin, but her tone sounds concerned.

"You again?" I rub my eyes a few times, knowing this is crazy.

Glancing at the clock, I see it's almost midnight. Mark's still not home from poker night, and I'm hallucinating that Lexi's in my bedroom. I wave my hand back and forth in her direction, willing her to disappear.

"You can't get rid of me that easy," she says as she sits on the edge of my bed. Her long, thick, burgundy hair cascades down her back in a tumble of loose curls. "Listen," she says. "I think we can help each other. We're both struggling in our relationships. Let's talk it out and see what we come up with. What happened when you came home the other night after we visited the townhouse?" Lexi leans closer to me, encouraging me to continue.

Feeling too exhausted to fight against this alternate reality, I give in. "I was fired up and ready to tell Mark what needed to change, but it didn't go well..." My voice trails off as I remember.

I arrived home well after bedtime. Mark entered our garage before I could even shut off the car.

"Where were you?" he demanded.

"I don't know. I just needed to drive around and clear my head. How are the kids?"

"Everyone's fine. I gave them cereal for dinner. I let them skip taking a bath. Emma and Ezra insisted we play several games of bingo. They fell asleep at about eight, except Baby G. He was awake until nine."

My pulse began beating wildly at the mention of bingo. *Had Mark and I filled in another space on our card?*

"You fed them cereal and skipped the bath? I'd love to take the easy way out most nights too," I barked.

"Relax, Faye," he snapped. "Everything got done. What does it matter?"

Neither of us spoke for a few moments. My head was spinning with disappointment. I was supposed to march in confidently and explain the things I needed to change. But we were already trapped in a disagreement about dinner and bath time.

"I read the letter you left under my pillow," he said, breaking the silence.

Finally. "It's about time."

His face contorted with annoyance. "I just don't think you get how much pressure I'm under. The multiple car repair shops, all the business decisions, supporting this family." I could feel his irritation beating around me.

"I wrote the letter because you don't understand how hard being at home is!" Furious waves crashed inside my chest. "I've tried to explain countless times. I'm on the verge of a breakdown. I need help with the kids."

As the memory of the other night overtakes me, a warm rush of tears streams down my cheek. Embarrassed, I turn my head away from Lexi.

She reaches out and grabs my hand. "It's okay," she says sympathetically. "Tell me what went wrong. Maybe I can help?"

My mind skips back to the way things ended the other night.

"I've totally lost myself," I snarled at Mark as I walked from the garage into the house. "I haven't picked up a paintbrush since the twins were born. I don't know who I am anymore, other than someone who changes diapers, feeds people, cleans, and does laundry!" My head pounded in fury.

"Well, it's impossible to help you, Faye. I've given up." Mark's hands sliced the air in sharp movements as he spoke. "You only approve if I do things your way. Let Milo do things on his own. He can pour his own goddamn milk. Don't you get that?"

"I do, but then he'll spill. And then Emma and Ezra will whine that they want a turn. And then Griffin will fuss that his bottle's delayed. I do what I do to keep things running smoothly, to be efficient, and avoid extra work, such as cleaning up a puddle of milk from the floor. Maybe if you lived my life for one week, you could understand that." The octave of my voice was too high. It sounded unfamiliar, even to me.

Mark glared at me but didn't respond.

"Why can't you see how I'm struggling?" I pleaded. "We live in this house together, but you can't see anything from my point of view."

Moving slowly from exhaustion, I shuffled over to our large, rectangular kitchen table and took my usual seat, closest to the heart of the kitchen. I noticed rows and rows of tiny holes in perfect lines of four, from where Ezra's constantly ramming his fork into the soft wood of the table.

"And it's not even just the logistics of the caretaking, Mark. I feel like I exist only for you to continue to live the life you had before we had kids." A heavy breath pushed out of me as I spoke my truth.

Mark's face took on an expression I'd never seen before. His chin pushed up and out. His eyes narrowed into slivers. "Are you crazy, Faye? How can you say that?"

"Don't you understand? Everything has changed for me since we've had kids. I've lost almost every single part of myself."

"What does that even mean?" He looked at me as if I was talking in a foreign language.

"What it means, Mark, is that you need to make some sacrifices and help more. I've lost myself, and that's exactly what's secured your freedom to live your life as you please."

I hear sobbing before I realize it's coming from me.

"It's okay, Faye," Lexi says. "First, you need to cry. Then you can move forward." She wraps me in a hug, and I'm struck by how long it's been since someone has taken care of me.

Catching my breath, I pull away from her embrace. "So, what should I do?" I ask, desperate to make all my hurt feelings disappear.

"The answer is obvious to me," she says. "I think you know."

"What?" I say, confused.

Her eyes look directly into mine. "Stop asking for permission from Mark. If you need a nanny, if you want to paint, read, or whatever else, do it. This relationship has been out of balance for too long. You and Mark should be equals."

My body shudders. She's right. My needs are just as important as Mark's. My desires are just as worthy.

"Here, let me get you a tissue." Lexi stands and walks into my bathroom.

But before she returns, I hear the rumble of the garage door. I spring out of bed to find her.

"Lexi?" Looking around, I confirm the space is empty. She's gone. Turning, I rush down the hall to talk with Mark. *We are equals*, I think as I step towards him.

CHAPTER 34

Harper Weiss

RYDER WALKS INTO the kitchen wearing a red Under Armour shirt, bright blue athletic shorts, and an American flag bandana wrapped around his head. "When are we leaving for the carnival?"

"You look very patriotic," I say as I put the finishing touches on his pancakes topped with strawberries and blueberries in honor of the Fourth of July.

"Where's the whipped cream?" he asks, taking his plate and sitting at our kitchen table.

Handing him a can of the fluffy topper, I push down the feeling of unease rising in my chest. "We're leaving as soon as Ben gets here. Probably in about fifteen minutes."

"Good, because Dad texted me five minutes ago. He's already on his way." Ryder stuffs a fork full of food in his mouth and chews.

An image of Noah standing in this very kitchen, staring at Ben and me, half-naked, flashes through my mind. And now, because Noah's planning to spend the Fourth with Ryder at Jupiter Cove's annual carnival, Ben and I have arranged a fake date to keep up the premise that we're in a relationship.

"They're here!" Ryder springs out of his chair and runs toward the front door. A moment later, Ben and Wyatt are standing in my kitchen. They look adorable in matching Vineyard Vines American flag whale pocket tees.

"Help yourself to some pancakes," I offer, as I try my best to steady my nerves. This whole thing was Ben's idea. He offered to take me on a "date" to the carnival after I complained the other day about Noah's plans.

"Wyatt and I are going anyway. It won't be that hard to pretend we're dating. I can even win you a stuffed animal from the ring toss to drive home the point that you're my girlfriend."

He laughed, but my stomach lurched. We still haven't circled back to the conversation we began to have in the kitchen when Noah interrupted us. I still don't know what Ben was going to say about our night together being a one-time thing.

"Everyone ready? It's close to eleven. We should go." I smooth my navy blue sundress as I toss sunscreen in my bag.

"All right, patriots. Let's go!"

Now that I've got a boot on, I can get around without crutches, but I'm slow. The boys blast past me, but Ben steps slowly, staying in sync with my turtle's pace.

Driving toward Main Street, I see throngs of people enjoying the day. Smears of red, white, and blue bounce along in every direction.

"Dad said he would ride the Gravitron with me!" Ryder squeals in excitement.

"I want to go." Wyatt mimics Ryder's enthusiasm. "Daddy, will you go with me?"

"No way," Ben answers. "I get sick just looking at those rides."

"Me too," I say.

Ben turns to me and grins as we get out of the car and walk toward the carnival.

"I should probably hold your hand," he says as he threads his fingers through mine. "So Noah sees," he adds with a conspiratorial wink.

The feeling of my palm against his sends a warm rush through my body. This is dangerous. I'm definitely going to end up with a broken heart, I think, as Noah approaches.

"Hi." Noah waves. "Happy Fourth." He looks ridiculous in his red Gucci t-shirt, navy shorts, and expensive loafers.

"Dad, let's go. I want to get in line for the Gravitron before it gets too long." Ryder pulls Noah's arm toward the area set up with thrill rides.

"Guess we're going," Noah says. "We'll meet up for fireworks?"

My face must wash over with annoyance, because Noah quickly shifts gears.

"Um, that wasn't what we talked about, I guess. You guys enjoy the fireworks. Ryder and I will catch up with you later."

I watch as Noah and Ryder push through the crowd on their way to spin around endlessly on a ride that I consider torture.

"Let's go check out the kid's rides," Ben says to Wyatt. "I think I saw bumper cars."

Wyatt runs ahead as Ben and I follow. It's hard not to grin as people walk by with giant clouds of blue cotton candy and enormous tubs of popcorn. Genuine smiles burst from every face like fireworks.

"Harper!" Hearing my name, I turn toward the familiar voice.

"Harper, hey." Ellory steps out from behind a group of teenagers.

"Ellory, hi." I'm surprised she's shown up to the carnival but thrilled she's saying hello.

"I just had to come." She beams. "I have so many memories of this event from growing up." She glances around as if she's looking into her past and smiles. "I wanted to talk to you about the chapters you sent me," she continues. Her eyes slide from my face and land on Ben. "Your girlfriend's a very talented writer."

Ben smirks. "My girlfriend *is* a very talented writer," he agrees as he squeezes my palm, acknowledging our little charade.

"Anyway, Harper, I hope you don't mind, but I sent your pages to my agent a few weeks ago."

"Huh?" I blurt, ever so eloquent.

"Yes, I get pages from people all the time. This is one of the best excerpts I've read. You're good. Really good." Ellory nods along as she speaks in a sing-song voice.

A rush of butterflies sweeps through my chest. The pages she read are from a book that encompasses all my hopes and dreams. *Is she really going to champion my cherished ambition?*

"This business is hard," she continues. "You have to know people. You have to be connected. I'm so excited about your writing, Harper. All my contacts are your contacts. All my connections are your connections. I got my start the same way. An established author blurbed me, and I'm going to do the same for you. You're going to be a published author."

Suddenly, tears are streaming from my eyes. To have Ellory Brayson validate my writing, to have Ellory Brayson commit to helping me, to have Ellory Brayson in my corner. For the first time, I consider that maybe this dream I've had of being a writer all my life is within reach. The emotions surging through me are like nothing I've ever experienced.

"I didn't mean to make you cry," Ellory says as she pats my shoulder. She looks to Ben for support.

"My girlfriend can be very emotional," he teases as he pulls me into a side hug. "I think she's just happy."

I nod my head in agreement and swallow hard. "Yes," I say. "I can't put words together to express how I feel. I'm just so appreciative. Thank you."

Ellory smiles again warmly. "All right, you two. Go have fun. Kiss on the Ferris wheel or something!" She turns and walks away.

"My body is literally shaking," I say as I hold out my hands and watch them tremble.

"I bet," Ben says. "That's amazing. You're going to be a published author!" His voice beats with excitement. "I'd love to read your book, if you'll let me."

"Really?" His offer both thrills and terrifies me.

"Yes, really. This is your big dream. What kind of boyfriend would I be if I didn't support you?" He winks playfully, not recognizing how his words encompass another dream of mine.

But before I can fully comprehend that Ben is everything I'm looking for in a partner, he grabs my other hand and wraps it in his large palm.

"Now come on. You heard her. We have to go kiss on the Ferris wheel." He pulls me forward a few steps and then scoops Wyatt onto his hip.

"We're going to kiss on the Ferris wheel," Wyatt sings as we walk toward the ride.

And although I know I shouldn't let myself get swept away in the fantasy of Ben and me, the logical part of my brain falls away. I'm going to be a published author. And I'm going to kiss Ben on the Ferris wheel. Happy Fourth of July!

CHAPTER 35

Ellory Brayson

WALKING THROUGH THE crowd, I feel a surge of positive energy. Helping Harper launch her career is exhilarating. There's no doubt she's talented. She just needs someone like me to bring her to the attention of the publishing world.

I've spent the better part of my life focused on my own desires. I neglected to realize how great it feels to help others. And although the moment on *This Morning America* was one of the worst of my life, it has loosened the grip of my celebrity persona. There's a whole part of my brain that's bubbling with pleasure at the thought of Harper getting her book published. And it's a wonderful distraction from the drama with Maxy. The momentum carries me forward as I step toward the booth Tabby has set up for Blast Off Books.

She's promoting a few local authors and asked that I come by to increase interest. I agreed to sign books for thirty minutes, but then will move forward with my plan. *It's time for me to apologize.* My fingers brush the charm bracelet in my pocket. I've brought it with me today as if it has supernatural powers that can heal our wounded friendship. It lies against the item that will launch my apology.

"Happy Fourth," I chirp as I walk into the booth for Blast Off Books.

Tabby, who is standing beside two people, smiles. "Ellory, perfect timing. These are my local authors, Lorna and Evan."

"Hi there." I inch closer to them.

"Wow, this is exciting. The one and only Ellory Brayson," Evan blurts. "My wife is a huge fan!"

"Oh, thanks," I say. My eyes sweep the display of books on the table beside him. "I'd love to hear about your book."

Tabby cocks her head, clearly bewildered by my interest.

"It's a children's book about a wacky daddy." Evan holds up the charming cover proudly. "I've got two boys of my own, so there was plenty of material to choose from." He chuckles.

I nod my approval. "And Lorna, what about yours?" I shift my gaze to the tall, slender woman standing next to Evan.

"It's a young adult novel about love, friendship, and heartbreak, all set in a coastal town in Florida."

"Ahh, a setting I've used myself. Jupiter Cove makes a great backdrop." I wink.

"I hate to interrupt," Tabby chimes in. "But we've already got a line forming, Ellory." She gestures toward a roped-off area I hadn't noticed. She hands me a red Sharpie and leads me toward the line. "I thought you could sign in red because it's the Fourth."

"Sure," I say as I take the marker from her. "You know I consider this our special holiday." My words hang in the air. I'm aware she may not want to acknowledge this.

She gives me a slightly puzzled look. She starts to say something, but then pauses. "Thanks for doing this." She steps away as I approach the first person in line.

"THIS WAS GREAT." Evan beams. "I sold fifteen books, thanks to you. And Lorna sold a bunch as well."

"My pleasure," I reply as he asks me to sign his wife's copy of *The*

Prince of Silicon Valley. "She's a one-day-and-done Ellory reader," he confesses.

As I hand Evan back my novel, Tabby puts the unsold books in a box on the table. I push aside the charm bracelet in my pocket and thumb the index card next to it. I'm trying to work up the nerve to follow through with my plan. *It's now or never.*

"So," I say as casually as possible as I pull the index card from my pocket. "I made our Fourth of July fireworks list."

Tabby glances at the index card and shakes her head slightly.

"I thought it might be fun for old time's sake," I stammer nervously.

She takes the index card from my hand and reads the list of items.

1. Eat funnel cake in under two minutes
2. Steal sparklers to shoot off at the beach
3. Scare little kids in the funhouse
4. Make a boy think you want to kiss him on the Ferris wheel

Her face tightens, but I'm unsure if it's because she's irritated or if she's holding back a smile.

"This brings back memories," she says, placing the card down on the table. She continues putting the last books in the box, dismissing the list.

My heart sinks, but I push forward. "Can we at least eat a funnel cake?" I ask. "My treat."

Tabby looks up at me, searching my eyes for clues about my motivation.

"Okay," I say softly, filling in the silence. "I get why you're hesitant." Stepping toward her, I grasp her hand. "I know you probably didn't want me coming here for the summer. And you're annoyed I've pushed you into helping me with the whole Ellory's Editors thing." I take an unsteady breath and keep going. "I haven't been a good friend to you, Tabby. Somewhere along the way, I lost myself. I'm trying to find my way back." As the words leave my mouth, I'm amazed by how easily they fly free.

Tabby's expression turns serious. She releases her palm from my hand and takes a step back. "I've wanted you to acknowledge this for years, Ellory. But now, I don't know. Maybe it's too late." Her eyes shift from mine and look out into the crowd of cheerful people around us.

Blood pumps heavily in my veins, making my neck throb. She's right. I abandoned her, and she owes me nothing. But if there was ever a relationship worth fighting for, this is it.

I gather all the courage I have. "Let's go find somewhere to talk. I want you to tell me about what happened with Maxy. I need to know, and I'm finally ready to listen."

Tabby takes another step back and crosses her arms around her body. "I told you everything already. Right after it happened. You didn't care."

There's a sudden twisting in my gut. I've come this far. Ignoring the sharp stabs in my core, I continue. "You're absolutely right," I say. "You told me, but it was like my brain shut off. I refused to listen. We can't repair what's broken in our relationship until I really listen." I can feel the hot swell of tears in my eyes. "I'm ready to listen."

CHAPTER 36

Tabitha Wilson

'VE SEEN ELLORY cry exactly three times. Once when she fell out of a tree and broke her arm. Then again, when she packed up her car and moved to New York for her writing career. And right now.

Looking at her, vulnerable and teary-eyed, I feel pulled by the significance of our history. Our shared past lives in my bones.

"El-Ellory…" I stammer. Swallowing, I move closer to her. "I'm not sure it's the best time for me to rehash everything."

Ellory's eyes widen in disappointment. "Okay," she says. Her voice is barely a whisper.

We stand under the shade of a tree for a minute or two in silence. I've envisioned this moment a million times. But now that it's here, it seems pointless. We've already lost twenty years and missed all the moments we should have been there for each other. Yet, the pull of the past is a force too intense to deny.

Clearing my throat, I force myself to accept her proposal. "Why don't we get funnel cake and find a quiet spot to talk."

Ellory looks at me with a hopeful expression. "Really? I mean, yes, great. Thank you, Tabby."

Ellory disappears for a few minutes behind a food truck. When she reappears, she's holding a giant-sized sugary treat and beaming. We make our way toward a picnic bench away from the crowd. Ripping off a small piece of fried dough, I dunk it into chocolate sauce. Ellory does the same and we sit for a few moments enjoying the pleasures of carnival food.

"Thanks for doing this." Ellory wipes gooey chocolate from her hands. "I wish I would have listened the first time, but I'm thankful you're giving me another chance."

My body tenses as I realize this is my cue to speak. My mind travels back to twenty years ago, the night of Ellory's bachelorette party in New York City. I was looking forward to seeing her and meeting Prince Maximilian Jacoby. Ellory had been living in Europe for the past year and just recently moved back to New York. We had so much to catch up on.

When I arrived at their swanky penthouse apartment on the Upper East Side, I was shocked by the noticeable change in Ellory's appearance. She wore garish designer clothes from head to toe. A thick layer of makeup covered her face, and she had perfectly styled her overly highlighted hair.

But more than that, there was something off about the cadence of her voice and the way she held her body. She seemed almost like a caricature of herself. She had just appeared on the *Today Show* and her books were flying off the shelves. It all was going to her head.

"Maxy's on his way home and excited to meet you!" She squealed as a butler refilled our champagne glasses. "We'll have to leave after you say your hellos. I don't want to be late for my party." She laughed haughtily.

Excusing myself, I went into the spare bedroom, where I would stay for the weekend. I changed into my favorite little black dress and freshened up. When I walked back out into the apartment's main area, Maxy was home.

"Maxy, meet my very best friend in the world, Tabby!" Ellory's eyes bounced with excitement between me and Maxy.

He stepped forward and kissed me on each cheek. "Tabby, I've heard so much about you. Ellory's excited to celebrate." He smiled, and I could see why Ellory fell for him so quickly. "Keep an eye on my girl tonight." He winked.

We spoke for a few more moments. His charm and good looks instantly cast a spell.

"All right, Tabby. We need to go. Don't be surprised by the paparazzi," Ellory said, looping her arm through mine. "My publicist leaked a few of the places on our itinerary. It will be great for book sales."

The night proceeded as expected. Ellory and her entourage paraded from high-end bar to posh lounge, celebrating her upcoming nuptials. The wedding was taking place at the palace where Maxy grew up. My plane ticket was a small fortune, but there was no way I was missing it.

"I think you'll need help to get her upstairs." The limo driver eyed Ellory from the rearview mirror as we pulled up in front of her apartment building.

"Ellory, we're home. Can you make it upstairs?" I gently pulled her forward, but she immediately slumped back into the limo's seat as if she was a boulder sinking to the bottom of the sea.

"I think you're right," I agreed. Fishing Ellory's phone out of her purse, I called Maxy. He agreed to meet me at the curb to help get Ellory inside.

As we entered their apartment, Maxy and I steered Ellory to their bedroom.

"My best friend and my prince," Ellory slurred. Her words dragged, and her head bobbed unnaturally as she spoke.

"That's okay, my darling," Maxy cooed as we stepped into their room.

My jaw practically dropped at the site of the luxurious finishes and deluxe furniture pieces.

"Let's unzip her dress and get her into some comfortable pajamas," I suggested.

Maxy nodded and disappeared into their palatial closet.

I pulled aspirin from my bag and picked up the glass of water Maxy had put on her bedside table. "Take these and drink this water," I instructed.

Ellory complied and promptly passed out.

Maxy and I tiptoed out of the room. "Can I get you anything?" he asked.

It had been hours since I'd eaten, and I needed food to help digest the alcohol swirling in my system. "I'd love some crackers, or a bagel. Something easy, if it's not too much trouble."

"Of course, Tabby. No trouble at all. Let's see what we've got."

Slipping off my heels, I followed Maxy down a long hallway until we reached the kitchen. He started rummaging through the cabinets. It was clear he didn't know where anything was.

"Oh look, a box of unopened Croccantini crackers." He held the package up and grinned. His smile was something to behold. It made me feel as if I was the center of everything.

"Let's see if we have any good cheese and perhaps some red wine." He handed me the crackers as he searched around the kitchen.

I wasn't in the mood to drink anything more but agreed to a half glass to be polite. Maxy spread our snacks and wine on the large marble island in their kitchen, then hoisted himself up. He sat with his legs dangling as he cut off a sliver of cheese.

I stood directly across from him, happy to be putting food in my stomach before bed. He asked me a few questions about the evening's festivities and seemed delighted as I recounted the highlights of the night.

He finished the bottle of wine and then poured himself a glass of bourbon. "Would you like some?" he asked, nudging his glass in my direction.

"I'm exhausted," I said, noticing it was close to four in the morning. "I'm going to skip the bourbon and head to bed."

Taking a step toward the hall, it surprised me when Maxy grabbed my hand. Turning my head toward him, I frowned in confusion.

"Ellory told me you were beautiful, but the pictures I've seen don't do you justice." His voice purred like a cat. He looked down at me as if I was prey.

I jerked my hand away from his, my chest tightening. Taking another step away from him, I didn't respond to his advance. I hoped if I went to bed, it would be over. But before I could exit the kitchen, he pushed me up against a long row of cabinets and began slobbering all over my neck.

"Get off me!" I screamed.

"Stop trying to hide it. You're desperate for me." He growled as his hands traveled up my thighs.

Shaking, I felt disoriented. But then, suddenly, a protective instinct kicked in. I kneed Maxy hard in his crotch. He pulled away, bent over in pain.

Running down the hall, I escaped into the guest room, locking the door behind me.

"I didn't sleep at all," I say now as Ellory's eyes spill with tears. "As soon as I heard your staff arrive in the morning, I grabbed my suitcase and left."

Clearing her throat, Ellory looks away from me, then meets my eyes again. "By the time you called me, Maxy had already told me his own version of the story." Her eyes are full of regret.

"Yes. You believed it was a misunderstanding, no matter what I said…" My voice trails as the betrayal I felt all those years ago comes flooding back.

"My future husband assaulted you, and all I cared about was protecting my fantasy world. I wish I could go back in time and support you, believe you, and make this right. I betrayed you, and I'll never forgive myself."

Each word Ellory speaks is heavy with remorse. "You should never forgive me. You should never, ever forgive me." Ellory shakes her head mournfully, and I can't help but wonder if she's right. Can I ever forgive her? Or is this the moment where we formally acknowledge the end of our friendship as if we are a couple who are parting ways for good?

But before I can process the swirl of emotions coursing through me, I see Ila walking toward us, waving. I'm still surprised by the recent improvement in our relationship.

"Hi," she says, smiling as she approaches the picnic table. "How'd the book signing go?"

"Good," I say, forcing myself to act as if nothing's wrong.

Ellory quickly jumps in, aware I'm having trouble switching gears so quickly. "I met a lot of great people and helped some local authors with book sales."

"Great," Ila says, shifting her gaze from Ellory to me. "I want to show you something." Her words leap from her mouth excitedly.

"Sure, what's up?" I ask, glad to be distracted from my relationship with Ellory.

"Follow me," Ila says. "Oh, and Ellory, you can come too."

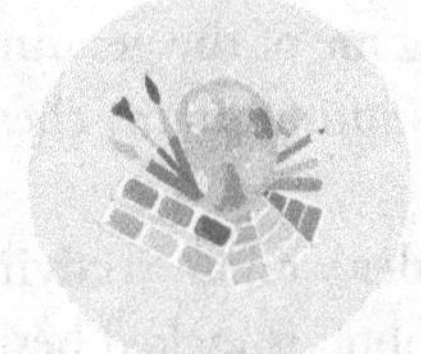

CHAPTER 37

Ila Wilson

MAYBE I SHOULDN'T *have interrupted them,* I think, as Tabby and Ellory toss the remnants of a funnel cake into the garbage can and follow me. As soon as I started talking, I could sense the heaviness between them.

Tabby quickens her pace and steps next to me as we walk. "My curiosity is officially piqued," she says.

I lead them to the small church that sits next to the carnival grounds.

"Jupiter Cove Artist Showcase," Ellory reads the large sign sitting on an easel in front of the weathered wood doors of All Saints.

"Oh!" Tabby lets out a small gasp. "Did you enter something?" Her eyes settle on mine excitedly. "Ila is a very talented artist," Tabby continues, directing her comment toward Ellory.

I can feel the grin spread across my face at the compliment. "Thanks." I push through the heavy oak doors and step into the arched entryway of the church. It was only an hour ago when I came here and found out the good news.

Making our way past the chapel, we step into a common room displaying the winners of Jupiter Cove's Art and Culture awards. Large screen panels line the room, sectioning it off into areas for paintings, drawings, graphic arts, poems, and short stories.

Tabby squeezes my hand as we walk toward the area of drawings. I'm not used to the warmth of her touch. Suddenly, a flood of memories rushes in, reminding me of the genuine care she has shown me over the years. A lightness springs in my chest. Maybe our paths were destined to intertwine?

Stepping beside an older woman studying the display, I point to my piece. A large blue ribbon is tacked beside it that reads "Second Place Overall."

Ellory steps closer to my pastel of the lighthouse taken from the view at Venus Inlet. "Wow, second place out of all the entries in all the different categories. Impressive." She turns her face toward mine, smiles, and then looks back at the figure of CJ sketched in the scene.

"There's something familiar about him," she says as her eyes soak up the image. "Reminds me—"

"Excuse me?" The older woman standing near us catches my eye. "Are you Ila Wilson?" She reads my name displayed under the pastel drawing.

Nodding my head, I suddenly notice her fashionable clothing and bold haircut, perfectly framing her heart-shaped face.

"I'm moved by your piece," she says, pursing her lips together as if she's hungry. "It's such an innovative take." Her eyes bounce from one corner of my drawing to another.

My body fills with a buzzy hum. Hearing a total stranger admire my work is exhilarating. "Thank you," I say hesitantly, not used to this type of praise.

The woman eyes me carefully for a moment as if I'm another piece of art she must deem worthy of her attention. She holds me in her gaze for a moment before she opens her large tote and fishes around. She pulls out a business card and hands it to me.

"My name is Dr. Anita Herrera. I'm a professor of foundational studies at FLAD. I'd love to see more of your work."

I can see Tabby grab Ellory's hand enthusiastically as Dr. Herrera waits for me to respond.

My knees suddenly feel like Jell-O. I shift my weight to steady myself. "I would love that," I say. Holding up the business card, I stare at the printed letters: *Anita Herrera, PhD, Art History.*

"Email me your portfolio tomorrow."

"Sure!" I blurt.

"I look forward to seeing more of your work." She turns and walks away.

As soon as she's out of sight, Ellory and Tabby huddle around me, hopping up and down with excitement.

"This is so exciting!" Ellory cries.

"I think you may have just been discovered," Tabby continues.

We all squeeze hands and hug. We linger, but then Ellory's phone rings, interrupting us. Pulling away from our circle, she reaches inside her bag and pulls out her phone. She looks at the screen. "It's Cade," she mouths as she steps away toward a window.

"Do you think I should tell Dr. Herrera I applied and was wait-listed?" I ask Tabby as Ellory takes her call.

"Hmm." Tabby looks out into the distance past my shoulder for a moment, thinking. "Not at first. Email her your portfolio and see what she says. That's my advice."

A mother's advice, I think to myself warmly. Why did I push Tabby away for all those years? "You're right," I say as a smile overtakes my face.

"Something's up with Cade." Ellory walks toward us, her nose pinched in concern. "Cade's my son," Ellory says, looking at me.

"What did he say?" Tabby puts her hand on Ellory's shoulder, concerned.

"It was weird. He said he needed to talk to me in person right away. He asked me to meet him at the pier."

"The pier? Why not just back at the Rutherford Estate?" Tabby looks at Ellory questioningly.

Shrugging her shoulders, Ellory's eyes scrunch together. "I don't know. He wouldn't say. He just insisted I meet him in fifteen minutes." Her voice wobbles with concern. "Can you drive me? I walked to the carnival." Ellory searches Tabby's eyes for support.

"Shoot, Andre dropped me off this morning. Ila, can you drive us?"

I glance at my watch. I'm supposed to meet CJ in two hours. The other night, when he said he had something to tell me, he begged me to let him do it over dinner on a proper date. "It's nothing bad," he promised. "Let's make a night out of it." He told me to wear a dress.

"Sure, I can drive you to the pier. I just need to be home in an hour."

As we pull into the parking lot, Ellory squints into the sunlight, looking for Cade. "He's not here yet." Her voice stretches thin with worry. "I'm going to go walk down the pier. I'm sure whatever Cade wants to discuss is private."

Tabby and I nod as Ellory gets out of my car and walks toward the worn-out wood slats that lead to an unobstructed view of the ocean.

A few minutes go by, and then a sleek black car pulls into a space on the other side of the parking lot.

"Good, he's here." Tabby sighs with relief.

I watch Ellory turn back toward the land as the passenger door to the car across the way opens.

Looking toward the sound of a slamming car door, my entire body suddenly constricts.

"CJ?" I say out loud in disbelief, turning to look at Tabby.

"Huh?" She looks at me, confused.

"What's going on?" I blurt. "Why is CJ here?"

"CJ?" Tabby asks again. "That's Ellory's son, Cade." She looks at me with a puzzled expression.

I stare out the window as CJ approaches Ellory on the pier. They begin to talk, and then she reaches for his hand.

Suddenly, anger boils through every inch of my body. I throw open the car door and bolt toward the pier.

CJ's back is to me, and Ellory's so invested in whatever he's saying, she doesn't notice I'm only a few feet away.

"He wants me to go to Europe with him until it's safe to come back to the States. He's not under investigation, but he wants to put as much space between him and those thugs as possible."

I can hear the cadence of his familiar voice. Yet, now, knowing what I know, his words sound like a strange, computerized synthesizer.

"Dad wants you to leave with him? For how long? When?" Ellory's voice is on the edge of panic.

"Tomorrow," CJ says just as Ellory notices me.

"Ila?" Ellory looks at me, confused.

CJ immediately swings around, his mouth hanging open at the sight of me. "Ila, what's going on? Why are you here?"

"Why am I here?" I snap. "Who are you? You've been lying to me this entire time!" My words tumble over each other.

Ellory stares at both of us, too confused to say anything.

CJ lets out a long breath. "I'm CJ, just like I told you." His voice is soft, as if he's afraid to speak.

"You're Cade! Not CJ," I bark angrily.

Suddenly, I hear Ellory's voice. "Cade. That's his name. But all his friends call him CJ. It's short for Cade Jacoby." She does her best to defend him, but I can tell she's confused.

"See?" CJ says with relief in his voice. "CJ."

He reaches for my hand, but I snatch it away. "But you're Ellory Brayson's son? You never told me. You said you were on your own here, staying with a friend."

"I was going to tell you everything tonight. I swear." CJ's words burst out in a rush. "I realized the other night you were Tabby's stepdaughter when I saw her name on your phone." He looks over my shoulder at the sound of feet running down the pier.

"Ila, what in the world is going on?" Tabby is taking quick strides toward us. She moves next to me and wraps her left arm around my shoulder protectively.

A moment later, we all swivel our heads toward the sound of a car door slamming. A man steps out of the driver's side of the black car.

Everyone is quiet as we watch his feet pound the pier.

"Maxy? What the hell are you doing here?" Ellory crosses her arms over her body and takes a step back.

"I'm here to bring Cade to Europe with me. I need to go home for a few months and wait out the investigation."

Tabby releases me from her embrace as soon as he's done speaking and bolts back to my car. I'm too upset to register everything that's going on around me.

"Cade, tell your mom," Maxy continues. "You're coming with me. We're leaving first thing in the morning." Maxy looks at Cade.

But instead of turning to Ellory, Cade turns to me. "Ila, you have to believe me. I was going to tell you everything tonight. At first, I didn't want you to know I was Ellory's son. People treat me differently when they find out. And I had just been arrested in Miami. Let's just go somewhere and talk. Me and you." His eyes widen like saucers.

"No!" My voice is shrill as I hold back tears. I need to get off this dock before I break down. I turn, taking hurried steps to my car.

"Ila, please! Let me explain!" CJ chases after me.

Suddenly, I stop and turn to face him. Maxy and Ellory are behind him, gaping at me.

"There's nothing to talk about," I say. "I don't know you, and I don't trust you."

CJ's shoulders slump, and he looks toward the ground.

And although my heart feels like it's breaking into a million pieces, I say exactly what needs to be said. "You should leave Jupiter Cove. Go with your dad. I never want to see you again."

CHAPTER 38

Faye Carter

"**M**ILO'S AT A playdate. The twins will want to play bingo. I also bought a bunch of art supplies."

Linda, my nanny, nods as the twins come barreling toward the kitchen with their new emoji bingo set.

"Lin-duh," Emma squeals with delight. She hugs Linda around the thighs and buries her head in the soft fabric of her leggings.

It's surprising how attached my kids have grown to Linda in just two weeks. But it's easy to acknowledge how much happier everyone is since she's become part of our routine. When Mark came home from his poker night, I did exactly what Lexi suggested. I told him I was moving forward with a nanny. I did not ask permission. I did not seek his consent or approval. I simply stated the facts. I need help and some time to myself. I'll be hiring a nanny three days a week.

Mark's eyes went wide, and I braced myself for an argument.

"Okay," he said evenly. "If that's what you think you need, then okay." He stepped past me and passed out in bed.

I stood in the hallway, motionless for several minutes. *That's it?* I thought. Years of fighting about this, and all I needed to do was pose my need as a statement rather than a question? Had I set myself up for the power struggles Mark and I have been having by constantly asking for his permission rather than declaring what I needed?

I felt a rush of goodwill about my marriage and hoped it would last. Maybe Mark and I were done filling in the squares on our marriage bingo card. Maybe we'd finally figured this thing out.

"Mommy, leave now." Ezra grabs my hand and leads me toward the front door.

"Wow," I say, lingering. "My kids really enjoy being with you, Linda."

"We have fun." She smiles. "And the Hershey kisses I bribe them with don't hurt either." She winks as I collect Ellory's manuscript from the table by the front door.

"Griffin will be up from his nap in about an hour. You can give them chicken nuggets and fruit for dinner. Mark has soccer tonight and won't be home until after I get back." I kiss the top of Emma and Ezra's heads and leave for my Ellory's Editors meeting.

As I drive away, my body feels light. Almost as if I could float away. I have four hours of kid-free time to interact with adults and focus on nothing but my own needs. The freedom is exhilarating.

When I arrive at Blast Off Books, I see Harper sitting in the café. She's sipping a large, iced coffee and smiling at a very good-looking man. Unsure if I should interrupt, I walk toward Tabby's office, ready for another round of editing.

"Faye!" I hear Harper call as I step past the café. "Over here," she continues.

I change direction and walk toward her. "Hi," I say.

Harper glances toward Tabby's office. "Tabby's not here, and no sign of Ellory." She shrugs her shoulders.

"Oh," I say. "Well, it's only five minutes past. Maybe they're coming?"

"Why don't you join us?" The man sitting with Harper gestures to the empty chair at the table. "I'm Ben, by the way."

"Oh, thanks." I smile. "I think I'll browse until we start. It's been years since I've been here without my kids, so it will be a treat."

"She has four kids, six and under!" Harper delights in filling her friend in on my crazy life.

"Wow, I can see why you want alone time." He emphasizes the word *alone* and lets out a joyful huff. His smile is warm and easy.

"Exactly," I say. "Harper, grab me when Tabby and Ellory get here. I'll be in the romance section."

"That's my girl," Harper says as I wander away unencumbered.

I'm not sure how long I've been combing through the selection of Taylor Jenkins Reid's books when Harper approaches.

"Faye, Tabby's finally here. But still no sign of Ellory." Looking at my watch, I see we are an hour behind schedule. It's close to five.

"That's weird," I say, grasping *The Seven Husbands of Evelyn Hugo*. "This book's been on my TBR list for a long time. I'm going to pay and then I'll come to the office."

Harper nods as I leave to make my purchase.

"So, where's Ellory?" I ask, walking into Tabby's office a few minutes later. As I step inside, I notice Tabby is teary-eyed and Harper's consoling her.

"Oh, do you want me to leave?" I say, wondering if I'm intruding.

"No, it's okay." Tabby sinks into her chair. She looks exhausted. "I'm so tired of hiding this," Tabby says in between sobs.

I take a seat in the chair next to Tabby and look at Harper for guidance. She catches my eye, and I can see the despair in her eyes. *Why is Tabby upset?*

She suddenly speaks up. "I was telling Harper. I just got a call from my doctor about an hour ago. My husband and I are going through fertility treatment for the fourth time." Tabby inhales deeply and pauses. "It didn't work out again."

Reaching my hand out, I grasp Tabby's palm. "I'm sorry," I say as I consider how unfair it is that I've had four perfect and healthy babies, and she so desperately wants just one. My chest bubbles with shame as I consider how happy I was earlier to leave them with Linda.

The remorse makes me realize that motherhood is a constant toggle between feelings of guilt, exhaustion, joy, crankiness, pride, fear, and love. And as terrifying and exhilarating as it is, when I look at Tabby, I understand I am the luckiest person in the world to be riding such a tumultuous wave of emotions.

"I'm sorry I'm unloading this on you," Tabby continues as she glances tentatively between me and Harper. "For so many years, I've relied solely on my husband. He's been wonderful. But it's hard for him to see me break down. Thanks for letting me." Her words drag out slowly, edged with pain.

I can't help but wonder why Tabby is leaning on Harper and me, rather than Ellory, her best friend. But instead of asking questions, I just stroke Tabby's hand as tears drip from her eyes.

"I know there's nothing we can say," Harper interjects. "But we're happy to sit here and talk with you." Harper looks in my direction, pursing her lips together somberly.

"Thanks," Tabby replies, sitting up in her chair. "You know what? I'm kinda hungry, and I'd love a margarita. It's been a tough week. Anyone care to join me?"

CHAPTER 39
Harper Weiss

MY BODY LURCHES forward as Faye swerves her giant SUV into a parking spot at Galaxy Gastro Pub.

"Sorry." Faye looks at me in the backseat through her rearview mirror.

Tabby laughs. "Faye obviously needs this impromptu girls' night as much as I do."

I peer at Tabby's profile from the back seat as she smiles. She's been through so much. I'm happy to be with her tonight and ease her pain, even if for just a few hours.

"Yes," Faye agrees. "I really need this."

Faye and Tabby open their doors and exit the car. Pushing aside a few sippy cups and several children's books, I unsnap my seatbelt. My shoes crunch against Cheerios scattered on the floor of Faye's car as I step out and join them.

The bar area of the pub is crammed with bodies. A Miami Marlins game plays on multiple large flat screens as fans crowd around anxiously watching a close game against the Atlanta Braves.

"Right this way." A young hostess grabs menus and leads us to a table on the other side of the restaurant.

As soon as we sit down, Faye's phone buzzes.

"Ugh, it's Mark again. He's not used to me having last-minute plans. The nanny just left, and he's drowning on his own with bedtime." I can tell Faye is somewhat pleased by her husband's struggle.

Suddenly, Faye looks panicked that she's said exactly the wrong thing in front of Tabby.

Tabby must sense the same thing, because she quickly speaks up. "Don't worry, Faye. I don't want you tiptoeing around me just because you have kids."

Faye nods agreeably, but I can still see guilt creep across her face. "Let me call him really quick, or he'll be texting every five minutes." Standing, she walks toward the restaurant's exit.

"I don't want us to dwell on my sad news," Tabby says as she reads the menu. "I mean that. I need a distraction."

"I understand," I say, as the waiter appears.

"I'll have a margarita with salt. Harper, want to join me?"

Although I'm not sure I'm up for margaritas tonight, I'm desperate to make Tabby happy. "Sure," I say.

Faye suddenly appears and jumps in as well.

"Maybe get a pitcher of margaritas for the table," the waiter says as the crowd at the bar cheers in unison. "We're running a special for the game. It's a better deal."

"Great!" Tabby says.

Five minutes later, the waiter is back with frosty glasses and a very large pitcher of margaritas. "Just let me know when you're ready to order," he says, walking away.

Tabby eagerly fills our glasses, and we all take a first sip of the tart, cold drink.

"Wow, that's strong." Faye pushes her glass to the side. "I'm driving, so maybe I should skip it."

"So, tell us, what's happening with your book?" Tabby looks at me as she takes a long sip of her drink.

"It's been about three weeks since Ellory sent it to her agent. Hopefully, I'll hear something soon." My face explodes with an enormous smile. I still can't believe Ellory passed my novel to her agent. It's as if I'm about to jump off a cliff into my wildest dreams.

"What happened to Ellory today?" Faye asks as my body continues to hum with excitement.

Tabby swirls her straw around in her almost empty glass. "She wasn't up to coming."

Both Faye and I look at Tabby, waiting for her to say more.

"I really shouldn't talk about her personal life." Tabby huffs. "But considering she wrote an entire book about our relationship, I shouldn't feel bad." She shrugs her shoulders.

My lips purse together. "I suspected the characters Tish and Emma were you and Ellory, but I wasn't going to ask."

"Oh my, is all that true?" Faye asks, concerned.

"The theme of betrayal is true," Tabby says, her words dragging slightly. "But the story is not an exact retelling of what actually happened."

"Oh, well, I'm sorry if Ellory hurt you." Faye slides her hand over Tabby's for just a moment. She clearly has a natural talent for mothering.

Tabby stares off into the crowd at the bar for a moment. "Despite everything, I still care for her. But it's complicated." She pauses and refills her margarita glass. "Her husband showed up here unexpectedly a few weeks ago on the Fourth of July. He convinced their son Cade to travel with him to Europe for the next several months."

"Prince Maximilian?" I ask, feeling a special thrill at the thought of Ellory's love story.

"He's not what you think," Tabby says. "And Ellory doesn't want Cade to spend time with him. She's upset he left with him so suddenly."

I pour myself another margarita, already feeling buzzed as Tabby continues.

"I think she's finally ready to file for divorce. But it's scary. She's depressed and overwhelmed. But I think it's the right thing to do."

Faye and I look at each other uncomfortably.

Tabby sees our faces and quickly switches gears. "Do you like her new book? It's a big change from romance to serious contemporary fiction."

"It was just okay," Faye admits. "I love my romance novels."

"Me too," I agree. "I liked it, but I just prefer the escapist fun of a romance novel. What about you? Do you like it?" I glance at Tabby, waiting for her to respond.

"I do," she says with a sigh. "But it was like someone jumped into my brain and captured my childhood on paper."

"That makes sense," I agree. "Are you upset she wrote an entire book about your relationship?"

Tabby pushes her hand through her long tight curls. "No, I almost feel like it's a three-hundred-page apology." She finishes her second margarita and smirks. "But I think it would surprise you both to find out what genre I enjoy reading most."

"What?" Faye asks, her interest piqued by the coy look on Tabby's face.

"*Smut*," Tabby whispers the word exaggeratedly.

"What?" Faye says again, surprised.

"Smut," Tabby repeats more assuredly this time.

"What exactly do you mean?" I ask.

Tabby huddles toward the center of the table, and Faye and I do the same.

"Spicy books. Lots of sex." She giggles, and then it turns into a hiccup.

"Really!" I gasp.

"Oh, yes, it's a guilty pleasure. I don't really sell too many in my store, but I follow TikTok to find the books that will get me going." She laughs between more hiccups.

Faye giggles, and I can't help but smile.

Tabby leans further toward the middle of the table, encouraging Faye and me to do the same. She attempts to lower her voice, but she's buzzed, and her words come out louder than she intends. "I'll send you a link to Emily McIntire's book, *Hooked*. You'll love it."

The waiter slides up next to our table as soon as she speaks, but Tabby doesn't notice and continues. "I'll also send a link to the vibrator I use after I've read a few chapters!"

"Oh, my!" The waiter takes a step back.

The three of us burst into uncontrollable laughter as his face turns bright red. "I'll come back soon." He quickly scurries away.

Happy tears stream down Tabby's face as we all try to catch our breath. "Wow, I've really spilled all my secrets tonight," she says as we settle down. "To be fair, you both should 'fess up about something." She looks at us playfully, bobbing in her chair. She's clearly drunk.

Feeling the courage of a warm buzz, I immediately volunteer. "I've got something!" I blurt.

Tabby and Faye eye me with excitement.

"Ben's not my boyfriend. We're only pretending!" As soon as the words escape my lips, I realize how sad they sound.

"Huh? Pretending?" Faye looks at me questioningly.

"Yes, it evolved into this weird fake relationship when my ex caught us the morning after an unexpected one night—"

Tabby immediately interjects, "Oh, sounds like one of my smut books!" She gasps.

"Yes, I'm trapped in a romance novel," I admit. A shaky feeling slides over my body as I think about the night Ben and I spent together. "The thing is, I really like him. I could see being in a real relationship with him. And to top everything off, we're both Jewish, so maybe it's *besheret*?"

Looking up, I notice Tabby and Faye look confused. "It's a Yiddish word that means destined to be together." I exhale deeply, trying to push away the arousal coursing through me as I picture him naked in my bed.

"I saw the way he looked at you earlier today in the bookstore. He's into you!" Faye gives me an encouraging look.

Shaking my head, I explain. "He's got a divorce that's dragging out. It's not even final yet. It's not the right time."

"Don't you remember what Ellory said at her book signing?" Faye pauses.

"No." I take another sloppy gulp of my third margarita.

"Everyone can have a great love story, but if you put any kind of constraint on it that narrows the possibilities, you're going to miss it." Her voice brims with enthusiasm.

"Such a hopeless romantic!" Tabby looks at Faye. "Your turn. What's your secret?"

I'm thankful Tabby has taken the focus off my feelings for Ben, and quickly speak up. "Yea, Faye, what's your something to share?"

"Hmmm." Faye's eyes move back and forth as she considers what to say. "If I tell you guys, you're going to think I'm crazy."

"Maybe?" I say. "But you're at a total advantage because Tabby and I are drunk, and you're completely sober."

Tabby looks at me, bobbling her head in agreement.

"But it's strange, like, really out there." Faye catches my eye, then looks away.

"Stranger than fake dating?!" I laugh.

Faye takes her turn, huddling toward the center of the table. She lowers her voice to a whisper. "You know the character Lexi from Ellory's romance novel?"

Tabby and I nod our heads.

"Well, sometimes, when I'm really upset and struggling with something, she appears and gives me advice." Faye pivots her gaze toward the table, afraid to look us in the eyes.

For a long moment, there's nothing but the hum of the crowd at the bar.

"That was unexpected!" Tabby squawks. "But I love it. I absolutely love it!"

Faye lifts her eyes and looks at us tentatively. "I mean, I know she isn't really there, but it's like a friend giving me advice. I've been so wrapped up in my life as a mom I've lost contact with friends. Sometimes I need support."

"We all need support sometimes," Tabby echoes back sincerely.

"Are you ladies still having an R-rated discussion, or are you ready to order?" The waiter steps up to our table slowly, clearly afraid of what he may overhear.

After we eat and leave the waiter a giant tip, we pile back into Faye's car so she can bring Tabby and me home.

I crawl into the backseat, and the car hums along the road. My mind settles on Ben and what Faye reminded me of earlier tonight. I think back to Ellory's advice when I asked if everyone could have a great love story.

…If you have rules about who this person is supposed to be, or a specific timeline it must happen by, or any kind of constraint that narrows the possibilities, your great love may slip through your fingers.

Grabbing my phone out of my bag, I give in to the warmth of my buzz.

Harper: I don't want to miss this…

A moment later, my phone flashes with a message from Ben.

Ben: ????

CHAPTER 40
Ellory Brayson

"TODAY IS THE first day of August. I plan to launch Ellory's Editors the weekend after Labor Day. We've got one month to make sure we've got all the images we need."

Nodding my head at Amber over a Zoom session, I hardly register her words. Cade's been gone for several weeks, and all I can think about is the terrible way everything unfolded on the pier.

At first, I was confused when Cade said Maxy wanted to take him to Europe. Why should Maxy involve Cade in his plan to flee the States? But before I could even ask Cade for more details about Maxy's reasons, Ila came storming down the dock.

"Ila?" I asked, wondering why she was so furious. But once she began talking with Cade, I could piece it together. Cade had met Ila somewhere in Jupiter Cove, and they were dating. Of all the people he could have met, what were the chances that he would end up in a relationship with Tabby's stepdaughter?

It stung when Cade admitted to Ila that he doesn't tell people he's Ellory Brayson's son. Is he ashamed? Is he protecting himself? Is there something so fundamentally wrong with our relationship that I can't even understand the reason he would feel the need to keep this information secret?

I could tell by the pleading look in his eyes as he spoke with Ila that he had fallen in love with her. I desperately wanted to wrap my arms around him and shelter him from his emotional pain. Affection, longing, and lust can quickly turn to doubt, fear, and obsessiveness when a new relationship stumbles. But in Cade's case, it was more than a stumble. His connection with Ila was plunging off a cliff.

As Ila made it clear she wanted nothing to do with Cade, Tabby appeared. But just as she was trying to get a handle on what was happening, Maxy came striding down the pier as if he owned the ocean. The sight of him made my stomach turn. Tabby quickly pushed past him and bolted for the car. Ila followed close behind. A moment later, they were gone.

"What are you doing here?" I barked at Maxy as I watched the taillights of Ila's car move into the distance.

"I knew you'd be upset." Cade gazed at me. "That's why I didn't want Dad to show up at your house."

Maxy focused in on me, his eyes like laser beams. "I'm going home to Europe. Cade's not in school right now, so the timing's perfect. He can come and live in my country for as long as he wants." Maxy's words thumped assuredly like the steady beat of a drum.

"No way!" I snapped. "I don't need Cade spending months on end with you as you gallivant around Europe, exemplifying all the reasons you're a terrible father and husband." My emotions were brimming over into a boil.

"What the hell do you mean?" Maxy sneered. His accent pushed up and over his angry words.

Cade moved his body between us as if he could disarm the bomb about to explode.

Exasperated, I continued anyway. "What I mean is that you let Cade meet your girlfriends. You expose him to shady people. You've taught him that there are never consequences!" My chest heaved as the words exploded from my mouth.

Maxy's face worked itself into a sinister grin. "But, Ellory, you've always known I'm someone who can't be with just one woman. Even before we got married."

Cade immediately sprang from between us and headed toward land. He didn't want to hear anymore.

Maxy continued. "Don't pretend you didn't know. Your friend Tabby told you firsthand that I had a wandering eye, but you didn't care. You weighed the benefits of our situation and accepted it. So don't tell me now that it matters." His tone was akin to a menacing villain's.

Regret consumed me as soon as Maxy said Tabby's name. My body burned as Maxy stood before me with his sickening logic. I stared at the living, breathing incarnation of my misplaced loyalty.

Without a word, I walked past him, determined to support Cade and beg for Tabby's forgiveness. But by the time the Uber dropped me at home, Cade was packed.

"There's nothing for me here," he said in a raspy voice.

"Because of Ila?" I asked as I placed my hand on his shoulder and guided him to sit down on the couch.

"Yes, because of Ila. I messed up." His words trailed off despondently.

"Ila should be angry," I agreed. "But I also think it could just be a knee-jerk reaction." I tried desperately to think of all the books I had written on broken love. I had a special talent for helping my characters find their way back to each other, even when logic would suggest otherwise.

My mind quickly flitted through hundreds of plot lines. And then a strange sensation spread through my body. My chosen genre, my career, and the place where I made my fame and fortune are based on the unicorn of happily ever after. *It does not exist.*

The truth is, a lifelong relationship is more of a *happily after.* Omit the *ever,* and you'll find the best relationships can find love again *after*—after disappointment, after misunderstanding, and after difficulties. The best relationships can come back together and find *happily* again, *after.*

"Ellory? Ellory, are you there?"

I shift my gaze from beyond my computer screen and focus back on Amber's face. "What did you say?" I ask, trying my best to focus on the here and now.

"You said there was something else you needed to tell me after we discussed the launch plan for Ellory's Editors."

My extremities immediately tingle with nervous energy. "Yes," I say as I clear my throat. "Maxy and I are announcing the divorce. I just thought you should know."

Amber's face collapses into a muddled expression. I'm sure she's had enough. How could she possibly save my career after the series of land mines that have exploded, starting with *This Morning America*.

"Ellory, I'm sorry. I'm sure this is difficult."

I nod my head, afraid words will fail me.

"You understand this will overshadow Ellory's Editors," Amber continues. "And it's going to kill the launch plan for your next book." Amber furiously writes on a piece of paper, as if her intense scribbling can save the onslaught of bad publicity headed my way.

Taking a deep breath, I respond with the truth. "For once, Amber, I don't care what happens with my book or my public persona. The only thing I care about is my son." It's at this exact moment that I realize all the ways Celebrity Ellory has failed me. I have abandoned myself and it's time to find my way back.

CHAPTER 41

Tabitha Wilson

ROLLING IN MY bed, I move my arm over, feeling for the warmth of Andre's body. My hand slides up our soft sheets, confirming what I suspected. I've slept late, and he's gone for the day. I love the comfort of our morning routine and feel disappointed I've missed it. We begin each day drinking Cuban coffee as we do the Wordle. The winner gets bragging rights for the day.

It's no surprise I overslept this morning. Faye, Harper, and I met up for another fun dinner last night. The cosmopolitans I drank have my stomach churning. Curling my body into a ball, I hope the discomfort passes. But it's not just the discomfort left behind by cheap vodka. I worry I've made a mistake telling Harper and Faye about my struggles with infertility. I barely know them, and they're both moms. *Have I made them uncomfortable? Have I saddled them with information too personal?*

I've spent years on this IVF journey, orbiting only with Andre. He's been my solo companion and outlet for an avalanche of emotion. And while he's been wonderful, he's suffering in his own way. And then suffering even more when he witnesses my pain.

What made me finally share something I've held close to my vest? I think about all the reasons I never tell anyone. Will they tell me to adopt? Will they tell me to just stop thinking about it, and it will happen? Will they tell me a crazy story about a friend of a friend of a cousin who finally had a successful IVF treatment after years of trying? Will they stop talking about their children with me? Will they pity me and look at me with teary eyes?

All of these fears have compelled me to bottle up the biggest battle of my life and fight as a lone soldier. But I'm exhausted. And an army of one can never be as effective as a battalion. What a relief it was to have Faye squeeze my hand and not say a word the day I told her. What a gift it was to have Harper say she's here to talk or to distract, whatever I need.

Stretching out my body, my stomach softens. As I make my way to the bathroom to brush away the sticky sweet taste overpowering my mouth, I hear Ila trot down the stairs. I quickly spit toothpaste into the sink, determined to talk with her about Cade. Ever since the evening on the pier, she's pulled away again. It stings, given that we were finally making headway in our relationship.

"Hey." I shuffle into the kitchen and find Ila sitting down, drinking a glass of orange juice.

She nods in response, but her eyes have a vacant look about them. When she stands to put her cup in the sink, I notice she's dressed in a black pencil skirt and a professional-looking top.

I look at her curiously. "Where are you headed?"

She smooths out her skirt and pauses in the doorway that leads out of the kitchen. "I'm meeting with that professor today. She looked at my portfolio and invited me to come in."

"That's fantastic." I beam.

But Ila shrugs her shoulders, uninterested in telling me more. "Well, I need to go." Her voice is lifeless as she turns away from me.

A moment later, I hear the scrape of the front door as she leaves.

My head scrambles, trying to recall the exact words she said to me when she came running down the pier.

"He's a liar!" she choked her words out through tears. "Just like my mom, he's a liar."

I attempted to talk with Ila about how she was feeling over the days following, but each time I did, she blew me off.

"Lying is the one thing I cannot tolerate. You have to be able to trust someone." Her face would cloud with betrayal as she spoke, and then she would walk away.

Ila's kryptonite was clearly sparked by Cade's betrayal. I wish Andre and I had done a better job of protecting her. My body suddenly ignites with heat. I'm furious about the explosion of problems that have erupted since the pier.

As Ila wrestles with her feelings for Cade, I'm also fighting to keep thoughts of Maxy at bay. But since seeing his face and glimpsing the brazen way he eyed me, I can't stop thinking about the night of Ellory's bachelorette party.

What if I hadn't been able to stop him? An image of Ellory's shaken expression on the Fourth of July, when I recounted the incident, flutters through my mind. She seems remorseful. And she's trying to repair our relationship. But because Ila interrupted us, and then because of the scene at the pier, we never finished our conversation.

Suddenly, I'm gripped by the strangest realization. Maybe some conversations are better left unfinished. Maybe I don't want to forgive her. Maybe I just can't.

CHAPTER 42

Ila Wilson

MY FEET TAKE quick steps as I turn my back on Tabby and walk out the front door. Everything in my life has been swirling downward since the night on the pier. And now, just when it seems like the door to the opportunity I've been dreaming about is going to blast open, my involvement with Cade may slam it shut.

Placing my portfolio bag onto the passenger seat of my car, I push my concerns away. Now is not the time to let my fears overwhelm me. I need to show up to this meeting at FLAD clear-headed and focused.

I was thrilled when Professor Herrera emailed with nothing but praise for the link I sent of my recent artwork. Taking Tabby's advice, I immediately let her know I was wait-listed for FLAD's program.

Then, as I waited for her reply, I felt queasy. I tried to eat, but the thought of swallowing food sickened me. Days passed and my stomach churned at the slightest odor. *Was I really this nervous about Professor Herrera's response?*

When her email finally came, I was in bed, having called in sick at the diner. My eyes bounced nervously on my phone's screen as I read her response.

I've reviewed your application and shared your most recent work with the admissions committee. The year off has given you the opportunity to expand your skill set and hone your craft. I would like to meet with you on August 9th to discuss your work. The admissions committee would also like to arrange an interview for this date.

But, instead of feeling overjoyed, I ran to the bathroom and dry heaved over the toilet. That's when it hit me. *Could I be pregnant?*

Pulling up my calendar on my phone, I felt relieved to see that I was only a few days late. But as a few days turned into a week, I grew more afraid. I was about to be accepted to FLAD, and Cade and I were no longer in touch. The thought of having a baby was unthinkable.

After reading and rereading the email from Professor Herrera, I promised myself I would not take a pregnancy test until after my interview. I didn't want to know if my dreams were going to go up in smoke.

As my car drives on I-95 toward Miami, I have Taylor's album *Lover* playing. The songs are lighter than *Reputation* and will put me in a better headspace for my interview today. My hands tap around to the beat of the music as I weave my way down the highway, trying to keep my head clear of minefields.

But as the song "Soon You'll Get Better" comes on, the anger I harbor toward my mom ascends to the top of my emotions like a layer of oil rising to the top of a glass of water. She lied to me. She abandoned me.

These past weeks, since cutting Cade off, have made me question if I am making him pay for her mistakes. Each night, I lay awake, wondering if I should have heard him out. But a rip of humiliation tore through my heart when I learned he lied. A wound first created by my mother. A wound that has never fully healed.

He called and texted multiple times after I ran from the pier. He begged me to just let him tell his side. But I was completely shut down and overpowered by his betrayal. I had trusted him, and he had shattered the ground beneath us.

But now I'm regretting my harsh judgment. I miss him. Yet I'm terrified to tell him and face the reality of what may lie ahead for us.

I want to lean on Tabby for support, but instead, I've pulled away. I can hardly face her, knowing that what's potentially happening inside of me is what she wishes for. I feel like a thief who has stolen her dream.

Suddenly, a car cuts me off. I quickly jerk my steering wheel to the left. A horn blows loudly, and it takes me a moment to realize it's my own. I was just inches from getting into a crash. Trembling, I pull off the highway. I need to relax and get into a better headspace before my interview.

I drive for another minute until I reach the next exit. Pulling into a grocery store, I park my car and take a deep breath. I feel so untethered. All the pieces of my life are floating away from me, carried by a current I can't control. I'm suddenly desperate for control. Instantly, I realize I have to know if I'm pregnant. The weight of what ifs are crushing me.

Pushing open my car door, I walk rapidly into the grocery store. It's time to take a test. I need to know if I'm pregnant.

CHAPTER 43
Faye Carter

WAITERS AND WAITRESSES rush past us, carrying trays piled high with perfect cuts of meat and twice-baked potatoes. I glance out the window, soaking in the water view. I hope tonight will be an enjoyable evening.

Mark and I sit across from each other at Butcher's House, the high-end steak restaurant Mark chose for us to celebrate our anniversary. I realize we always go to steak places when we have something to celebrate. Steak and potatoes are Mark's favorite. I prefer Mediterranean.

Things have been better since I hired Linda. The time to myself has been of the greatest importance. I registered for an online course at our community college that begins in the fall. I want to complete my associate degree. Maybe I'll start on my bachelor's degree after that.

I have also used the time to get back into painting. I've been dropping into an open-session class at the Jupiter Cove Art Co-Op for the last month. I forgot how sitting in front of a blank white canvas, surrounded by blobs of brightly colored paint, ignites my soul. Many days, I rush over to the studio the moment Linda arrives, impatient to find my salvation.

As I paint, I get lost in the swirl of colors, the feel of the brush in my hand, and the way the light hits the bright blues, making them shine as if they are illuminated. My free hours go by in a blink. I have to tear myself away to make it home and relieve the nanny.

I haven't told Mark or anyone about the painting. It's just for me, a way to reclaim my existence as someone other than a mother and wife. I've even had a few dinners and coffee dates with Harper and Tabby. Ever since Tabby revealed her infertility struggles, the three of us have become a supportive squad. And since gaining their friendship, Lexi has stayed locked in the pages of Ellory's book where she belongs.

The waitress appears and places two plates with perfectly cooked filet mignons on our table before refilling our wine.

Mark lifts his glass. "Happy Anniversary," he says.

"Yes, Happy Anniversary," I repeat. "I've got something exciting to share with you." I can feel my body flutter with nervous energy. I'm planning to reveal to Mark that I've been painting again. Picking up my wine glass, I ingest a small sip of the burgundy liquid. The flavor is sour, and my lips pucker in response.

"Oh really? I've got some news too," he says. His eyebrows shift upward as he speaks. I can tell he's excited.

"You go first," I say.

"Me and my brothers are going to see FLA-U play Notre Dame and visit other college football towns in the Midwest. We're going to make a week out of it." Mark bounces in his chair excitedly.

Suddenly, my body floods with rage. I've been trying to get Mark to commit to a family trip to Disney World, but he's been unresponsive. Forcing my anger down, I quickly consider how I can use his football trip as an opening to discuss a family vacation.

"That sounds like a lot of fun. Did you look at those hotel options I sent you for Disney during fall break? There's the Grand Floridian. But the Caribbean Beach Resort might be fun. It has an amazing pool with a water slide. The kids would love that." I make my lips curl into a grin.

"Oh, right. No, I haven't looked at any of that yet. What were the dates you were looking at again? I've just committed to a soccer tournament the week of October 15th."

I slam my fork down. A couple close by looks over, surprised by my interruption. But I'm too furious to care about what others think. "That's the week of fall break. I sent you the email over a month ago. You never even bothered to look at it?"

Mark's face stiffens as he hunches toward me. "Calm down, Faye. I've just been busy."

I can't help but roll my eyes in exasperation. "You're always too busy to take the time when it's something you're not interested in. You certainly weren't too busy to plan this trip to Notre Dame."

"I'm sorry. You're right. Can we move on? Why would you pick a fight on our anniversary?" He waves his hands around as if my anger is a pesky bug he's pushing aside.

"Ugh!" I bark. "I'm not picking a fight for no reason. I'm hurt and trying to convey those feelings." My voice is too loud for the restaurant's intimate setting.

"Okay, okay," he says. "Can you please just let this go right now? We can talk about it more later." He glances around timidly, wondering if other people are looking at us.

"I'm not sure," I say honestly as I take a huge gulp of the red wine Mark chose.

His eyes look at me pleadingly, but it only confirms his vision is faulty. He can only zoom in on his desires. He cannot bring anything else into focus.

"Please, Faye. It's our anniversary," he continues. "We've been through a lot over the past months. Things are just settling down. I'm not going to let plans to visit Disney ruin our night. I apologize. I will look at the emails this week. I promise." He leans forward and reaches for my hand. His palm feels cold.

Suddenly, the fight goes out of me. I turn my gaze toward the coastline beside us, looking deep out into the horizon. I'm not in a relationship of equals. I'm fooling myself. This is not a partnership. I am at the bottom of the food chain.

Mark has consistently pushed my needs aside as if meaningless. My desire to return to work, my request for a nanny, my preference for a minivan, my wish to have him take care of dinner occasionally, and my pleas for a family vacation.

He has disregarded the requests I have made to incorporate things I value into my life time after time after time. And each time he casts a need of mine aside, it's as if he is declaring I am small, I am worthless, I am not important. I see an image of a bingo card in my mind. Our card is almost full, I think. My heart thumps sluggishly in my chest.

"Faye? Earth to Faye."

I pull my eyes away from the horizon and look back at Mark.

"You said you had something exciting you wanted to tell me. Let's hear it."

"I've been painting again," I say, but my voice sounds far off. Almost as if someone else is talking.

"Yes, I thought so," he says as he slices off a piece of meat with a pink center. "I found a painter's smock in your car when I borrowed it a few weeks ago."

A small crack breaks open in my heart as the words escape his lips.

"You knew?" I say, my facial expression warped in surprise. If roles were reversed, I'd waste no time asking about his rediscovered passion. The crack in my heart widens into a deeper groove.

Mark looks at me, confused. I quickly swallow another sip of wine and try not to let the cavern forming in my chest overtake me.

"Yes, I leave my smock in my car. I'm surprised you didn't ask me about it." I keep my voice steady. Our anniversary celebration has already been disastrous. I just want to get through it and get home.

"I think I meant to," he says casually. "I must have gotten side-tracked by something before I got around to it."

I'm too exhausted to give in to the depth of my despair. I'm grasping for a way to get back to stable ground. Closing my eyes for a moment, I search for a way to avoid discussing my disappointment. An idea comes to mind. "My instructor has been encouraging. She wants me to take one of my paintings to a local gallery. She says they may consider putting it on display for purchase."

"Wow, that's exciting for you." Mark smiles.

My shoulders relax. I did it. I moved past that awful moment of disappointment without Mark even realizing how his disinterest broke my heart. My body slumps forward. I'm completely depleted.

Mark sits back and looks at me carefully. "Wait? Are you mad I didn't ask about the smock?"

"No, not at all," I say, trying my best to sound easygoing.

But Mark isn't buying it. His eyes shift back and forth quickly as his body stiffens.

What can I say to bury my hurt and just finish this conversation?

"In fact," I say. "I'd love for you to drop by the art co-op on your way home from work this week and look at my paintings. I'd love to know which one you think I should present to the gallery."

Mark relaxes after he hears my request. "Sure, I'd love to. I'll stop by tomorrow."

CHAPTER 44

Harper Weiss

"**I** NEED THAT REPORT so I can submit the claim to the patient's insurance." Jill tilts her head, waiting for me to respond. She should have left to pick up her husband twenty minutes ago, but she's stalling.

"I haven't finished it yet. I'll give it to you tomorrow. Go on and leave. There's nothing left to say on Ben." I force the corners of my lips up, hoping this will convince Jill I'm fine.

Her eyes focus on mine, seeing right through me. "I know your parents are coming back tomorrow and you'll no longer need Ben's help. But there's a difference between need and want." She looks at me pleadingly and continues. "You want him in your life, and I think you should tell him."

Walking over to Jill's desk, I pick up her bag and hold it up. "I appreciate you, Jill. You know I do. You're like a second mom to me. But it's time for you to go. You're going to be late picking up Howie."

Nodding, Jill pushes out from her chair and stands. "If you insist." Her words sound like air going out of a tire. "Tell Ben I say hello," she says as she leaves the office.

As soon as she's gone, I rush to the bathroom to freshen up. I asked Ben and Wyatt to celebrate Shabbat with Ryder and me tonight as a thank you for everything. The boys' presence will prevent Ben and me from any further physical complications.

Fluffing my curls, I suddenly see an image of Ben and me wrapped up in each other's arms on the Ferris wheel. The moment was sweet. And our lips barely touched to keep things kid-appropriate in front of Wyatt. But there was something about the way Ben grasped my shoulder, digging his fingertips into my back when he leaned into me, that reminded me of our night together.

Tilting toward the mirror, I wrap myself in emotionless hard steel. He's going through a divorce, and his ex said they're working toward reconciliation. It all ends tonight.

"Anyone here?"

As I exit the bathroom, I hear Ben's sexy voice travel down the hall.

Stepping around the corner, I see Wyatt bouncing around the waiting room, exploring our new toys. Ben's wearing a fitted navy pocket t-shirt and jeans. I can feel my breath quicken.

AS THE SHABBAT candles flicker out, Ben smiles. The boys are outside enjoying one of the last weekends before school begins. I planned to confirm the end of our fake relationship as soon as the boys wandered away to play, but I've been putting it off.

"That was delicious," he says. "Your matzoh balls are fantastic."

Swallowing, I try to say the words I practiced earlier. But before I can say anything, Ben's talking again.

"What's the latest with your book? It's been over a month since Ellory sent it to her agent. Have you heard anything?"

I jump at the tangent. Anything to avoid talking about our impending "breakup."

"I don't know what to think?" I say honestly. "Ellory's disappeared. She hasn't shown up to our last two Ellory's Editors meetings. I've emailed her twice about my book, but she's completely ghosted me." My heart sears as if it's being sliced with a knife. Ellory made it seem like my dream was going to become a reality, but clearly, it's pure fantasy.

Ben must sense my turmoil. He quickly grasps my hand in his and folds his fingers around mine. The warmth of his touch shoots through my body, making my insides quiver. "Ellory is one of the most famous authors in the world. If she saw promise in your work. I'm sure others will too." He sits back, releasing my hand.

I nod, wishing I had the same confidence. "I don't know. I've been sending it out to agents, but it's just rejection after rejection. Maybe I'm just not good enough."

He reaches back across the table and tucks a loose strand of hair behind my ear. The gesture is caring, inching toward the edge of sensual. "I read your book in three days. It's fantastic. You're talented. Don't give up." His fingertips brush my cheek as he pulls his hand away from my face.

On impulse, I grab his hand. I'm unwilling to let go. I'm unwilling to let *him* go. And this gesture, something that seems so insignificant, suddenly seems monumental. I've exposed myself. Ben fully understands that I need him. That I want him. That I don't want to end this thing between us.

Scrambling quickly, I release his hand. The words I promised I would say earlier fly from my mouth. "With my parents back tomorrow, you don't have to worry about any of this anymore. Getting me around, my book." I gulp in air and continue. "You've been such a mensch, just like your dad." I use the Yiddish term, trying to lighten the moment, but he just stares at me.

I quickly continue through the awkwardness. "And a good sport to pretend we're dating. But the truth is, I don't need to pretend for Noah's sake. He's my son's father. It ends there."

Ben leans back in his chair, crossing his muscular arms over his chest. He tilts his head to the side, studying my expression.

"I like worrying about you," he says softly. "I like getting you your vat of sugary Starbucks in the morning. I like driving you around." He pauses for a moment, dropping his chin slightly, glancing down at the table, and then meeting my eyes directly. "I like you."

It doesn't matter what he says. He's not ready to be in a relationship. I don't want to get hurt. My mind is searching for what to say when I feel his leg push against mine under the table. My entire body vibrates.

I stand abruptly, afraid of where his touch will lead. "I'll get the black and white cookies you brought. Meet me outside and we can have dessert with the boys."

Ben's eyes cloud with hurt. "I think when you texted me that night that you didn't want to 'miss this,' you meant us. Whatever it is that's happening between us."

My body freezes as I step toward the kitchen. I think about the lame way I explained my drunken text to him, telling him it was for someone else. Turning my head, our eyes meet, and we hold each other's gaze for several moments.

"Let's not miss this," he pleads, lightly grasping my arm and pulling me toward him. "Cassidy is ready to sign the papers. My divorce is almost final."

A montage of images fills my mind. Seeing Ben for the first time after Wyatt knocked me over. Confessing my attraction to Ben in a medicated stupor. His smile when he hands me my coffee in the morning. The way his fingers tap the steering wheel to the beat of a song on the radio. His enthusiasm about my book. His love of family and Jewish culture. The sweet kiss on the Ferris wheel. His naked body over mine.

But the eleven years I've spent shielding myself from heartbreak and abandonment suddenly consume me like a protective instinct. "I can't," I whisper. "I just can't."

CHAPTER 45

Ellory Brayson

THUMBING THROUGH THE paperwork my divorce lawyer sent over, I flip to the end and sign. My hands shake as I push the legal documents to the side. Once Maxy receives the filing, his parents will pounce.

Thankfully, I've kept the money I've made from my own career separate. I suppose, in my heart, I knew I couldn't trust Maxy. It's a shame I wasted so many years refusing to let that reality travel into my head.

And although I know divorce is the right course of action, there's an ache deep inside my soul. I'm grieving for the relationship I should have had. I'm mourning the years I can't get back.

Anger seethes through my every fiber. Not just at Maxy, but myself. I put blinders on to secure the life I thought I wanted, letting my celebrity persona take charge. I never asked questions I didn't want the answers to. And in the end, the deceit I feel is born from within. I've become someone I don't like. I've betrayed myself.

Pulling out my phone, I dial Cade's number. He's the one thing I've done right. He's the bright spot in all of this.

"Hi, Mom." His voice strains over the thumping of loud club music.

"Hi, baby. Where are you?" I make my voice sound breezy, even though it sounds like he's in the midst of a party at the Playboy Mansion.

"Dad and I are in Monte Carlo. We're staying at a hotel. I'm at the pool."

I can hear lively voices chattering in the background. A wave of fear consumes me as his words travel through the phone line. I don't want Cade to turn into his philandering father. Maxy's already left his pregnant girlfriend. I'm terrified Cade will treat women like shiny decorative objects that can be easily cast aside when something bigger and brighter comes along. But instead of sharing these thoughts, I take a different approach.

"When do you think you'll come home?" I ask, trying to keep my voice even.

"Not sure. Dad and I may spend a week in Paris after this. We're still figuring it out."

Fueled by feelings of concern, I can't help but burst with the truth. "You've been gone for six weeks, Cade. You're traveling around Europe as if you don't have a care in the world. Summer's almost over. You need to think about what's next." My words are tight with tension.

Cade lets out an exaggerated huff. "I'm not talking about this right now."

Desperate to steer us back to pleasant conversation, I abandon my need to get Cade to agree to come home. "Okay, that's fair. You're at the pool relaxing. We can pick it up another time."

Suddenly, I hear the chirp of a young girl. "Cade, there you are. I was looking for you."

Cade's voice fills my ear. "Saved you a chair." He pauses, then speaks again. "Hey, Mom, I've got to go. I'll talk to you soon."

The phone goes silent before I can hang up. A deep sense of unease works its way through my body. I can't let Cade go down this path and become his father. My brain scrambles for a way to convince him to come home. When the idea crashes through my mind, I laugh out loud.

Yes, this is a plot right out of one of my novels. The only thing that may convince Cade to return home is love. Maybe I can convince Ila to pretend she needs a serious operation, or that she's pregnant. This story arc worked in my third bestseller.

I jump in my car and speed toward Tabby's house, hoping Ila's home. Knocking on the door, adrenaline pumps through my body. I don't care what it takes. I don't care what I have to say. I'm going to use Ila to get Cade home.

But, just as these thoughts swarm through my mind, I realize this is the same agenda that lead me to betray Tabby. I'm only thinking about myself. I'm only thinking about my needs. My pounding fist quickly deflates into an open palm as I lean my body against Tabby's front door.

A moment later, I hear the shuffling of feet. I stand up just as Tabby opens the door.

"Ellory, hi." Her voice sounds hesitant. "What are you doing here?"

Looking at her, I see my past. I see her face with the round fullness it had when we were kids. I see her crimped hair from our teen years. I see the person that means the most to me in this world next to Cade. Words bubble from within my gut. I may have come here with self-serving intentions, but my reason for being here is suddenly crystal clear.

"We never finished our conversation from the Fourth of July," I say.

Tabby's forehead scrunches in confusion.

"I mean, I never got to finish saying what I wanted to say before Ila appeared, and we ended up on the pier." I pause, knowing exactly what I need to say. "I told you I wouldn't forgive me if I were you. I told you I don't forgive myself."

Tabby nods cautiously. "I'm not sure what you're trying to say, Ellory. You made your regret clear. You apologized. What else is there to do?"

"But don't you see?" My words tumble out quickly. "That's not enough. I want to repair our relationship. I want you back in my life. I'm trying so hard to change."

Tabby looks down at her feet, uncomfortable with my vulnerability. "Like I just said—" she lifts her face back up and looks at me, "—there's nothing else to say."

Grasping her hand, I ask the question burning a hole in my heart. "Yes, there *is* more to say. I told you I could never forgive myself. But I'm standing here in front of you now to ask you. Can *you* forgive me? I know I don't deserve it, but I'm ready to put aside all the things that have failed me—my ego, my narcissism, my selfishness. I'm praying that my willingness to be completely vulnerable and take full responsibility will be enough."

Tabby stares at me with an expression I can't read. A long silence looms between us. After a few minutes, I realize I'm too late. Some mistakes cannot be absolved.

CHAPTER 46
Tabitha Wilson

ELLORY'S EYES BULGE in desperation as the corners of her mouth fall. A part of me is glad to see her suffer. But another part of me, equal in force, wants to soothe her pain.

I have complicated feelings about our friendship. Anger, grief, love, jealousy, and happiness swirl together like a tornado in my heart. Looking at her, I say the words I know to be true. "I don't know if I can forgive you. I want to. But what I want and what I'm capable of is not the same."

Ellory's eyes immediately glisten with tears. "I understand," she says. "It's hard for me to accept this, since I've made a career out of resolving fictional relationships that had little hope of mending. But this is real life. And maybe this thing between us will always be unresolved." Her voice shakes slightly, then suddenly, she's coughing. She hits her fist against her chest to relieve her hacking.

"Come in. Let me get you some water." I pull Ellory by the arm and lead her to my kitchen.

She takes a seat at the island as I fill a glass. She gulps the water down quickly.

"Thanks, Tabby. I think I'm okay." After she places the cup down, she works her hands together, kneading them back and forth. "I know

I should go. I'm just not sure what to say. I keep thinking, is this the last time I'll ever be in a room with you? I keep wondering if this is where our story ends. I'm a wordsmith, but I can't seem to come up with the words to put closure on the most important relationship of my life." Ellory pauses and her words hang over us. Before I can say anything, she's talking again.

"Did you know I've been walking around with our charm bracelet in my bag since coming to Jupiter Cove? I dug it out of a box before I left New York, thinking maybe it had some magic that could repair us."

My eyes widen as Ellory digs through her designer tote, searching for the bracelet.

"Here!" She pushes the bright pink plastic chain-link piece of jewelry toward me. Charms that represent our past dangle haphazardly.

My eyes settle on the obnoxiously bright plastic trinkets—a pink waffle cone with a white swirly ice cream top, a gray unicorn with a rainbow-colored mane, a teal blue roller skate with moving wheels, a fire engine red fake lipstick.

Running my fingers over the lipstick charm, I laugh, recalling how Ellory earned this adornment. "Was it worth it? Kissing Wayne Lester?" I tease.

Ellory brushes the charm with her finger and smiles. "It was worth it because you didn't think I would do it! He was kind of smelly and his teeth were awful."

An image of Ellory locking lips with him on the Ferris wheel at the Fourth of July carnival all those years ago pops into my mind. "You always loved a good dare." I snicker at the memory.

"Do you still have your bracelet?" Ellory's blond eyebrows rise as she looks at me.

"I do," I say evenly. I can't help but wonder if I should cut this trip down memory lane short before I get sucked in. But it's hard to ignore the thread pulling me toward this moment. "I think it's in the guest room. Let's go see."

We stride down the hall with purpose, as if we're seven-year-olds about to play with our Cabbage Patch dolls. Opening the door, I flip the light on. My throat tickles from the musty air. "No one ever comes in here." I wave my hand around to freshen things up.

As I walk to the closet, Ellory plops onto the bed. "Is that the bridesmaid's dress from my wedding?" She jumps up and peers into the closet. "You still have it?" She looks at me, confused.

My face flushes. *Why do I still have it?* "I can't seem to get rid of anything," I say. "Marie Kondo would have a heart attack if she came to my house." I force a laugh and quickly change the subject.

"Here!" I point to a bubble gum pink Caboodles case. Pulling it down, I set it on the bed. "I think the charm bracelet's in here."

Digging my hand around through trinkets from my past, I find the bracelet. I hold it up excitedly as if it's the winning lottery ticket. As the plastic charms clang against each other and straighten out, my heart sinks. There's a blue plastic baby carriage, a green teddy bear, and a pink rattle.

My face collapses. "I always wanted to be pregnant and have a baby." The words wobble out of my mouth.

Ellory puts her hand on my shoulder and squeezes. "I wish I knew the right thing to say. You've been a great mom to Ila. She's got a good head on her shoulders."

I appreciate Ellory's words, but I know Ila doesn't feel the same. "When Ila was young, I truly felt like her mother. But when Andre and I decided we wanted a second child, my relationship with Ila fell apart. I'll never forgive myself."

Ellory's face flushes. "I think I've just proven it's never too late to apologize."

A soft smile pushes my lips outward. "And by the way, I was just as shocked as you were to find out Ila and Cade were dating."

Ellory's face flashes with a mischievous grin. "What are the chances that those two would get together?"

"Sounds like something out of one of your novels." I clasp my bracelet on my wrist as I speak. The plastic on one side has almost completely disintegrated, and the baby rattle charm is practically falling off. My fingers methodically stroke the charm, my heart breaking at all it represents.

Ellory must sense the pain seeping through my body, because she squeezes me into her side. "Tabs, I know this is hard. The hardest thing ever."

I wait for her to say what everyone always says—that it will happen. That one day I will get pregnant. Not one person I know has the courage to tell me what I know is true. Not every woman gets to have a baby just because they want to.

But instead of insisting that there will be a baby in my future, she hugs me tighter, acknowledging the heartbreaking truth of my infertility.

"I'm here for you if you want me to be." Ellory's words hang in the air.

I want to tell her she missed her chance. I want to tell her it's too late. The anger I feel about our past is like a powerful hand pushing me underwater, drowning me.

But, suddenly, I realize I don't want to keep struggling to breathe. I want to push through what's swallowing me and gulp air. My forgiveness will not change what has happened in our past, but it will open an opportunity in our future. My forgiveness will not exonerate her. *It will liberate me.*

I exhale from deep within my heart. "Thanks," I say. "It's hard to describe the feeling of loss surrounding something I've never had. But I'd love your support." A stream of hot tears rolls down my cheeks. "I'm going to grab a tissue. Be right back."

Standing, I step into the guest bathroom. As I reach my hand toward the Kleenex box, something clangs into the garbage can. Looking at my bracelet, I see the baby rattle charm has fallen off. Stooping down, I move the toilet paper bunched in the garbage can, looking for the charm. As my hand pushes the wad aside, it unravels.

My body stiffens when I see the words on the exposed box. *This can't be happening.* Is this why Ila has suddenly pulled away? I lift the box out of the garbage—First Response pregnancy test. My hands shake as I slip my fingers inside, hoping it contains the test, but the box is empty.

CHAPTER 47

Ila Wilson

OPENING THE MAILBOX, I pull out the contents. I grin widely when I see an envelope from FLAD. I received an email acceptance from the admissions committee just two days after my interview. Tearing open the letter, I'm thrilled to see a congratulatory note from Professor Herrera. My body floods with positive ions as I step toward the house. But as soon as I look up, I notice Ellory's car parked on the curb.

I can't face her. It will stir up my feelings about CJ. I quickly stride to my car and drive away. Rounding the corner at the end of my block, I pull into the neighborhood playground's parking lot. I'll wait for thirty minutes before I go back home.

Opening my text messages, I read the last text CJ sent. It was a few days after he landed in Europe.

CJ: Please reach out when you're ready to talk

The sadness I feel about how our relationship ended pulses through me in a slow, painful wave. Maybe I would have responded if I wasn't terrified I was pregnant. I didn't know what to say.

I recall the day at the grocery store when I took my first pregnancy test. I sat in the stall and waited for two minutes for the test to reveal my fate. The seconds dragged as if Father Time had to yank each moment forward. When the test came back negative, my chest filled with a buoyant relief.

I practically skipped to my car, continuing my drive to Miami. I walked into my interview at FLAD as if I was soaring into my promising future. The admissions committee could not rattle me, even with their most challenging questions. The relief I felt about the negative test made me indestructible.

It wasn't until later, as I drove home, that I realized the negative test didn't mean I wasn't pregnant. It was still a possibility. For the past week, I've woken up each morning and fled to the guest bathroom. I don't want to risk taking the test in the hallway bathroom by my bedroom. It's terrifying knowing my dad or Tabby could walk by as I discover news that will change my life.

After each test, I carefully wrap the box and results in toilet paper and hide them in my purse until I can dispose of them outside of the house.

Seeing the garbage can by the park's edge, I search through my bag. I should dispose of this morning's test. As I pull out the wad, I'm confused. Where's the box? I have the negative test, but I must have left the box in the bathroom.

My stomach somersaults as if it's trying to impress judges on the Olympic committee. I need to get in the house and get the box. My nerves settle as I consider that no one ever goes into the guest room. I should be okay. Plus, the box is wrapped in toilet paper.

All the sneaking and test-taking seem dramatic when I think about it now. I finally got my period this afternoon. I'm not pregnant. The moment it happened, a cool calmness penetrated my bones. I can move forward with FLAD and my life. Nothing is going to interfere with the plans I have for myself. But, more significantly, I can look Tabby in the eye knowing I have not stolen her dream.

Getting back in my car, I glance again at CJ's text message. Perhaps I'm ready to talk now. A space has opened in my mind now that I know

I'm not pregnant. A space that was formerly crowded with images and thoughts about how my life would change if I were.

My fingers quickly punch the letters on my phone as if driven by a force all their own.

> **Ila:** I'm ready to talk. When is a good time to call?

My stomach constricts into a pit of nerves as I stare at my phone's screen, waiting for a response. A few minutes pass, but he doesn't reply. I pick up the pile of mail sitting on my passenger seat to distract myself.

Thumbing through the stack, I see a letter addressed to me. I hold it up. The writing is precise and unfamiliar. Shifting my eyes to the return address, I see it's from Brighter Times Rehabilitation Center in Albuquerque, New Mexico.

A letter from my mom. My thoughts rush forward, as if running uncontrollably down a hill. How strange to get a letter from my mom on the exact day I find out I will not hold this role, at least for now. Opening the letter, my eyes read the words.

Dear Ila,

I am sorry I missed your call in July. I'm ashamed to admit I was using. When I returned and realized you'd reached out, I instantly committed to sobering up. There is so much I want to tell you. There is so much I need to explain. The regret I feel about leaving you and missing out on your life is something that makes it hard for me to breathe. I don't expect you to forgive me, but I wonder if there is a way we can connect and grow something from this broken place. For the last month, I have been sober. I know a month is not that impressive, but I have not been sober for this amount of time in years. I feel as if I have turned a corner. I'd love to hear from you if you feel open to reaching out again. While I know my problems won't magically go away now that I'm getting sober, I am starting to believe that, somehow, the universe will work things out between us.

Holding the letter to my chest, I can't help but let out a discordant sob. Maybe the timing of this letter is a coincidence. Or maybe it is the universe trying to heal the wound my mother has left. But before I can formulate another thought, my phone pings. It's a message from Cade.

Cade: This is Cade's new girlfriend. He's over you. Don't text him again.

CHAPTER 48
Faye Carter

S EVERAL COPIES OF Lucy Score's next release teeter on a rolling cart next to the table where Harper, Tabby, and I are sitting. White flowers dot the pink pastel-colored book covers and it almost looks as if the cart is a garden with full blooms.

"I need to get these on the display table in the front," Tabby says as she glances at the cart.

The café at Blast Off Books overflows with people sitting on cozy couches and at tables perusing books.

"Order for Michele." A tall woman with dark curly hair, wearing large red glasses grabs a mug. She walks by our table carrying Rochelle B. Weinstein's, *What You Do To Me*. I can't help but chuckle at the words on her t-shirt—*Sorry I can't. I have book club.*

"So, how was your anniversary dinner?" Harper glances at me.

Tabby looks off into the distance, distracted.

"Fine, good," I say, knowing this is far from the truth.

Tabby snaps back to attention. "Oh, let me treat you to a book as a gift." She pushes back her chair and walks over to a display near the café. A moment later, she's handing me a bright yellow hardback.

"It's not exactly romance in the traditional sense, but I have fallen in love with this author."

Glancing at the title, I read the words, *The Dinner List*. "Rebecca Serle, yes, I've heard a lot of great things. Thanks, that's kind of you."

Tabby smirks. "But if I had known it was your anniversary, I would've ordered you a spicy book!" I'm glad to see Tabby suddenly filled with enthusiasm. She's been off today. She seems preoccupied.

Harper and Tabby giggle as I force myself to join in. They don't know that my marriage is a struggle. I put the book in my bag. Suddenly, I'm overcome with emotion. "I need to get home. See you both soon for our last meeting with Ellory."

Harper's mouth immediately tenses. "It's strange how Ellory disappeared," she says. "But I guess we need to finish what we started."

Tabby nods. "The announcement of her divorce and Cade leaving with his dad put her over the edge. But she's doing better."

Harper shrugs her shoulders as if she's hurt. I'm not sure why she's taking Ellory's desertion so personally.

As I make my way out of the store, my chest rattles with unease. *An anniversary gift for a marriage that's barely hanging on?*

Driving away from Blast Off Books, I realize I have another hour before Linda leaves. It's a beautiful afternoon. *Why not read?* Instead of driving home, I go to the pier and park my car. Stepping out in the thick ocean air, I find a bench and crack the spine of *The Dinner List*.

Immediately, I'm absorbed in the story. As the main character wrestles with intense emotions, she imagines gathering around a dinner table with people she cherishes, some of whom are no longer living.

The magical realism strangely validates my visions of Lexi. My spine tingles. Looking up, I stare ahead at the soft lapping waves. The sound is hypnotic and puts me in a meditative state.

"The anniversary dinner was a bust."

Hearing Lexi's voice, I shift my gaze away from the water. She strolls toward me wearing a gauzy indigo-blue bathing suit coverup. Her long auburn hair rustles in the light breeze.

"Mind if I have a seat?" She takes a place on the bench next to me before I can answer.

Desperate for someone to talk to about my relationship with Mark, I give in to the moment. "It was awful," I agree. "Mark and

I are always fighting. He doesn't understand me, and I guess I don't understand him."

"Go on," Lexi encourages me to continue.

"He ignored my email about family vacation plans, and he wasn't interested enough to ask me about taking up painting again."

"So, where did you leave things?" Lexi moves her body closer to mine.

"I asked him to go see my paintings. I only did it to shift our conversation out of dangerous territory. But now that my request is out there, I'm terrified he won't follow through."

"Why do you think you're terrified?"

Taking a deep breath, I search for the answer to Lexi's question. "Because if he doesn't follow through, it will mean he's uninterested in me—that he's indifferent about my passions. I want to be with someone who is excited about me. I want to be with someone who makes me feel cherished."

Lexi takes my hand and sighs. "Do you think Mark will ever be able to make you feel this way?"

Hot tears streak my cheeks. "No. I am devastated to admit it, but no."

Lexi lets my words hang in the air for a few moments. "You have a long life ahead of you. You can still find what you're looking for." She brushes her hand over the cover of *The Dinner List*. "You deserve your own love story," she says. And then she's gone.

CHAPTER 49
Harper Weiss

"**T**HANKS FOR AGREEING to talk with me," I say, as I walk carefully in my boot toward Tabby's office. Ellory still hasn't responded to my follow-up emails about my book. I'm hoping Tabby will have a suggestion to help me get Ellory's attention.

"What did you want to talk about?"

A wiry girl as tall as a circus performer brings us fresh lattes. Tabby winks at the girl before she walks away.

Swallowing hard, I try not to let disappointment overwhelm me. "As you know, Ellory sent my book to her agent. She made me believe a dream that's flowed through my veins since childhood would be a reality. But it's been almost two months and I haven't heard back."

Tabby's eyes cloud. "Yes, she told me she's never sent someone's book to her agent before. Your pages impressed her. She says you have real potential."

"I know. She raved about my excerpt. She said it thrilled her to discover a fresh new voice." I wrap my fingers around the tall mug in my hands, trying to keep them steady. My voice wobbles, giving away my emotions. My eyes well with tears, but I blink rapidly to keep from crying.

"Oh, no. Don't be sad." Tabby looks at me with concern. "The publishing industry is notoriously slow. Two months is not a long time."

"Agreed," I say, gaining back some composure. "But it's more that Ellory has completely lost interest. It's that she went from being enthusiastic about helping me to falling off the face of the earth. It's clear she doesn't want to pursue this any further." I take a deep breath, unable to explain the thoughts bouncing around in my head. Ellory voluntarily scooped up my dream in her palm. I didn't ask her to. But instead of searching for a place where my dream could fly, she threw it down and walked away.

Tabby nods in understanding. "I get what you're saying, but to be fair, Ellory is busy and going through a difficult time personally. I understand you're disappointed, but she went to bat for you. She did something for you she's never done for anyone else. I don't think it's fair for you to be angry with her for not continuing to pursue it. I get the sadness and disappointment. But maybe anger isn't exactly the right response?"

Inhaling deeply, I carefully consider her words. "I-I never thought about it that way," I stammer. "But it hurts so much. To feel so close to my dream, but then to have it dissolve into nothing."

Tabby nods and I continue.

"I think it would help if I could get closure. Maybe her agent read it and didn't like it. Maybe Ellory could give me advice on how to improve. Anything would be better than feeling like my manuscript is spinning out in space, unread, forever."

"That makes sense," Tabby agrees as she brings her steaming mug to her mouth. "You should ask Ellory for closure."

Suddenly, it feels like the weight that's had me pinned down vanishes. Ellory tried to get my manuscript in front of her agent. She's not responsible for anything more. Surely, if her agent had read it and responded, she would have let me know. My anger unexpectedly fragments into tiny shards. I need closure and I will get it at the last Ellory's Editor meeting.

"Thanks, Tabby. Your words have helped."

"Good." She smiles widely. "It's almost impossible to get published," she adds. "There are so many nontraditional avenues to explore. Small presses and even self-publishing. If this is your dream, keep at it."

"You're probably right," I agree.

"I know I'm right," she insists. "The only difference between a published author and an unpublished author is that the published author didn't give up!" Her voice suddenly rises for emphasis.

"True, but it's overwhelming and scary to think about putting my work out into the world on my own." Looking down at the table, I notice the feathery ring left by my coffee mug.

"But," Tabby continues, still filled with excitement, "the best things come from the situations we fear the most."

"Wise words," I say as I finish the last sip of my latte.

"Not to change the subject," Tabby continues. "But whatever happened with Ben? Did you tell him how you really feel?" She looks at me with a coy expression.

"We're officially not fake dating anymore." My words sound soft and sad.

"Boo." Tabby scrunches her face together. "Same words I just said apply here. The best things come from the situations we fear the most."

Leaning back in my chair, Ben's face bursts into my mind like a shooting star crossing the sky. I can't ignore it or the way it makes me feel. "You know what? You're right. I need to tell him how I feel." My chair scrapes the floor as I abruptly stand.

"Um, right now? You're going right now to talk to him?" Tabby looks at me. Her face fills with anticipation.

"Yes, right now," I say confidently. "What am I so afraid of? I'm hurting without him. I might as well see where it goes. I will not let fear keep me down."

"Good luck," she calls as I shuffle toward the door. Getting into my car, I carefully remove my boot and hit the gas pedal.

Driving toward Ben's house, my body buzzes like a live wire. My admission to Ben will either burn us to the ground or ignite us into the relationship I've always dreamed about.

As my car pulls onto his block, my thoughts explode with images of us ripping each other's clothes off. But as I inch closer to his house, my body fills with dread. Ben's standing outside with his almost ex. *Are they trying to make it work?*

I was so pumped when I left Blast Off Books, I didn't consider I might come at a bad time. I quickly push my foot on the gas pedal and zoom by, praying Ben doesn't notice my car. As I speed away, I watch as Ben and his almost ex collide in a passionate kiss. My heart pounds with sorrow. The image blurs and fades away.

CHAPTER 50

Ellory Brayson

"**N**OW THAT YOUR impending divorce is public knowledge, we need to amend the launch plan for your next release. And as we discussed last time, we'll hold off on Ellory's Editors." Amber's perched back at her desk in her office overlooking Madison Avenue.

Her words rush out, practically tripping over one another. It's a sure sign she's stressed. I glance away from my computer, so her nervous energy doesn't swallow me. Shifting my eyes back toward the screen, I stare at Amber blankly. She looks remarkably well-rested and put together for a new mom. The awkward silence propels her into a rant about her reasoning.

"The Ellory's Editors idea is gold. I don't want anything to taint the positive attention. Let's let the divorce news settle before we move forward." She takes a quick breath and continues. "And we're going to have to push back the publication date on the new release." She scratches some notes on a notepad in front of her, but I remain silent.

"Ellory? Do you have anything to add? Any concerns?" Her eyes widen, waiting for me to respond.

"How's the baby?" I ask.

Amber's forehead creases in confusion. "My baby? How's my baby?"

"Yes," I say. "Now that you're back in the office, I don't get to see your recent addition on these calls. How's he doing?"

Amber leans toward her computer's camera. "Are you okay, Ellory? I'm worried about you."

My eyes squish together at her question. "You're asking if I'm okay because I want to know about your baby?" I say, surprised. But maybe I shouldn't be. I've never taken a personal interest in Amber's life. I've never cared to discuss anything with her that didn't center on my success. It's understandable that she's confused.

Her cheeks flush with worry. "Um, no. That's kind of you to ask. The baby is doing great. Sleeping through the night and smiling all the time."

"How wonderful," I say with heartfelt enthusiasm. A comforting warmth envelopes me as I recognize Celebrity Ellory's grip loosening. "It's such an amazing time for you and your wife. Enjoy it…" My words trail at the end as I consider how much I missed when Cade was a baby.

"We are," Amber replies happily. She pauses for a second. "Getting back to my recommendations. It's almost September. My team hashed out a launch plan for February. We'll capitalize on Valentine's Day and replace the media's need to rehash *This Morning America* with news about your new book. Does that work for you?"

"Sure," I say.

"I'm confident my team can solidify your status as the world's most famous romance author."

"Okay, whatever you think," I say, finally knowing my title as the world's most famous romance author should be secondary to my title as mom and friend.

Amber's eyes practically cross. I always push back. Especially on book release dates.

"Okay." She smiles hesitantly, still unsure if I'm about to throw a crazy demand at her.

"All right," I say, "I think we're done here."

As I click off Zoom, my screen populates with a search bar. The blank field begs me to fill in my name. I've been avoiding the internet.

These past weeks I've cared less and less about what the world is saying. I type in my name and scroll down the results.

> *World's Most Famous Romance Author, Who Shamed Fan,*
> *is Getting Divorced.*

I click the link for Buzz Feed.

> *Just months after the romance queen melted down on live television, she shocks the world by filing for divorce from her husband, Prince Maximilian Jacoby. It seems her own fairy tale has ended. Although her divorce filing showed irreconcilable differences, a source says the true reason for the split is Prince Maximilian's infidelity. Three women have come forward since the announcement, claiming to have had an affair with the European prince. The announcement has stunned her fans who read Brayson's books to get a dose of happily ever after.*

Suddenly, I'm the Titanic. But instead of spiraling with concern about how all of this will affect me, I'm anxious about how Cade's coping.

Pulling out my phone, I try calling, but it goes straight to voice-mail. I haven't been able to reach him since that day at the pool. *Is he avoiding me?*

I open Instagram and scroll through his posts. Cade and Maxy are on a yacht clinking champagne glasses. A tiny blond in a bikini has her arms wrapped around Cade's waist.

My heart thumps as if I'm standing on the edge of a cliff, about to jump. The only thing that matters right now is making sure Cade doesn't follow in the footsteps of his despicable father. I don't care if my career implodes. I must help Cade. I quickly search for flights. I need to get Cade home.

As I consider my options, there's a knock at my door. Standing, I shuffle to the entryway. I'm surprised when I peek through the side window and see Tabby. The last time I saw her, there was that moment in her guest room when I felt she was softening. It seemed, for a brief second, that she was opening a space for us to move forward.

But something changed when she walked out of the bathroom. It was as if she reconsidered and confined us to the restraints of our past. My heart burns as I recall how she announced she had some things to do.

"I think you should leave," she said. Her voice sounded robotic.

I've reached out several times since, but she keeps blowing me off.

Opening the door, I wonder exactly what's prompted her visit. "Hi." I fill my voice with as much fervor as I can.

I can see her red-rimmed eyes as she pushes past me. She rushes toward the living room, and I follow. She drops her body down into the cushions of the large red couch as if they are firefighters, catching her with a safety net twenty floors down.

"What's going on?" I can feel heat creeping up my neck.

Tabby swallows hard and looks at me. She holds my gaze for a moment before speaking. "I think Ila's pregnant."

CHAPTER 51
Tabitha Wilson

ELLORY'S EYES PRACTICALLY fall out of their sockets after I say the word pregnant.

"Pregnant?" she says in a tight voice.

Nodding, I cross my arms around my shoulders to settle my nerves.

"Cade's?" Her eyebrows arch vigorously.

"I'm assuming, Cade's. I don't think there's anyone else in the picture."

"Oh no, this can't be." Ellory's face crumples as she takes a sluggish step toward one of the modern wood chairs next to the couch and sits. "Why do you think she's pregnant? Did she tell you?"

My body pulses with pinpricks. I shift around, trying to ignore the sensation.

"That day we were in the guest room. I found an empty pregnancy test box in the bathroom."

"When I was there, with you? Is that when you found it?" Ellory cocks her head.

Nodding, I stare at her blankly. My inner voice has been relentless since finding out about Ila's potential pregnancy. I don't want Ila to be pregnant, because I know I'm not strong enough to manage the intense jealousy boiling through every fiber of my being. I don't want

Ila to be pregnant with Ellory's son's child. And more than anything, I don't want Ila to be pregnant just when her adult life is about to begin.

Ellory nestles her elbows in her lap and drops her head into her hands. Her shoulders scrunch up as she exhales. After a moment, she looks at me, her face flushed with a pink tinge. "So, the only thing we know right now is that she took a test. Nothing else. Maybe we shouldn't jump to conclusions."

Pushing my hand nervously through my curls, I take a breath. "True, but it's not just the test. Ila and I were finally connecting, and then she suddenly pulled back. She's been acting off ever since Cade left."

Ellory's mouth twists. "Okay, but that could be because of Cade leaving and all the drama on the pier. Not necessarily because she's pregnant."

Staring past her, I focus on the sunlight pushing through the floor-to-ceiling windows like a sharp blade. We sit in silence for several minutes. My mind tosses around images of Ila with a swollen belly. My imagination mocks me, and my chest fills with sadness.

"I know this will be hard." Ellory interrupts the silence. "But I think you need to ask her. Maybe she's not pregnant. But, if she is…" Ellory pauses for a moment and inhales deeply. "If she is, she's going to need your support. She'll have a decision to make."

The pulsing sadness in my chest feels like it will rip me open. Suddenly, I hear sobbing, and it takes me a moment to realize it's me.

Ellory rushes over, encircling me in her arms. "This is hard for so many reasons," she says as we bob back and forth in a hug.

I let the devastation overtake me. All the despondency that's lived in my body pours out. I am vibrating with emotion. It feels as if I am going to burst into a million tiny pieces.

"I'm here," Ellory says in a whisper.

When the wave of my emotion breaks a few minutes later, I pull out of Ellory's arms. "I…I'm…It's just that…" Each time I try to speak, my mind goes blank. There's no combination of words that could accurately capture my thoughts and feelings. There's nothing but a deep ache swallowing me whole.

"You don't have to say anything," Ellory says, filling the gap. "I understand." She places her hand on my shoulder.

My body sinks into itself. The tension I feel around not having to justify my breakdown releases. "Thank you."

Wiping my eyes, I feel stronger than I did only moments ago. "I know I have to talk with Ila," I say. "All week, I've been acting like nothing's wrong. I've been trying to fool myself into forgetting about what I found."

"I can understand why," Ellory agrees.

"That's why I came here. That's why I told you." My words rush out.

Ellory's forehead creases in confusion. "I'm not sure I follow."

"If I tell you, I can no longer pretend. If I tell you, I have to face this situation."

"What about Andre? Have you told him?" Ellory leans toward me.

"No," I say, shaking my head. "I didn't think it would be fair to tell him before I asked Ila. Just in case she's not pregnant. But I had to tell someone. And you are that someone." I reach for Ellory's palm and wrap our hands together.

She gently squeezes my hand. "I'm glad I'm that someone." A light stain of tears streaks her cheeks.

"This may be the hardest thing I've ever had to do," I say honestly. "But I can't ignore it any longer. Ila needs me. I can't abandon her again."

"You are a wonderful mother," Ellory says.

"Thanks." A warmth fills me as I consider her words. Ila may not be my flesh and blood, but she is my heart. "I need to go find Ila."

I push up from the couch, and Ellory stands. We embrace tightly in a hug. Our hearts beat against each other. Ellory has done so many things wrong. But today, starting now, I only want to focus on all the things she's done right.

CHAPTER 52
Ila Wilson

SHUFFLING IN FROM my shift at the diner, I realize I forgot to remove my uniform's Martian-themed headband from my hair. No wonder people were staring at me in my car as I drove home. The silver orbs suspended on a wire over my head bop around as I pull off the accessory.

My mind jumps to an image of CJ wearing the headband the first time he picked me up after work. I loved his silliness. I loved how his lightness balanced my heaviness. I found his boyish charm captivating rather than immature. His lightheartedness was even more endearing when I realized he could be serious when he needed to be.

But this was not the real CJ, I remind myself. The real CJ lied to me. The real CJ has already moved on to a new girl. None of it was real.

Suddenly, I feel desperate to see an image of his face—his luscious hair with hints of gold, his sapphire-colored eyes. Luckily, I was smart enough to delete every remnant of CJ from my phone and social media. I even blocked his number. The text his new girlfriend sent slayed my heart, but at least it proved that CJ is a fraud.

Relief washes through my core as I consider what would have happened had I been pregnant. The anxiety that consumed me over the last few weeks has finally subsided. But the ache in my heart has only intensified. I keep trying to get my brain to explain to my heart that CJ is nothing but a liar. But my heart will not listen. It beats with a naïve longing, casting away all logic.

Placing my hand on my chest, I push lightly, hoping to infuse my heart with the truth. My fingers dig into my skin a bit too aggressively. The word *stop* blares in my mind on repeat. *Stop missing him,* I plead as I continue to push my palm into my body.

As I stand in the entryway, physically attempting to jolt the longing out of my heart, I hear the thunder of the garage door. My dad has a double shift today. It must be Tabby. I take a long stride down the hallway and disappear into my room to avoid her. Things have been weird between us since my pregnancy scare.

I've thought a lot over the last few weeks about how confused she must be. We were just getting on smoother ground when I completely pulled away again. Every time she looks at me, her eyes fill with uncertainty. Her face tenses, as if she's trying to figure out the answer to an impossibly hard question on a final exam.

My guilty feelings have inspired me to make a move toward reconciliation. Tomorrow night, at dinner, I will tell my dad and Tabby about my acceptance at FLAD. I'm hopeful this piece of news will wipe away the strained atmosphere suffocating Tabby and me and allow us to move forward.

Since reading the second letter from my mom, I have thought less about her and more about Tabby. Tabby has been the one encouraging me, guiding me, loving me, and supporting me all these years. Tabby is the one who has believed in me when I have not believed in myself. *Tabby is my mother.*

As I pull off my work clothes and change into shorts, there's a knock at my door.

"Ila, it's Tabby. You in there?"

I'm surprised she's attempting to talk with me. Maybe she's feeling the same desire to repair our relationship that I am.

I pull on a t-shirt and crack open the door. "What's up?"

"I was wondering if you had a few minutes to talk?" She stands hesitantly in my door frame, looking like she's afraid to move. I notice her eyes are puffy, as if she's been crying. I wonder if she's upset about this last round of IVF. My dad told me it didn't work. But Tabby and I have never once talked about her fertility treatments.

I turn my body sideways and motion for her to enter my room. Our eyes lock for a moment as she steps toward my bed and sits on the edge. I walk to the other side and sit across from her with my back against the headboard.

Tabby reaches for one of my fluffy throw pillows and nestles it in her lap. She looks down at the pillow as she smooths the fabric.

"Are you okay?" I ask.

She lifts her eyes and looks at me directly. "I have to ask you something. I hope you will be honest."

"Okay." Each letter comes out of my mouth slowly, as if trying to give me extra time to wrap my head around what's coming.

"I found a pregnancy test box in the guest bathroom garbage."

As soon as Tabby speaks, my body floods with a tidal wave of humiliation. My fingers burn as if they're hot.

Tabby continues. "I left the box in the garbage, because I didn't want you to know I found it. I was hoping you would come to me and tell me. But you didn't. And I can understand why. But I want you to know I'm here to support you, Ila. You don't have to deal with this on your own." She places her palm on my knee.

"Oh my God," I blurt as I shoot up off the bed.

Tabby's hand falls off my knee as I stand. I pace the small area between the dresser and my door. Words escape me. I'm like a jack-in-the-box that must expel my energy in a discordant burst before I can relax.

"Oh my God," I say again as if the crank of the toy is winding. Then the words explode from my mouth. "I'm not pregnant." Looking at Tabby, I repeat myself. "I'm not pregnant." I can hear the sharpness of my voice.

Then, suddenly, I'm filled with fear. "Did you tell Dad? Please tell me you didn't say anything to Dad." My body folds into itself, and I sit on the floor in front of my bed, shaking.

As Tabby shakes her head, tears pour from my eyes. It's a cry encompassing the betrayal, fear, sadness, rejection, and loneliness I have felt over the past weeks. Moving from the bed to the floor, Tabby wraps her arm around my shoulders and lets me cry fat and forceful tears into her neck.

"I didn't tell your dad," she reiterates. "I only found the box, not the test itself. I didn't want to say anything until I spoke to you."

"Thanks," I whisper in a breathy sob as I pull away from her embrace. "I was late. It was scary. But I got my period the other day. I just wanted to move on from it without telling anyone."

"I can understand. But I hate to think you don't trust me to help you. I'm always here for you."

"But there were so many layers to this," I say. "CJ is Ellory's son. Ellory and you have a difficult relationship. And…And you and I," I stammer. "Our relationship hasn't been easy."

"Yes." She nods.

"I didn't want to upset you. It felt so unfair that I could be pregnant." My heart sinks. I hope my words haven't caused Tabby distress.

Tabby looks at me for a long moment. "Your empathy for my feelings is what makes me love you," Tabby says. "But this is part of parenting. You accept that sometimes the things your kids struggle with are going to push your own buttons, highlight your own struggles, rip out your own heart. But as a parent, you still want to help your child."

As we rock back and forth, hugging for several moments, I feel love, warmth, and support. I feel the connection between Tabby and me. A connection that supersedes the obligation of genetics and is born from our own wanting.

"I love you," Tabby says in a voice shaky with emotion.

"I love you too," I say as my entire body swells with happiness.

CHAPTER 53

Faye Carter

BLAST OFF BOOKS buzzes with moms who have brought their children for story hour. I watch as a young mom gently pulls a toddler as she pushes a stroller with a sleeping infant. Her hair is greasy from being ignored. A stained burp cloth sits over her shoulder. A trail of exhausted moms drags behind her as if they are an army of soldiers who barely survived a war.

For a moment, my heart pangs with guilt. I should be with my kids instead of meeting Tabby and Harper for coffee. I never realized hiring a nanny would come with feelings of remorse. Motherhood—damned if you do and damned if you don't.

"She's where?" Harper looks at Tabby, confused. Harper's puzzled tone forces me to get out of my head and focus.

"She flew to Paris to get Cade. She wants him to come home." Tabby crosses her arms and leans back. "The thing is, Maxy is a terrible influence. Ellory doesn't want him corrupting Cade."

Harper drops her voice. "I've read the media coverage since they announced their divorce. Maxy was awful. So many women are coming forward claiming to have had an affair. There's even one saying that Maxy is the father of her child."

Tabby nods while her eyes brim with distress. "I'm worried about Ellory. She's strong, but this is difficult. The entire world knows her marriage was a sham. I can't think of a worse situation for a romance writer."

"Well, she's better off getting divorced," I say, a bit too enthusiastically. My body tenses. *Have I given my feelings about my marriage away?* The word divorce has been clanging around in my mind at regular intervals ever since my last run-in with Lexi.

"You're absolutely right," Tabby agrees.

My strange zeal around Ellory's divorce suddenly appears appropriate and I relax.

Looking at her watch, Tabby lets out a small sigh. "I've got to get story hour started. Sorry, we don't have more time to chat."

"Enjoy," Harper says.

Tabby stands but turns back toward us. "You know, I always let one of my staff members run story hour. But I'm actually looking forward to it."

I smile at Tabby, unsure of what to say.

"I guess I'll see how it goes." She walks toward the brightly decorated children's section and sits in a chair nestled in a corner designed to look like a rocket ship.

"So, what else do you have going on today?" I ask, looking back at Harper.

"My first patient is coming at noon. I should probably get going." She stares off into the distance for a moment too long.

"Are you ready to talk more about Ben?" I ask, trying to be supportive. She told Tabby and me about Ben kissing his ex-wife. She's devastated.

"No, there's nothing to say. Glad I followed my gut and didn't get involved. I knew he wasn't ready." Her shoulders slump.

"But he's been calling and texting nonstop. He wants to talk to you."

Harper shakes her head defiantly. "He finally stopped," she says. "I told him to leave me alone."

"Aren't you the least bit curious about what he has to say?" I ask.

"Nope," she says with emphasis. "I'm not." Her words sound emphatic, but her face looks unsure. "Anyway, I've got to get going." She pushes her chair back and stands. "I'll see you at the last Ellory's Editors meeting. I guess Tabby will tell us if Ellory doesn't make it back in time."

"I'll walk out with you," I say. "I want to go to the art co-op and spend a bit of time painting before I have to be home to relieve the nanny."

LATER THAT EVENING, as I lay chicken breasts on a sheet pan and sprinkle them with parmesan cheese, my phone rings. It's Mark.

"I'm in the middle of cooking dinner. Can I call you back?"

"I just wanted to tell you I'm going to go by the art co-op now. I'll be home in about forty-five minutes."

My stomach rolls at the mention of the art co-op. It's been weeks since I asked Mark to look at my paintings. He had time for a work happy hour and a card night but has mentioned nothing about going to see my paintings.

"Okay," I say just as Griffin lets out a sharp cry.

"Sorry it's taken me this long to make it over."

There's no way he can understand how devastated I've been by his lack of interest in my paintings. The groove in my heart has widened into a gaping hole. I pause for a moment too long.

"Faye?"

"I need to go. Griffin is fussing. See you soon." I walk over to Baby G and pull him out of his swing. He smiles at me, his perfect little smile. "Did you just need some attention?" I coo as I rock him on my knee.

"Where's Daddy?" Ezra says as I move Griffin back to his swing.

"Daddy will be home soon. Give Mommy a quick hug." I walk back to the kitchen, open a box of angel hair pasta, and dump it into a large pot of boiling water.

At six o'clock, I hear the garage door announce Mark's return home. He walks into the house as I pull the chicken out of the oven. I turn my face up to look at him. I feel vulnerable. *What's he going to say about my paintings?*

Walking over to our kitchen table, I sit down. "So, what did you think?" I say hesitantly.

"I liked the big one that was all different shades of blue. You should show the gallery that one." He leans against the kitchen wall for a moment as he pushes his hand through his hair.

"I like that one too." I suddenly feel a jolt of affection for Mark. I'm excited to sit here and talk with him about my paintings in more detail.

But instead of sitting down and joining me at the table, he walks past me and turns toward the hallway. "I'm going upstairs to shower. What are we having for dinner tonight?"

The hole in my chest bursts open, and my heart explodes into a million jagged pieces.

THE NEXT AFTERNOON, while Mark is at a soccer game with Milo, I decide to do a cooking project with the twins while Griffin naps. Standing over Ezra and Emma's small bodies, I pull out a mixing bowl and wooden spoons. I purposefully let the twins take control of our baking activity so they can feel pride and accomplishment. Ezra tries to read the instructions on the red and white box of instant cupcake mix.

"Water," he says, pleased with himself.

"Yes, Ezra, exactly right. We need to add one-fourth cup of water. Emma, can you pour this into the bowl for us?"

Emma's shaky hand dumps the water into the bowl, and both kids watch intently as the brown powdery substance inside turns into a gooey concoction.

Ezra stirs around the wooden spoon a few times and looks up at me. "Finished. Now what, Mommy?"

I glance into the bowl filled half with wet dough and half with powdery dry mix yet to be included in the fold. "Let's try stirring it up one more time," I say in my most encouraging voice. "Emma, will you help us out?"

She grabs the spoon and does her best to mix everything. Once she's done, I hand them a small scooper so they can collect the batter and drop it into the paper liners in the mini cupcake pan. The movement of scooping and dropping is awkward for them, and much of the mix ends up on the pan in the area between muffin cups.

"My hands hurt," Emma says after just a few scoops.

I hold myself back from lecturing her on pushing through and not giving in so easily. "That's okay," I say. "It's hard to do. I'll finish up and put them in the oven. How about we play bingo while we're waiting for them to bake?"

"Sure!" Emma shouts with delight. She runs over to the game cabinet, pulls out the Hello Kitty bingo set, and plops it down on the kitchen table. She immediately plays a game of bingo by herself.

Opening the oven door, a waft of hot air tickles my face. The warmth feels good on my skin. I put the cupcakes inside, set the timer for fifteen minutes, and absent-mindedly sit on the floor. Ezra side-eyes me, confused. I'm sure he is wondering why Mommy is on the floor sitting in front of the oven. I'm also unsure of why I've positioned myself here. Ezra comes over to me and wraps me in a hug. He can sense my sadness. He doesn't ask me any questions. He just sits, his little body over mine, embracing me.

"I love you, Ez," I say. I just want to stay right here in this moment. The smell of chlorine lingers in his hair after yesterday's swim. Stroking his back, I kiss his little cheek.

"Mama, Ez, come play bingo. I set up cards." Emma jumps down from her chair and walks over to Ezra and me. "Come play," she insists.

Her adorable smiling face nudges me to shake off my feelings of self-pity.

"Yes, let's play," I say as I walk over to the kitchen table and take a seat in front of one of the bingo cards.

"I keep calling the numbers," Emma says, as Ezra and I gather our pink chips and review the numbers on our cards.

"2…7…10…4…" Emma's sweet voice slowly announces each new number.

The game continues, but I'm far from the present. My mind is flying with all the emotions I've experienced during my eleven years of marriage. I feel so disconnected from the man I married. He cannot grasp my point of view.

My heart sinks as I realize his inability to understand me is not because he's a cruel and uncaring man. It's just who he is, for better or for worse. Wanting or even expecting him to change is akin to asking him to make his blue eyes brown. It's not possible.

"Mama, win. Mama, look at card." Ezra shakes my arm, and my mind lands back in the moment.

I look down and see a line of hot pink chips. "Yes, I guess I won," I say, startled.

"Mama, check the numbers," Emma says.

I slide the bright pink chips off my card to compare them to the numbers Emma has called out. However, as I peer down at the card, the numbers morph into words. Each square contains a feeling I have experienced over the years.

Pain, disappointment, worthlessness, loneliness, fear, disregarded.

"Bingo!" I scream out in a frantic, shrill voice. "Bingo!"

CHAPTER 54

Harper Weiss

"I'LL SEE YOU tomorrow. Have fun with Dad." Hanging up the phone, I stroll toward my desk, happy to have the entire weekend to myself. Noah picked Ryder up from school and is spending the entire weekend with him before he heads back to LA.

Opening my latest draft of *The Broken-Hearted Barista* (BHB_WIP_Ver43_Draft7), I feel equal parts excitement and dread. Writing a novel is a form of self-flagellation that defies explanation. And when you add in a constant stream of rejections, mixed with agents disappearing after enthusiastically requesting pages, and editorial comments that reveal those who've read your pages have actually just skimmed through them, you have the recipe for psychological torture. Why do I keep going?

It's a question I don't have a logical answer to. I look up at my favorite motivational quote by Elizabeth Gilbert. She reminds me the outcome cannot matter. I should keep going, regardless of the outcome. There's magic in the process and it feeds my soul.

Her words wash over me and remind me I do this to nourish something deep inside my heart. Period. My fingers peck at my keyboard. My body fills with pride, knowing I have beaten down self-doubt and all the negative feedback once again. I keep showing up for myself, regardless of the outcome.

As I kill unnecessary adverbs, reduce my passive voice, and eliminate meaningless dialogue, I hear a car door shut. Trying to focus, I continue moving through my 300-page Word document, determined to finish this round of editing over my free weekend.

Suddenly, I hear a familiar harmony blaring outside my window. Standing, I hobble on my boot toward the music, confused. The song stirs up a well of emotions as the melody of the music repeats.

Peeking through the glass panes that face my front lawn, my eyes focus on the image before me. Ben is standing in a beige trench coat, holding a Bluetooth speaker overhead as the song "In Your Eyes" pulses with its hypnotic melody.

The pace of my heart quickens. Ben's eyes connect with mine, and he nods his head assuredly. Walking toward my door, I fumble with the lock and step outside. I watch him for a few moments but say nothing.

After the chorus plays, Ben talks. "You wouldn't talk to me, and I needed to get your attention."

I tilt my head to the side, feeling both charmed and lovesick. "You have my attention now," I say as I step toward him.

"That day you saw me kissing my ex. She saw you coming. She kissed me to make you jealous. She was putting on a show." Ben yells his words over the loud music.

"She kissed you to make me jealous?" I ask, confirming his words.

Ben lowers his arms and turns the Bluetooth speaker's volume down. "Yes, she's the worst. I ran after your car, so I could tell you, but you sped away so quickly you didn't see."

"Oh," I say, surprised by the truth of what I witnessed.

"I tried calling, texting, everything so that I could explain, but you refused to talk to me." He pauses for a moment and looks at the ground shyly. "So here I am, making my big romantic gesture, like we're in a romance novel." He lifts his head and beams at me. "I've been reading romance novels by Jewish authors all summer."

"Really?" My heart swells.

"Yes, really. Meredith Schorr, Heidi Shertok."

I take another few steps until our bodies are only inches apart. "We could start our own book club," I say, bursting with pleasure. "But why would your ex-wife kiss you?"

Ben pushes the speaker into his pocket and reaches for my hand. "She can't handle that I've moved on." He begins to say something else, but then pauses.

"Oh," I say again, overwhelmed by emotion.

He leans into me and cups my face in his other hand. "She knows I'm falling in love with you."

"Oh," I say for the third time, at a complete loss for words.

"Let's not miss this," he whispers.

As he wraps his arms around me and kisses me softly, I feel like Emily Henry has magically inserted me into a dreamy storyline that ends with my happily ever after.

"Let's go inside. I can hardly wait another minute," I whisper into Ben's ear as I gently release myself from his embrace.

He scoops me up in his arms, and his warm, muscular body surrounds me. The sun glints around us and leaves rustle in a gentle wind. As Ben steps toward my front door, it feels like we're floating. The moment is perfection, and the scene could easily be the cover of the latest best-selling romance novel.

As he bends over and kisses me passionately, I finally understand that real love, the kind that endures, evokes the same feelings as a romance novel. There are obstacles to overcome, and there is heartbreak. But there are those occasional moments that carry us away to a fantastical place where dreams become reality.

CHAPTER 55
Ellory Brayson

"**A**RE YOU SURE you want to do this?" I look at Cade's profile as he drives us to Tabby's bookstore.

His square jaw tenses. "I need to see Ila. I really messed things up. I've never felt about anyone the way I feel about her. She has to know."

My stomach clenches as I consider the risk he's taking. "You understand she may want nothing to do with you."

He exhales. "Yes. I could kill that girl for lying in that text. She wasn't my girlfriend."

"But you kissed her?" I say, confirming the story he told me earlier.

"It was a stupid kiss. It was a rebound thing. I regretted it the second it happened." He bobs his head around slightly as he talks, as if his muscles have tensed up.

"Okay," I say. "Tell her the truth. At least Ila will know how you feel. You'll need to respect whatever decision she makes after that."

As Cade pulls into a parking spot, I can't help but wonder if Ila will tell Cade about the pregnancy scare. Ila doesn't know Tabby told me, and I certainly will not tell Cade.

Stepping out of the car, Cade grabs a dozen roses and a bag of peaches.

"Why the peaches?" I ask.

He smirks as we walk toward the store's entrance.

Putting my arm around his shoulder, I hope to infuse him with the courage he'll need to confront Ila. "I'm so glad you came home," I say.

The simple words I speak fall grossly short of the gratitude I feel for the choice Cade made when I showed up in Paris. It didn't take much to convince Cade to return. Six weeks of watching his father party and hook up with women half his age was enough.

"I'm not sure who's the adult in this relationship," Cade had grumbled when we talked. "And I miss Ila."

Swinging the door open, Cade enters the store and finds Ila sitting at the coffee bar. "Wish me luck," he says as he walks toward her.

My heart stops for just a moment as I consider he may get crushed. I watch as he approaches Ila and then leads her to a quiet corner of the store where they can speak in private.

Walking in the opposite direction, I head to Tabby's office for the last Ellory's Editors meeting. Amber has sent a professional photographer to get photos for the social media campaign. Ila, who agreed to read my book, has stepped in as my younger editor.

As I approach the door, I hear boisterous laughing followed by Tabby's voice. "I don't even think that sexual position is physically possible." She snorts.

Harper and Faye are curled over, hysterical with glee.

"Right, I was thinking the same thing," Harper says, barely able to get the words out.

"What's so funny?" I interrupt.

Tabby, Harper, and Faye turn to look at me, suddenly aware I'm in the room.

"Oh, boy!" Faye says. "Tabby had us read one of the erotic books she loves, and we're having a little chat about it."

"Erotica?" I ask. My voice tinged with surprise. "You like to read erotica?" I look at Tabby as she nods enthusiastically.

"Cat's out of the bag!" she says with vigor. "I love sexy books, and I'm not ashamed of it."

"Interesting," I say, intrigued. I glance at the book lying on the table and notice the title, *Craving,* by Helen Hardt. Picking it up, I read the blurb on the back.

Dark mysteries and spicy romance.

"Take it with you," Tabby suggests. "I think you'll enjoy it." She winks.

"Now may not be the best time, with the divorce," I admit.

"I'm also getting divorced," Faye blurts. Her face immediately flushes. "I don't know why I just said that. I'm sorry."

Taking the seat beside her on the couch, I grab her hand as she tears up. "No need to be sorry."

"I haven't told anyone yet. I know this is the right thing to do, but I'm terrified."

"I understand completely," I say.

"We're here to support you any way we can," Tabby adds.

"Thanks, I appreciate that. I don't want to talk about it now, but I'm glad I told you. I will need people to lean on." Faye glances at each of us gratefully.

"Yes, of course," Harper agrees.

As soon as Harper speaks, I remember her emails that sit in my inbox, unanswered. A gust of discomfort fills my chest. I owe her an explanation and an apology. "Harper, I've been meaning to talk to you. Do you mind if we talk privately for a few minutes before the photographer gets here?"

Harper's body stiffens. She's clearly unnerved by my request.

Tabby glances at Faye. "Why don't Faye and I step out? We'll get some snacks and be back in a few minutes."

Harper swallows hard as soon as Tabby and Faye stand to leave. She seems like she's about to cry. My body burns with guilt. I know she's disappointed.

"Listen, I want to apologize. I voluntarily took your book under my wing, so to speak, but then never followed up. I'm sure I got your hopes up. I should've circled back with you." Pausing for a moment, I allow Harper to speak.

But instead of responding, she just looks at me wide-eyed.

"My agent never responded," I continue. "I reached out to her about it once but never heard back. Then my life kind of blew up…" My words trail off.

Harper nods but remains quiet.

"The world of publishing is impossible," I tell her. "Agents receive books every minute. It's hard to understand what makes one rise to the top and get their attention. I thought if I put your book forward, it would be enough to get my agent's attention, but I guess it wasn't."

Harper shifts in her chair uncomfortably. "Do you know if she read it?" Her voice shakes slightly, and I suddenly remember how vulnerable I felt as I tried to find an agent for my first book. It would devastate me if a famous author's attempts to get my work noticed went unanswered.

"I don't," I say honestly. "I'm sorry."

She shifts her gaze to the floor, unable to meet my eye.

"But, listen," I say. "I loved what I read, and I know you have an audience out there. I'm extremely busy but will make time to read your book and provide some general edits. Why don't we start there?"

Harper tilts her head. She seems unsure if she wants to take me up on my offer. All creatives struggle between wanting their work noticed and protecting themselves from the pain that comes from rejection. I can understand her hesitation.

"Just think about it," I say, not wanting to push her.

"Where is everyone?" Ila breaks the tension in the room as she walks in. I search her face for clues about her reaction to Cade's apology. She doesn't appear upset or angry. I'm left wondering how their conversation went.

"Those are beautiful roses." Harper beams. "Looks like someone has an admirer."

"Just a friend," Ila says. "But we'll see." She turns and looks directly at me, understanding my desire to know how things went.

"We're back." Tabby walks in with a tray of pastries.

Faye follows close behind, carrying a carafe of coffee. As she sets it down on the table in front of us, the photographer arrives. She's older than I expected.

"Hi, I'm Helen, I'm here for the photo shoot." Her eyes land on mine. The wrinkles around her eyes bunch up as she smiles. "Ellory Brayson," she says excitedly. "What a pleasure to meet you. I've read all your books." She reaches her hand out to shake mine, and I notice the purple veins peeking through the thinning skin on her hand. She must be in her mid to late sixties.

"It's always great to meet a fan," I say sincerely. As I take in the sight of her, I think of my grandmother. Helen has a similar look. A bit frail, with powdery white, short hair, and a timeworn smile. Yet she exudes dignity with her stylish and mature presence.

"Your publicist sent me a list of shots she wants me to get today. Some will be by the bay window I saw when I walked in, but some will be outside."

"Sounds great," I say. "Would you like a snack or some coffee before we get started?" I gesture to the food before us.

Helen's eyes glance at the spread of treats on the table but then move to the spicy book.

"Oh," I say, embarrassed, as Tabby grabs the book and flips it over.

Helen's eyes widen. I shuffle back and forth on my feet for a second, afraid of what she's going to say.

"*Craving* is good, but the next one in the series is better." Helen winks as she smiles slyly.

The room immediately erupts in laughter.

"Erotica is my favorite," she adds. "You should follow me on TikTok for reviews of the best titles—@hotspicygrandma68."

I glance around the room. Ila's face is bright red. Faye and Harper are holding hands, giggling. Tabby's arm crosses over her chest as she inhales deeply between laughs.

My heart warms as my body fills with a feeling of peace. This summer has been the hardest of my life. But I am finally feeling like myself again. My happily ever after starts now.

EPILOGUE

Ellory Brayson

One Year Later

TABBY WAVES ENTHUSIASTICALLY the moment I enter her store. Walking past a display table filled with copies of my latest release, *Charmed*, I smile. I pick up the light pink cover and graze my fingers over the whimsical drawing of two hands clasped tightly. Each wrist has a bracelet with charms dangling in an array of sunny colors.

"How was the house hunting?" Tabby approaches me and smiles.

Placing the book down, I look at her excitedly. "I found a nice property on the beach over by Venus Inlet. I think I'm going to make an offer."

"Wow! I know you're only going to be a snowbird, but it will be great having you back in Jupiter Cove." Tabby's face softens into a warm expression as she speaks.

"I'm looking forward to escaping from New York during the winter. Plus, now that I'm living solo in a smaller apartment, I need extra storage space. My home here will double as an extra closet."

My stomach clenches thinking about how difficult it was to pack up the grand apartment Maxy and I owned on the Upper East Side.

Divorce is an unpaved path. And sometimes it feels less like a path and more like a thick, muddy sludge. But I keep moving forward. I've come a long way over the past year, but I know I have so much further to go.

"Follow me. I want to show you something." Tabby's voice jolts me back to the moment. Staying present is the best way to avoid a downward spiral of emotion. I quickly push the thoughts about my divorce aside. I'll save it for my next therapy appointment.

As soon as we walk into her office, I practically jump. Cade is sitting on the couch. Ila sits beside him.

"What a surprise!" I beam. "I thought you were going to be in Las Vegas covering the Bar and Restaurant Expo." Cade's been working tirelessly at the *Miami Tribune* since the fall as an assistant for the paper's lifestyle section.

Cade smiles at me with a sheepish grin. "I just got promoted. They want me to be here for the Miami Food and Wine Festival this week." His face overflows with pride.

"He's so excited," Ila interjects happily. "And did he tell you his short story about the sailor was just accepted into a magazine?"

"What? I had no idea." My voice beats with excitement.

Cade shrugs shyly. "I wanted to tell you in person."

Stepping over to the couch, I pull him up and wrap him in a hug. "I'm so proud of you." I hold him tightly for a minute longer than necessary, but he doesn't seem to mind.

As our bodies pull apart, I turn toward Ila. "How are things going at FLAD?"

"It's hard. My professors are tough. But I'm learning a lot."

Cade grabs her hand and my heart soars. They've worked through last summer and have been dating steadily for a few months. Tabby and I have all our hopes and dreams pinned on them ending up together. But we are doing our best to play it cool.

"Sorry, I'm a few minutes late." Harper steps beside me and looks at Tabby. "Ben's pulled up in front of the store with a box of books. Where should I get everything set up?"

Tabby stands. "I put a display table for you next to Ellory's for the event. Let me show Ben where to put everything."

Tabby and Harper turn to leave, but Harper stops right before walking out. "Thank you," she mouths to me silently as she takes a step toward Tabby.

"It's going to be fantastic," I reply. My heart bumps happily in my chest with excitement for Harper. She's promoting her book, *The Broken-Hearted Barista*, before I do a book signing for *Charmed*. Both books are the first to be released under my publishing imprint—*Blast Off Books*. It thrilled Tabby to incorporate her store's name.

After several months of trying to help Harper find an agent, I became disillusioned with the entire industry. My imprint focuses on representing first-time authors like Harper. I'm thrilled to support her and looking forward to taking a break from writing to help new authors break through. *The Broken-Hearted Barista* is a fun and heartfelt book. I know it has an audience. I'm excited for her to find her following.

Now that I've broken away from traditional publishing, a heavy weight has lifted. The pressure of having to write bestseller after bestseller was the beating heart of my celebrity persona. Now that this pressure has fallen away, I feel like myself again. I'm no longer interested in social media schemes and other ploys to gain success. I make my own decisions, always staying true to myself.

I'm curious to see what happens with *Charmed*. I'll be okay if it doesn't become a bestseller. The book is an authentic reflection of who I am. And that's my new beating heart.

"I'm here!" A moment later, Faye enters the office.

I jump out of my chair and give her a warm hug. We've gotten close as we navigate the realities of divorce together. "How are the kids?" I ask, understanding a divorce with four young children adds another level to her split.

"Everyone's doing okay. We have our moments. It's not always easy," she answers honestly.

"You're doing great, Faye," I say encouragingly. "I love the cover you did for Harper's book."

She smiles as she lowers her body into a chair. "It came out great. I think I can build a side hustle with this book cover business as I work on my graphic arts degree."

"I don't know how you do it all," Ila says admiringly. "You're a mom, you're a student, you're running a business. It's impressive."

"I drink a lot of coffee," Faye teases. "And my nanny is the absolute best."

"The store is filling up." Tabby strolls back into the office, pumping with adrenaline. "Oh, Faye, when did you arrive?"

"A few minutes ago."

"Thanks again for all those hand-me-downs. I went through everything the other day. There are so many adorable, tiny dresses. I can't wait to get Liu home."

Tabby and Andre leave for China in two weeks to bring their baby girl home. I've already told Tabby I expect to be called Auntie Ellory.

Faye winks at Tabby. "Enjoy all the pink."

Tabby places her palm over her heart. "I will. Stop by to see the mural Ila painted in the nursery. It's spectacular."

Ila's face lights up at the compliment. "Aww, thanks. I can't wait to meet my baby sister," she says with heartfelt sincerity.

"I think it's time." Tabby motions for all of us to stand. We walk in a line out toward the large crowd gathered in the store.

"LET'S HEAR IT again for Harper," I say as I adjust my microphone. "I know you're going to love her book." I nod toward Harper as she takes a seat next to Ben in the front row.

"Well, I have to say. No one shows up quite like the hometown crowd." Glancing around the store, I can't even see the faces of the people crammed into the back. "I really appreciate your support and everyone coming out tonight to get a copy of my new book, *Charmed*. I also want to say a special thank you to Ellory's Editors. We never launched the campaign on social media, but I truly could not have done it without you." My eyes sweep the faces of the Ellory's Editors team, and my heart fills with love.

The crowd applauds, excited to be involved in my new book's launch event.

"We love you, Ellory," a random voice in the crowd shouts. Everyone in the store begins to hoot and holler.

When it's quiet, I speak again. "Wow. I feel humbled to have this town's support and affection." Heat rises to my cheeks as I continue. "Love. I've built my career on it. Attraction, courtship, intimacy, passion. The stories that surround romantic love are some of the greatest stories out there."

Pausing, I swallow nervously. "As you read my new book, I hope you will take a journey with me to explore a different kind of love."

The audience stills, their eyes widening.

"I'd like to start by reading the dedication."

"Dear Reader, thank you for allowing me to tell you stories about romantic love over the years. We have explored heartbreak, second chances, fake dating, and so much more. And it has truly been my greatest pleasure to write these stories."

"This new book is also about love. But a different kind. It's about acceptance. It's about trust. It's about a deep feeling of belonging. It's about forgiveness. It's about love that makes it easy to believe in yourself."

"It's about the love of a best friend. Tabby, this book is for you."

THE END

Thank you for reading **Moms Who Read Romance Novels!** I'd love for you to leave a review on Amazon and Goodreads. Ratings drive book sales and rankings. Thank you!

The title reveal for my third book is coming soon! Sign up for my newsletter at authorjenifergoldin.com so you don't miss it. It's another book about friendship, motherhood, and relationships mixed with a dash of snark.

Follow me at

jenifergoldinwrites

Author Jenifer Goldin

jenifergoldinauthor

Acknowledgments

First and foremost, I must thank my husband and children for allowing me to disappear into my head for a second time as I wrote and edited *Moms Who Read Romance Novels*. Writing is all-consuming. It's difficult to find the right balance as I get swept away. The house got messy, the laundry piled up, I missed important school emails, and we ate more fast food than we should have. Jon, Anna, Micah, and Luna- thank you for allowing me the time and space to write.

I'd also like to thank Micah for helping to come up with the title of this book. One Saturday night, when we were brainstorming ideas for my next mom-focused book, Micah said "what about romance books?" SHAZAM⚡⚡⚡It was a lightning bolt moment. Yes! I screamed. "Moms Who Read Romance Novels! That's my next title." My son is excited to take all the credit and I'm happy to let him have it.

And to Anna, you are the bravest person I know. You are confident, smart, and friendly. I've seen you fight through fears and try new things even when they scare you. I'm so lucky to be your mom.

Thank you to my family. Mom, thanks for your willingness to pick up my kids, watch Luna, and help in any way you can. To my brother, Andrew, I love our relationship and the unwavering support we provide for each other. Allison and Carrie, how did I end up with the two best sisters-in-laws on the planet? Joel, thanks for being my attorney and always offering support. Dad, thanks for always being the first to like my social media posts. And to all of my extended family, thanks for your interest in this crazy hobby of mine.

To my first readers and Beta readers. Thank you so much for your time and willingness to read. Michele Blondheim, it's pretty awesome when your best friend since second grade is a voracious reader and is also willing to provide honest feedback. Stacy Brown, I'm lucky to have the support of an intelligent and thoughtful person like you. And it helps that you are a published author! Heather Carlin, remember that year you read over one hundred and fifty books and didn't think it was a big deal? Keri Halpern, I love that you don't sugar coat and hope we can meet in person one day! Sam Katz, you provided amazing edits when *Moms Who Read Romance Novels* was in its infancy. I'm consistently awed by your intelligence, mothering skills, and cooking! Laurie Rubin, you are the world's biggest cheerleader. I'm so lucky to have you on this journey. Lorna Sherwinter, my writing buddy and emotional support person. And, Stephanie Tavani, Feldani's forever.

Thank you to Melinda Carter, BSN, RNC, Reproductive Biology Associates Director of Clinical Compliance and Research Coordinator. I could not release this book without ensuring the details about fertility treatment were correct. I appreciate your feedback and expertise.

A big shout out to "the people I should pay!" You know who you are and I thank you.

Sexy mamas who haven't been mentioned yet. Everyone needs the support of a mom text chain and ours is hilarious. Lori Cahill, you are one of the most genuine people I know. I couldn't make it through play practice without our open-ended carpool. Robyn Klugman, the most well-connected person in Atlanta, and always willing to cheer me on. Jodi Loar, the very first person to read my very first unpublished book. So happy our stars crossed. Heather Lourie, you are a kind soul through and through. And Amy Rosen, who shouts my book out on every social platform. Thanks so much for believing in me.

Also, thank you Genyee Feldman, for connecting me with the expert reader I needed to finalize this book. And to Meredith Lee, I love having you on my team. Thanks for your amazing feedback on the cover.

To all my friends who ask about my writing and support me on this journey. There are so many of you. My friends from growing up in Miami, my friends from camp, my friends from college and graduate school, my friends from my early adult years, and the friends

I have made since becoming a mom. I am so blessed and appreciate and love all of you.

To all of my advanced readers. Thank you for your final edits. You are a big piece of this puzzle. I could not do this without you!

To the Bookstagrammers who have posted and reviewed my books. I love getting glimpses into your life on Insta, and I'm happy to be part of this awesome community of book nerds!

Thank you to my developmental editor, Laura Silverman. I enjoyed your positive approach and the razor-sharp suggestions you made to improve *Moms Who Read Romance Novels*.

Thank you to my copy editor Shannon Cave. This is our second time working together. You make the difficult part of writing easy.

Thank you to Stuart Bache from Books Covered for the amazing cover.

Thank you to Stephanie Anderson from Alt 19 Creative for the beautiful interior pages. It's also our second time working together. I love your creative eye.

Finally, there are a few authors who took a chance and agreed to read my debut, Anonymous Mom Posts. Thank you Rochelle B. Weinstein. I had no expectations when I blindly reached out to you. Not only did you respond, but your continuous support has been beyond amazing. You are the best cheerleader! Thank you

Jean Meltzer. What a thrill to have a best-selling author review and recommend my book! Thank you Sara Goodman Confino for always answering my questions and rooting for me. And thank you Samantha Greene Woodruff for all your feedback. I'm excited to incorporate your input into my work in progress.

And last but certainly not least, thank YOU! You purchased my book and are holding my dream in your hand. My writing is my heart and soul put into words. Thanks for reading.

About the Author

Jenifer Goldin, a Miami native, graduated from the University of Florida and Gallaudet University. An audiologist by trade, Goldin specialized in pediatric cochlear implants. However, writing has always been her passion. Some of Goldin's stories reveal her truest emotions, and sometimes her emotions are just the  jumping-off point for a fictional tale. Her favorite books always go beyond storytelling and shine a light on the human experience. Goldin now resides in Atlanta with her husband, two children, and her very furry dog. She loves mom life (#momming), her mini goldendoodle, Yacht Rock music, spending time with friends, and making fun of her husband's love of sappy holiday romance movies.